THE

SUBPRIMES

ALSO BY KARL TARO GREENFELD

THE

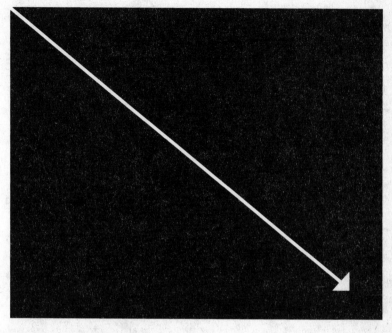

SUBPRIMES

A NOVEL

KARL TARO GREENFELD

HARPER PERENNIAL

NEW YORK • LONDON • TORONTO • SYDNEY • NEW DELHI • AUCKLAND

HARPER ⬤ PERENNIAL

A hardcover edition of this book was published in 2015 by HarperCollins
Publishers.

HarperCollins books may be purchased for educational, business, or sales
promotional use. For information please e-mail the Special Markets Department
at SPsales@harpercollins.com.

FIRST HARPER PERENNIAL EDITION PUBLISHED 2016.

Designed by Michael Correy

The Library of Congress has catalogued the hardcover edition as follows:
Greenfeld, Karl Taro.
The subprimes : a novel / Karl Taro Greenfeld. — First edition.
pages ; cm
ISBN 978-0-06-213242-0 (hardcover)
I. Title.
PS3607.R4536S83 2015
813'.6—dc23   2014036100

ISBN 978-0-06-213243-7 (pbk.)

16 17 18 19 20 OV/RRD 10 9 8 7 6 5 4 3 2 1

For the 99%

"Thou shalt support the repeal of all taxation."

"Thou shalt oppose all personal and corporate income taxation,
   including capital gains taxes, all criminal and civil sanctions
   against tax evasion should be terminated immediately."

"Thou shalt support repeal of all laws which impede
   the ability of any person to find employment, such
   as minimum wage laws and child labor laws."

"Thou shalt condemn compulsory education laws . . . and call for the
   immediate repeal of such laws. Government ownership, operation,
   regulation and subsidy of schools and colleges should be ended."

"Thou shalt favor the repeal of the fraudulent, bankrupt,
   and oppressive Social Security system."

"Thou shalt support the abolition of the Department of Energy."

"Thou shalt support the abolition of the government Postal Service."

"Thou shalt support the abolition of the Environmental Protection Agency."

"Thou shalt support the abolition of the Food and Drug Administration."

"Thou shalt call for the repeal of the Occupational Safety and Health Act."

"Thou shalt call for the abolition of the Consumer Protection Agency."

"Thou shalt oppose all government welfare, relief projects, and 'aid to
   the poor' programs."

—THE NEW COMMANDMENTS OF THE FREEDOM PRAIRIE CHURCH (AN EXCERPT)

When a majority of the people are hungry and cold
they will take by force what they need. And the little
screaming fact that sounds through all history: repression
works only to strengthen and knit the repressed.

—JOHN STEINBECK, *THE GRAPES OF WRATH*

THE

SUBPRIMES

TWO DOZEN BODIES LAY IN duct-tape-patched nylon sleeping bags atop cardboard folded for padding against the pebbled, cigarette-butt-and-bottle-cap-littered earth. Empties were discarded around the sleepers, duffels and packs were torn open, contents spread in the dark, waiting to be gathered at first light. Animal tracks wound around the packs and the bedding; a stray dog had been sniffing around last night. Above was the roar of automobiles on a crumbling freeway, so dilapidated and overdue for resurfacing you could glimpse through cracks the sooty undercarriage of cars passing overhead; and higher, on reinforced pylons straddling the old road, was the elevated skyway, one of the new toll roads that whisked the wealthy from mansions to airports. Smog rose in crowning layers and somewhere up there, presumably, was blue—had to be—though most days you saw only brown smudge.

The horizontal figures were mostly men, but among them, blanket or nylon rising in shorter breaths, were a few women and children, bundled against the night chill. This was the best sleep, in the minutes before dawn, after the fears about food and money and shelter that had prolonged wakefulness among the adults had finally been worn through and even those most prone to worry could drop off into blessed nod.

The sleepers stirred, the auto roar and exhaust awakening them. First a woman in sweats stood up from her blankets, rubbed her eyes, and at the same time reached for a pot, sniffing at it to make sure it was clean. She felt around in her pack and rooted out a half-dozen square chunks of scavenged one-by-four, a squirt can of gasoline, and two cans of refried beans. The blocks were arranged into a small pyramid and beneath them she built a mound of balled-up flyers into which she shot a stream of gasoline and then sat back, struck a match, and tossed it into the combustible pile. The flame shot up, subsided, was fanned by the woman into a steady burn; then the woman set upon the fire an iron grate, once part of a barbecue grill. The cans of beans clugged as she shook them into the pot.

She had graying hair. She could be anywhere between thirty-five and fifty; it was hard to tell because, like so many subprimes, she had stopped dying her hair. Her hands moved in a steady blur—there was an easy efficiency to her actions; she did not need to think about each step of preparing this meal—she flipped open a lock-blade jackknife and chopped onions, cilantro, and half a tomato she found in her pack.

The beans came to a boil. She shook the narrow figure next to her awake and then reached over him to rouse a slightly larger form. The sleepers resisted until she shoved them again and then both sat up and rubbed their eyes, the larger of the two, a teenage girl, stretching.

"I'm hungry," said the smaller, a boy. "We have any eggs?"

The woman stirred the beans and chopped up vegetables. "Beans."

"We have any tortillas?"

"Finished them last night."

"Aw," the boy said, looking down at his bowl of beans.

Near them, a man in a sleeping bag sat up. "Don't give your mom a hard time. That's good food."

The boy nodded and took a mouthful.

Now other women were waking, smelling the fire, glancing over at the family to see if they had finished cooking.

"You mind?" said a Latino woman who wore jeans and a bra. She held in front of her a pot with dried oatmeal in it.

The first woman shrugged. "All yours. But do my family the courtesy of putting on a shirt."

The Latino woman looked down at herself. "Oh my God. I'm sorry."

The husband, drinking from a jug of water, watched the Latina as she walked back to her pack. The woman threw a stick at him. "You dog!"

He laughed. "Bailey, honey, I was just making sure she listened to you."

The whole encampment was rousing. Mothers and fathers trying to figure out how to get their children fed, how to divide scarce water for drinking, cooking, and washing up, and then escorting the youngest to a pit dug behind a pylon so they could make their toilets.

They'd been here three days. A rough spot, but convenient to day labor for the men, and close to an open water tap behind a gas station. Bailey had developed an internal clock for how long a Ryanville might last before they were run off. That first afternoon they had set off from their Riverside house, sleeping bags, clothes, and cookware piled into the rear cargo area and atop the roof of the creaking, bald-tired Ford Flex, duct-taped rear panel windows and six dashboard service lights pegged CHECK, she had not known what they were riding into. Her husband, Jeb, said they should head east, get out of California and into Nevada, Colorado, Texas, states where there were rumors about suburbs with abandoned houses stretching to the horizon and anti-immigration legislation had driven out the Latinos. "We can work picking fruit," he reasoned. "They still have to get the crop in."

Bailey did not want to remove the kids from school, but what choice did they have? They were broke, had nowhere to live, and it was impossible to imagine a scenario in which they could make it in California. They had to go east. But first they needed a stake, so they headed into Los Angeles, to Mayweather, near Vernon, where every day five thousand men stood in quiet rows beneath the Vernon Gate Towers and marched forward according to orders broadcast from a loudspeaker—"Farmer John needs twenty-four to swab out rendering vats"; "Freezinhot needs sixty to load the freezer"—and Jeb took his place among the men every morning shortly after dawn.

Now he dressed quickly, pulling on jeans, work boots, old Carhartts. In a way they were lucky, thought Bailey. Her husband had always been strong enough for backwork. Her own job, routing claims forms for a dental insurance company, had long since become redundant through a combination of better software and cheaper labor. Before that, she was an elementary school teacher, until the state stripped the unions of collective bargaining rights in the Right to Learn Act, subcontracting public school education to for-profit corporations. She still missed teaching, but that was strictly an hourly-wage temp job now, for those lucky enough to get hired.

That left Jeb to work for whatever the bosses offered under the National Right to Work Act—the minimum wage having been abolished—enough to keep them fed and the car gassed but not enough for a roof or to save much more than coins. The kids were out of school all day, playing with other subprime off-spring in whatever Ryanville they parked in for the night. Her daughter, Vanessa, was already being noticed by the boys and young men hanging around the camp; Bailey could tell she was enjoying the attention.

But Bailey was busy lugging buckets of water to do as much laundry as she could, mending the kids' clothes, and trying to maintain basic hygiene; it pained her to look at them, out of school, going feral with the other kids.

Jeb walked down the hill, slipped through the gap in the fence to the road at the base of the culvert beneath the underpass and down the street to their parked car. He would make the rounds of as many work spots as he could afford on two gallons of gas and be back before nightfall. Bailey had fifteen dollars left; she would have liked to buy Jeb some steak or a piece of chicken but knew she could only buy bulk canned beans.

She pushed the money into her jeans. "Vanessa, Tom, come here. Take that bucket and before you go wandering off go down to the Mobile and fetch some water."

THIS SCENE WAS REPEATED IN every previously uninhabited nook, elbow, spit, lot, and underpass throughout the foreclosed and abandoned suburbs and exurbs and trailer parks of America, now squatted by the millions who had walked out on mortgages, been foreclosed upon, or simply could no longer afford a fixed address. They were all lumped together by the media into a category called "subprimes," a less descriptive label, perhaps, than "homeless," but one that in this era of raw, rapacious capitalism gave all the information anyone needed: the credit rating of the men, women, and children who inhabited these Ryanvilles was subprime. Their credit rating made them unemployable; they were fugitives from warrants for collection and summonses to appear. Their immediate goal was to avoid imprisonment in Halliburton-, Bechtel-, or Pepper Industries–operated Credit Rehabilitation Centers.

To stay out of these debtors' prisons, the subprimes kept moving. The percentage of the population that lived in Ryanvilles was impossible to calculate, but in certain parts of certain cities it seemed as if one in every five folks was living rough, in tents or parked cars, under a freeway or next to a river. The American economy had shifted from being consumer driven to energy exporting—Saudi Arabia, only with bacon on every menu. Big oil didn't need the American consumer, so why should American industry pay enough for Americans to keep on consuming? Denied government assistance, the poor had gone past being poor. The recent American Empowerment Act cut benefits to a onetime $250 in vouchers to fast-food outlets. They were cut off from health insurance. And they were denied any federal housing subsidy—the National Housing Freedom Bill had changed that program to a onetime $500 voucher for any of several major hotel chains. Millions had taken to the road, living in the last valuable possession any of them had, their SUVs, as they traveled across the country looking for work and a squat for the night.

THERE WAS, AMONG THE SUBPRIMES beneath the highway, a woman of medium height with black hair, copper skin, and blue eyes. She had full, deeply grooved lips that made the men grin and the other women distrust her, but she was cautious, keeping her distance from the married men and making a point of helping the women with kids or cooking. She kept a motorcycle just inside the fence, and during the afternoons she tinkered with it, spending the better part of three days removing an intake valve cover and replacing the valves. It was dirty work, the grease streaking her forehead, and in the evening, when the men were coming home, one or two thought about lending the pretty girl a hand.

Sargam had been going from Ryanville to Ryanville with nothing but a small pry-bar for protection, only she was different from the families in that she had been wandering her whole life, ever since she left her third foster home at puberty. She had never known her parents, never even known her race, which had been listed on Child Protective Services forms as "other/mixed." She was often confused for African American, sometimes for Indian, occasionally for Native American, once in a while Indonesian or Sri Lankan. She was all of those things, so bewildering a mélange that she gave up trying to parse the sixteenths of this or the eighths of that. She said she was everything, all of it, people and countries and ideas and dreams all rolled into one so that she could dream bigger and talk louder and fight harder than all the rest. "What this all means? All of the me in me?" she would say. "It means don't fuck with me, me, me, and me."

The few days they had been in camp, Bailey and Jeb, and the other families, accepted Sargam as one of their own, inviting her in the evenings to share their fire and pleased that she was so quick to help when a pot needed cleaning or a blanket airing. She spoke in stolid, unaccented English, and her narrow, appraising eyes projected experience yet not judgment. They were usually wary of singles, men or women, but the families found Sargam's presence reassuring. If a smart, capable single woman was here,

well, hell, then anyone could end up in a Ryanville. It wasn't
their fault they were here.

Most of the camp would gather around a fire, the kids huddled in their own shadowy circles, daring one another and telling stories, the men sitting up smoking. There were families on
each flattening in the rise, dug into terraces, stretching up to
the bases of the pylons to the roadway. Sixty or so faces glowing
orange in the early night.

Sargam shook her head. She told them she had seen thousands, tens of thousands, living like this. Families spread up and
down the California coast, east into Nevada, south to Arizona,
all living rough and makeshift, out of cars or in encampments.

"There's something wrong in the world," Sargam said, "when
good people, honest people, can't sleep under a roof or share a
meal around a table."

Bailey nodded. "You said it, sister."

"Something needs to change," Sargam said. "What happened
to this country? We have people living in mansions, flying private jets, building their own sanctuary islands in the ocean, and
decent families don't have a place to live? What happened?"

There were a few murmurs of assent from the surrounding
campfires, as well as a few grunts.

"Don't get all political," said one man. "Keep your politics to
yourself."

"It doesn't bother you that because of your credit you can't get
a real job?" Sargam said.

"You a politician?" another man said. "This is the greatest
country in the world, or it was until the politicians and media
ruined it, made it hard for business."

"Hard for business?" Sargam said. "Do you really think it's
hard for business in America? How much are you getting an
hour? Five dollars? Five fifty?"

There were murmurs of assent from around the hillside.

"You're barely making enough to eat on and pay for the gas to get you to the next day's work."

"Lady, we're working all day, we don't need to hear you going on about socialism when we want to get some rest."

Bailey took Sargam's hand. "Darlin', complaining don't feed our kids."

Sargam nodded. "I know. It's just . . . there's something broken here, been broken for a while now, and whenever I see kids out of school and men working all day for thirty dollars, or a woman like you who has to sleep out in the open, I wonder why it is we all just sit here and take it."

"Lady, give it a rest, will ya."

Sargam sighed. She'd heard the same thing everywhere. Her ideas weren't complicated. It was a simple sense that something was wrong, the system was unfair, that lives were being crushed and no one was saying anything about it because there was no money to be made by saying anything about it. She was not an educated woman. She just felt she had to speak her mind. Not like so many subprimes who seemed too intimidated or frightened or defeated to wonder about their circumstances or how they might make things right.

The roar of traffic followed a predictable pattern, from constant to heavy to regular to sporadic. She could become accustomed to the cars and fumes, but the way the overpass blocked the stars was confusing to her. If she opened her eyes in the night, she was bewildered by the black above her until the ambient light from distant streetlights and passing cars would let her reestablish her sense of place.

Sargam was lying awake when she heard a murmuring, a shuffling of feet, the pepper-mill percussion of boots on gravel. She sat up and looked down the hill, where she could see a line of uniformed men making their way through the gap in the fence. She crouched and ran over to where Bailey was sleeping, shaking her.

"Girl, get up."

"What?"

"Trouble," Sargam said, and then went back to her sleeping bag, which she began quickly rolling, stuffing it into her backpack.

Harsh white lights were now turned on, the beams cutting through the dark in whirling columns of motes. The men were marching up the hill, kicking awake the sleeping men and women. "Get up, subprimes! This is private property."

"Dirty bums got to go!"

The young girl near Sargam screamed as a boot made contact with her stomach.

Jeb leaped up from where he had been rolling up his pack and knocked down the man who had kicked his daughter. The security guard was reaching for his holstered sidearm when with surprising quickness, Sargam jumped over the prone, terrified children still in their sleeping bags and brought her pry-bar down onto the back of the security guard's head. He went limp immediately, his arm falling from his holster.

Jeb rolled away, stood up.

"You run, girl," Jeb said.

"Is he dead?" Sargam whispered.

"We're not waiting to find out."

Everyone in Ryanville was grabbing possessions and scrambling down the hill toward the gap in the fence. The security guards pushed them along as they stumbled, children crying, women screaming, the men trying to salvage what they could.

"Can we at least pack up?" someone asked.

"It's all junk anyway. Just get out."

In the commotion, none of the other guards had yet noticed that one of their own had fallen.

Sargam ran down the hill, dodging security guards.

"Hey!" a guard shouted. The other guards turned to where their colleague was standing, waving his flashlight.

"Man down."

The crowd surged, pushing through the gap in the fence. Sargam joined the swelling crowd. She turned to Bailey. "I'll see you at your truck. One hour." And slipped through the fence and on to where her motorcycle stood. She tossed her pack into a saddlebag and leaped to straddle the seat, taking the handlebars, opening the fuel valve, turning the key, and kickstarting the bike.

"Stop her!" one of the rent-a-cops shouted. "She's the one that did him."

But the security guards had begun tossing what the families had left behind over the fence. Sleeping bags, T-shirts, jackets, shoes, pots and pans all flying over or catching in the tines at the top, and the crowd was so thick on the sidewalk against the fence that none of the guards could get through. Sargam roared off along the avenue beneath the underpass.

JEB AND BAILEY'S LITTLE GIRL, Vanessa, was bent over double, sitting in the backseat of the Flex. A large octagonal bruise had formed, blue and black, where the boot had made contact with her side. She was running a fever, and Bailey sent the boy, Thomas, to the convenience store to get ice, which she wrapped in a plastic bag.

"Keep this against your sister's ribs. She's hurting."

Tom nodded. Jeb secured what remained of their possessions in the cargo area of the Flex. He studied the dipstick; he didn't need to crawl under the car to get a look at the brake pads, which he knew were worn through. He was keeping himself busy so that he did not have to look at his daughter.

While Bailey was showing the boy how to gently keep the ice on the bruise, a police car rolled up beside her. She felt the policeman's gaze without looking over and quickly put the ice away and lowered Vanessa's shirt.

The officer, wearing mirrored sunglasses and a hard-shell helmet, stepped out of the car.

"You subprimes were sleeping in the underpass?"

Jeb nodded.

"A security tech was badly injured there last night," the officer said. "A gang of subprimes jumped him."

"I didn't see nothing like that," Jeb said.

"Beat him up pretty bad. He's in critical condition."

"Like I said, we just rolled up our stuff and got out of there. Didn't see nothing."

The officer looked inside the rolled-down window at the girl asleep on the rear seat of the Flex. "What's wrong with her?"

"Fever," Bailey said.

The officer walked around the vehicle, noting the bald tires, sagging suspension, missing rear bumper. "License and registration."

Jeb had a valid license, but the vehicle's registration was long since expired.

Jeb handed the license to the officer who returned to his squad car. Soon he was back, saying there was a warrant out for an unpaid citation for driving an unregistered vehicle.

"Officer, can you give me a break? Just, look, I need every dollar to feed my kids and for gas to get to a day's work." Jeb shook his head. "I'm sorry that I couldn't pay that ticket."

"I can arrest you, impound the vehicle," the officer said. "Put you in credit rehab."

"I know. But then what about my kids?"

"Subprimes and their kids." The officer snorted. "Did you think about your kids before you stopped paying your mortgage? Or maybe thought about your circumstances before you even had kids?"

He looked around. "Tell you what. How much money do you have?"

Jeb turned to Bailey.

"Fifteen dollars," she said.

"Give it to me," said the officer.

"How am I gonna get to the lineup? Feed my kids?"

"You can walk."

Bailey handed over the dirty bills.

The officer pocketed the money, pointed at Vanessa lying with her eyes closed on the backseat. "You should take her to a doctor, get that checked out."

When he was gone, Bailey lifted the girl's shirt and applied the ice.

"What are we gonna do now?" Jeb asked.

"You don't think I'd give him our last money, do you?"

Jeb smiled. "How much?"

"I have a twenty in my bra."

"That's not gonna get us far."

"It'll get us fed, and you to work."

He looked down the dusty road, the battered vehicles parked alongside it, the dried eucalyptus leaves, borne by hot, dry wind, scratching at the pavement. There was a narrow strip of cracked sidewalk lined by fencing, and beyond that, litter-strewn land owned by the Department of Public Works, a patch similar to where they had been sleeping. They had to get away from there.

A battered SUV pulled up alongside them; they recognized the wide eyes and dirty faces of a fellow subprime family from the underpass.

"How is your little girl?" the mother asked from behind the wheel.

"She's feeling it, that's for sure," said Bailey.

"I'm sorry about that. Who would kick a little girl?"

The father leaned over from the passenger seat. "Where you headed?"

"Not far. We don't have the fuel to get anywhere."

The man nodded.

"Heard they're looking for that girl, the one that talked politics. They're saying she's the one that did the tech."

Jeb kept quiet.

The man continued: "Well, we're going to try for Nevada. It has to be better than here. They got abandoned houses where you can squat, thousands of them, you can just move right in."

The mother revved the engine.

Their children were in the backseat, staring over. They waved to Tom, and he waved back sadly.

"It makes you think," the father shouted as they drove away. "That woman was right, about this all being messed up, the unfairness . . ."

"You don't need to tell me," Bailey said, turning back to her daughter.

"What are we waiting for?" Jeb asked. "Let's get moving. We have to find a spot for the night."

"We're waiting for Sargam," Bailey said. "She said she'd turn up back here."

"She can't," Jeb said. "If that tech dies, that's a murder rap. She's probably halfway to Mexico by now, or should be."

"You're right," Bailey said. "No point in waiting, I suppose."

Vanessa sat up. "I'm hungry."

Bailey smiled. "Thank God. Let's get you some food."

Jeb started the Flex and the boy ran around to the rear passenger's-side door and climbed in. As they were about to pull away they heard a thumping on the rear tailgate. In his rearview Jeb saw a helmeted figure on a motorcycle.

"Sargam!" the boy shouted.

She was on the idling bike in her white leathers, her blue eyes visible beneath the flipped-up visor of her helmet. She came forward, pulling even with the driver's window.

"Follow me," Sargam said, and tore off on the bike.

Jeb mashed the accelerator and the Flex lurched forward. He followed her down the paved arroyo and out of Huntington Park, past the Vernon walls and through the subdivisions in the shadows of the Vernon Natural Gas plant. They rode over the tracks, Jeb slowing down to spare his flattened suspension, into Maywood and Bell and then down toward the 710 Freeway, where she pulled up into the parking lot of an abandoned tire store next to the on-ramp.

Jeb stopped his vehicle beside her.

She removed her helmet and shook her hair loose.

"Girl, they are after you!" Bailey said.

"I know. I'm leaving. You should, too."

"Where can we go? We can't afford a tank of gas."

Sargam reached into her jacket and removed a hundred-dollar bill. "Here. Fill her up. Get the kids fed. How is Van?"

"I'm sore," Vanessa said.

"I gave her a Tylenol. She says she's hungry. That's always a good sign," Bailey said.

"It is," Sargam agreed. "Get some gas, and let's get out of here."

"Where to?" Jeb asked.

"Let's try Nevada."

THE EIGHT-LANE PUBLIC ROAD ROSE up over the exurban sprawl that stretched from the Pacific to Barstow, letting up only where the windmill vanes—vestiges of the era of legal rewewable energy—still cut their lazy spins through the hot air. The late-afternoon orange light woke the children, and Jeb adjusted the windshield visor while he drove. Sargam was on her motorcycle just ahead of them. They'd filled up on rice-and-bean burritos and bought a tank of gas, and they were all optimistic about the road ahead.

"They got houses there!" the boy was saying. "Can I have my own room?"

Bailey smiled. "Maybe. Now, these aren't mansions we're talkin' about. They're squats. Someone's old house that they didn't want anymore."

"Why didn't they want it?"

"Well, they *did* want it. But like us, they couldn't pay for it."

Tom thought back to the morning his family had loaded the Flex and driven west from Riverside. They'd still had Griff back then, the long-haired half-Lab. It had been a hot morning, but gray, overcast, unusually muggy for the high desert. His neighborhood looked much as it always had: carefully tended one-story homes with scant vegetation and yellowing lawns, streets without sidewalks, cars parked in driveways. The boy hadn't noticed the signs that the neighborhood was emptying. The lawns going brown, the weeds rising in cracks, the empty driveways, the padlocks on front doors. They weren't the first to leave, and by the time they did, driving out before the marshal chased them, their neighbors on either side had already abandoned their homes. As they were leaving, Tom saw his friends, Daniel and Terry, seated on their bikes in Daniel's driveway. He waved, and they waved back, and the boy thought about a blue hoodie he had left at Daniel's that he would never get back, and how Terry's mom had once taken them ice skating.

And now they were leaving, and his mom and dad didn't even know where they were going. They would be staying in a hotel for a few nights, he had been told, and he was excited about that, imagining a swimming pool. But after that, where would they go?

His parents had no answers for that. They offered a vague reassurance that they would get by, that they were strong, that as long as they were together they would be okay. But why couldn't they just stay in their house?

How long ago had that been, the boy wondered. He couldn't guess. He had not been to school since, and he had trouble keeping track of the days. The hotel had been for just a few nights, and then there were a few nights with one of his uncles, and then a few more nights sleeping in the car, and then a few Ryanvilles, as his father drove the Flex around Los Angeles looking for work and a place to sleep. Griff had gone missing a few Ryanvilles back. He wandered off while they were sleeping, and the boy had cried when they had to pack up and leave without him and did not find consoling at all his mother's belief that Griff had "found a better home." How could there be a better home than with them?

At first it had been fun, sort of like camping, or like being in an army on the march. You packed up every few days and moved out, but if you made any new friends, you left them behind and might never see them again. He missed his old friends, Daniel and Terry, and he never stopped missing Griff. They no longer had Internet access or cell phones—those had been cut off before they even moved out—and since free public wifi had been banned (in the National Right to Internet and Telecommunications Freedom Act), he had no way to stay in touch with his old friends or his new ones. The first few days they took their meals in fast-food restaurants, but since then they ate what they could cook on a fire, or, if they were in a Ryanville where fires weren't allowed, they had cold sandwiches. The boy thought of his old house, and of Daniel and Terry and Griff, and dreamed that maybe in the next place, in this Nevada, they would have a little house and there would be kids there, not Daniel and Terry, he knew, but boys just like them, that he could have friends to go to school with.

"Mom, can we get a dog when we get our new house?" he asked.

THE TRAFFIC SLOWED COMING OUT of Mountain Pass. There was nothing on either side of the road but washed-out scrubland and dry canyon, yet Jeb had to keep tapping the brakes to slow down until finally the line of cars came to a halt, moving ahead just a car length at a time. Coming back toward them were more battered SUVs, filled with families with sad, angry expressions. A few were parked on the side of the road, men and women talking in small huddles.

The front passenger window on the Flex was broken, so Jeb rolled down the rear passenger window and shouted to a man wearing a backward Los Angeles Angels of Anaheim cap, "What's going on?"

"They're not letting anyone with California plates cross into Nevada if you can't show a confirmation e-mail from a Vegas hotel or have a credit score over 650."

"Credit score?"

"They're running your credit right there."

Jeb shook his head. Cars were turning out of the lane, making U-turns and heading back into California. He was about twenty cars from a police roadblock—four squad cars, a half-dozen officers, and a black command post that had been pulled out by a semi-tractor.

The police were checking IDs and then running licenses through handheld devices, checking credit scores.

"What are we gonna do?" asked Bailey.

Jeb pulled forward slowly. "What *can* we do?"

Sargam had turned her bike around and was now at Jeb's window, facing the other way. She flipped up her visor.

"I don't have any ID," she said.

Jeb and Bailey nodded.

"They're checking credit. I never heard of that before," Jeb said. "I guess they don't want Californians in Nevada. Don't want subprimes in all those houses."

Sargam pursed her lips, weighing her options. "I can't cross here. I'm going to find a back road in, take my bike down a trail if I have to."

"You do what you gotta do. We understand."

"You head back down to Mountain Pass, toward Barstow, find a cat road and see if you can back-door it into Nevada. Here." Sargam handed over another twenty dollars.

"We can't take this," Bailey said.

"Take it. You need it more than me. There's four of you."

"God bless you," Jeb said.

"Not God. It's just people. People helping people. That's all we got."

There were a few car lengths open ahead of Jeb. The traffic behind him was honking impatiently.

Sargam smiled at the young girl and little boy, then flipped down her visor.

She popped the bike into gear and was gone, a blur of white growing distant in the early-evening gray light.

THE BOY WATCHED HER GO. Again, he thought. Again. We make a friend. And then they're gone. And you never see them again, and that's because we don't have the Internet anymore, and how can you find someone without that?

You can't, the boy thought. Sargam was gone.

CHAPTER 2

GEMMA HAD NOT DRIVEN TO the Hamptons in years. Everyone she knew flew the HeliJitney. Still, apparently, there were enough service workers, locals, subprimes, and out-of-season tourists that the Montauk Highway was bumper-to-bumper once she exited the Sunrise Highway. Dusk was slipping; in a few minutes the light would pull back, leaving them in the passing headlight wash and the LCD dash displays. The girls watched their movie, the most recent iteration of the *Frozen* saga, on fold-down screens while the Range Rover idled forward. No wonder no one drove out to the Hamptons anymore, the trip had become impossible, a six-hour ordeal that took them through suburban and exurban wasteland—off-ramp America—Wendy's, Subways, Taco Bells, and cell towers as far as she could see. Only the plutocrats and their hoarding of acreage and local development ordinances had kept the Hamptons somewhat green—otherwise it would have been private airstrips right on the dunes. As it was, the roadside had been denuded of native dogwood and poplar, those species driven out by the hardier, invasive Kamchatka pine, which not only withstood aggressive pine beetles but actually thrived as it hosted them. The symmetrical, white-trunked, and spiney-needled trees proliferated, the Christmas-tree shape identical from sapling to full-grown tree—the prolific species took just eighteen months to grow to full forty-foot height. Their sap was particularly pungent, a turpentine-like odor that had been the subject of numerous comments on local websites. The K-pines were everywhere, a monoculture that was ruining the glens and dales of all but the wealthiest of plutocrats who could afford private botanists to introduce genetically modified strangler vines that could fight the K-pine invasion but then went on their own ecosystem rampage, driving out native vines and bushes. You missed these details when you flew.

The girls hadn't realized how odd it was to take the car to the Hamptons. They still had not fully recognized their reduced circumstances. Former necessities such as the HeliJitney, or, for that matter, the house on Nearer Lane, even the brownstone on Eighty-first—these were all slipping away, or had already slipped. Gemma had decided early on that she could either look at her girls and feel pity, or look at them as the reason she needed to be strong—and she forced herself to act the latter despite the truth of the former. They would suffer, more perhaps than Gemma, who had herself come from modest means and could, if she had to, return to them.

But the girls had only been wealthy; for them, this would be traumatic, and maybe that was why she had never sat down and had a talk with them about what they would and would not be doing going forward. When she had tallied up how much they spent in an average week—excluding tuition, books, uniforms, activity fees, security fees, athletic fees, and, the most inscrutable of all, hall fees—it was $2,100 per week on dance lessons (hip-hop, jazz, and ballet), piano lessons, math tutor, gymnastics, art, French, dressage, and cotillion. Per kid.

And there was the longer-term tragedy, the fact that they might never be able to escape from this life but would have to fend with the rest of those who had been left behind. She and the girls could never afford a sanctuary.

She would let them down gradually, she decided, as the school year ended, after which dance and gymnastics would simply not be renewed. She would tell the girls they were going to spend more time together, more family time. There would be fewer of everything, lessons, outfits, horses, dinners out, just, well, every-thing. But they would be fine, Gemma kept reassuring herself, they would be—

What was that?

They had turned off the Montauk Highway onto Nearer Lane after the sun had sunk, leaving only a faint residue of light. As she took the big elbow right along the ocean, she saw what seemed like some kind of giant podlike structure built right on the sand, in clear violation of all local ordinances, even if this was Padma Cohen's estate. Nobody can build a large, black-gray building right on the beach.

"Mommy, look—a whale," Ginny said from behind her.

And that was what it was, Gemma realized, a beached whale. Enormous. Flat-headed, gawking-eyed, battleship-gray flesh mottled and ribbed, almost grinning mouth swung open, tail bobbing in the shallow tide. It looked nothing like Melville's monster, more like a huge wind sock in a gentle breeze, alive. A reflective shine from her headlights bounced from its nose, if that's what you called the front of the beast.

"We have to help it," said Franny.

What they had to do, Gemma well knew, was clear out the beach house so they could rent it. Get the Range Rover cleaned so they could sell it. But they couldn't just leave this whale. Nobody else seemed to have noticed it yet. In season there would have been a crowd around it, of course: TV crews and jiggle-bellied billionaires snapping cell-phone photos and T-shirt hawkers already monetizing the incident. But now?

Gemma scanned the beach. Nobody.

What could they do?

She slowed down and pulled over, yanking the brake handle and then sitting for a moment. She dialed 911.

"East Hampton PD. Would you like premium or standard emergency services?"

"I need to report a whale."

"Ma'am, you've dialed 911. Premium or regular?"

"Um, I'm reporting an emergency."

"I take it you want standard. Please hold."

She had to wait three minutes until finally she heard, "Is this a police or fire emergency?"

"It's a whale. It's on the beach."

"On the beach? Is anyone injured? Is there a fire or medical or rescue emergency?"

"It's off Nearer Lane, about, oh, two houses from the inlet."

The operator said, "Hold on while I connect you to a lifeguard."

"A lifeguard?"

"Do you have any other suggestions?"

"Can you send an officer?" she asked, but the line was already ringing and soon connected to a voice-mail message saying there was no one to take the call but if this was an emergency she should hang up and dial 911.

"We have to help it," Ginny and Franny were insisting.

"How?" Gemma asked, before realizing her daughters were unlikely to know aquatic mammal resuscitation.

She removed a flashlight from the glove compartment, opened the door, and stepped out, unlocking her daughters' doors and helping them out. The girls argued briefly over who should hold the light before deciding they would switch every thirty seconds.

She left her headlights on and they walked in the bright field until they crossed the narrow bridge over the channel connecting the ocean to the shallow swamp inlet. They made their way down the public access path that Padma Cohen had been trying to have closed down for years, the sand tracking into their shoes. It was dark, the only illumination the half-moon, the Rover's headlights, and the flashlight. She walked gingerly along the path, her girls behind her, hand in hand in hand.

They reached the beach and removed their shoes. From an animal that big, Gemma found herself anticipating ear-trembling decibelage, a moist elephantine harrumph, or a Chewbacca-like moaning, but there was silence. Next to the crashing of the waves and the sizzle of breakwater receding over sand, there was a noticeable absence of noise coming from the beast. As they approached, this breathtaking silence shut down the girls' chatter about whether this was a sperm or pilot whale. They crossed the channel, the freezing water making them gasp and Gemma clinging tightly to the girls as they waded in up to their knees.

Gemma stopped about twenty feet from the beast. It was even larger than it had seemed from a distance, its weight and bulk now giving it a dimension that she had not felt from the road. She shined her light against the gray, bumpy, divoted side of the beast. About halfway down, the flesh was rougher, the ridges and bumps more pronounced, barnacles clinging to the skin until five feet above the sand, where they vanished. There, blubber eddied in cellulite-like patches as the flesh rose and then curved gradually out of sight, like the fuselage of an airplane. She could see where there were chunks taken out, healed wounds from a life spent at sea.

There was a smell, like ocean and seaweed and fish and kelp and sweat and meat and rot and blood and feces and dirt, an odor both obscene and attractive, like sniffing your genitals.

Ginny grabbed the flashlight and ran toward the animal, walking alongside and moving the oval of light up along the beast until she came to the eye.

They all gasped.

It was the size of a grapefruit, and black, with thick, catenary lids on top and below. Then it blinked. Once. A reaction to the light, apparently.

So it was definitely alive.

"Mom, can we keep it?" Ginny shouted.

Gemma saw flashing lights coming up Nearer Lane and a squad car parking after the bridge over the channel, then two illuminated cones of light emerging and bobbing over the sand, coming closer to the whale, Gemma, and the girls.

"Holy shit," said one of the police officers.

He shined a light on Gemma, then on the kids. "Excuse us, ma'am, didn't see you and the girls."

He turned his beam back on the whale and walked around the animal. "Wow. I've never seen anything like this."

"It's alive," Franny told them.

"It is?" the officer said. "How do you know?"

"It blinked."

"Here, look." Franny took the light from Ginny and walked over to the eye, directing the beam against it. Another blink.

"Holy shit!" said the officer.

In the dark, with their gray uniforms, it was hard to distinguish the officers from the whale, especially as they walked up close to it. But Gemma could locate them by the squawks and beeps their radios were making.

"Unit 6, Unit 6, what's your signal?"

"Unit 6, copy, uh, we have a 10-something. Signal—I don't know what this is. We need someone out here who knows what to do with a whale."

"Unit 6, ten-nine?"

"A whale, okay? I don't know the code for that."

"A whale?"

"Yeah."

"Like Orca?"

"Copy."

"What's the forty?"

"At 617 Nearer Lane, on the beach in front."

"Jesus. Right on the beach?"

"Copy."

"Well, we'll try to find a vet, like an expert."

"Tell him: He's gonna need a bigger boat."

"Ten-nine?"

"Nothing, a joke."

"Copy, over."

The officers walked back to where Gemma and the girls were standing in their light sweatshirts. Gemma was worried the girls would catch cold in the early-evening chill; their legs were exposed.

"Damn, that's a big fish," said one of the officers, who Gemma could now see was an Asian man with a dark mustache.

"Maybe they can just push it back in," said the other officer, a taller Caucasian. "Get a bulldozer or something and shove it."

"You can't do that," Ginny said. "It came here because it's sick. That's what we learned at school. They beach themselves because they are sick, or they're confused."

"From summer," Franny said.

"What?" Gemma said.

"From sonar," Franny corrected herself. "The sonar from the navy gets them confused."

Within a few minutes, a black, tubular aircraft appeared overhead, a news drone of some kind, shining a harsh, white spotlight on the whale, then on Gemma and the girls, and soon a few more headlights were making their way down Nearer Lane. Local reporters monitoring police-band radios wanted to be the first on the ground.

Gemma grabbed the girls. "Let's go, girls, the police will be able to handle this."

"We can't just leave," Franny said. "What about the whale?"

"Well, what are *we* going to do—"

"Holy shit!" both officers shouted almost at once. The drone's searchlight had swung out to the waves, where it illuminated a black mass that was bobbing there, a vast, undulating dark wall rising from the shallow water, its shape apparent by the black absence of stars and clouds. It was a second whale, heading onshore, seemingly riding the tiny breakers in an attempt to beach itself.

Gemma grabbed the girls and pulled them up the beach, behind the first whale. She wanted to run but Ginny and Franny held her hands. They had both started crying.

"Why is this happening?" Ginny said.

For some reason, one of the cops, the Asian, ran down toward the water and began waving his arms, as if the whale were a truck attempting to park illegally. With the next set of waves, the Leviathan bobbed up for an instant and then lunged forward, wiggling once against the sand, making the sound of boots on gravel. The cop turned around and ran away from the water, stumbling and falling into the sand and then scrambling on all fours to get away from the whale.

It felt like an invasion, Gemma thought, an army of monsters storming the beach. The second one was not as large as the first but shared the same flattish front end, the rough skin halfway down. The tide must have gone out since the first whale beached itself because the second whale stopped about half a body length from the first.

Coming from up the beach Gemma could hear the shouts of more folks running down toward them. The white spotlight now caught parts of both whales at the edge of its illuminated circle.

"We're going to have to cordon off the area," the Asian cop said, standing up and brushing sand from his trouser legs.

"What do they want?" Gemma asked.

The cop looked at her. "Who knows what a fish is thinking."

"They're not fish," Franny and Ginny both said simultaneously. "They're mammals."

A small crowd had gathered, reporters, more cops, a few housekeepers who had come out to see what was causing the commotion, and even the occasional owner out for an off-season weekend.

"Gemma?" a familiar woman's voice called out to her.

Gemma cringed. She did not want to run into anyone she knew, anyone from her old life with Arthur.

She turned to see Trudi Katz, a brunette who'd had so many plastic surgeries the only way to figure out her true age would be to carbon-date her. She was on her third husband, a private equity partner at The Carlyle Group.

Considering the recent news, Trudi would never have risked speaking to Gemma in public. But under cover of darkness she felt perfectly safe.

"Oh my God, isn't this something?" Trudi said, shining her light at Gemma instead of at the whales.

"It is."

"What are they going to do? They can't leave them here," Trudi said. "This side of the channel is private beach."

Gemma nodded, waiting for the inevitable turn in the conversation. Which came now.

"So sorry to hear about Arthur," Trudi said. "That was a surprise. To all of us."

"It certainly was," Gemma said. "Nobody was more surprised than me."

"Of course, dear. What are you going to do?"

"Nothing."

"But you can't just stay—"

Gemma pulled the girls away, mumbling that it was late. They had a long, full day tomorrow.

As they were walking up the beach, they heard panicked shouts, more screaming.

Another whale was beaching itself.

GEMMA CAUGHT HERSELF THINKING, "WELL, I've been through worse." But no, she would stop herself, she hadn't. This was the worst. This was the most difficult. Two daughters, two private school tuitions, the mortgage on the house in the Hamptons, the rent on the brownstone, and now, a husband going to prison.

The facts of the prosecutor's case for securities fraud, grand larceny, scheming to defraud, and forgery were starkly laid out, making it clear that Arthur had cheated their friends, colleagues, acquaintances, their doctor, mechanic, and even—really, Arthur?—their nanny and *their daughters' classmates' parents*. He had been portrayed in the *Post* as a uniquely sleazy scoundrel— "Arthur Ponzerelli"—and in the *FT* and *Wall Street Journal* as a particularly incompetent and unsophisticated financial amateur who had evaded detection as long as he had because he scammed his closest friends.

In the days after his arrest, the rest of his miserable subterfuge had come into focus, the mistresses, the apartments he kept for them, his managing to swindle even his mistresses and *their* parents. Gemma shuddered as she thought about her own mother and how close she had been to taking out a mortgage on the house in Santa Monica and investing her life savings with Arthur.

She refused to visit him at Rikers. And had to explain to Ginny, their oldest, when she came back from first grade asking "What does 'slammer' mean?" that it meant prison, but that her father was not in prison but away on an extended business trip.

If Arthur had spirited many millions into offshore accounts in the Cayman Islands or Hong Kong, he was denying it. When investigators found only a paltry few million, a fraction of what had been lost by Arthur's investors, they concluded he had not only been running a scheme, but that he himself had been suckered by schemers only marginally more legal in their operations than he had been. This made perfect sense to Gemma: Arthur was feckless and inept in every area of life. The idea that he was a criminal mastermind was as preposterous as the notion that he could be a financial wizard. How their friends had fallen for it, Gemma had never understood. But Arthur talked a good game, with his professed expertise in carbon credits and emissions certificates and the various financial instruments that allowed global companies to pollute and belch forth the noxious fog that gave New York's skyline—every skyline—its perpetually gray tint. Arthur, or so he claimed, was the middleman, buying up the polluter rights of small companies and selling them for a handsome profit to Indian, Chinese, and Brazilian corporations. He would then sell hedges to these same companies so that the credits themselves would not devalue before they were used, and then sell these hedges to investors who were looking to go long in the carbon credit market without actually owning the under-lying carbon credits, and then allowing those investors looking to hedge their long positions to issue yet more instruments, the so-called C3DS3s—Carbon Credit Credit Default Swap Swap Swaps.

Eventually he was buying and holding instruments the workings of which he had absolutely no understanding. Gemma felt a twinge of guilt for not asking more questions about Arthur's business, for wanting to believe that her simpleton of a husband was an idiot savant of energies and commodities trading when she knew full well it could take him a good ninety seconds to calculate twenty-two percent of a restaurant check. She had enjoyed the perks, the real estate, the sense that the planet was turning to shit but that their family would be among the lucky ones with money enough, some-day, for a sanctuary homestead on a private, hydro-rich island, an option all their wealthy friends were planning.

Arthur had quite a run, and whenever Gemma caught a clip of him on the news, going to or from the lower Manhattan courts, he always appeared defiant and dapper. His attorneys were couching his defense in terms of Arthur running afoul of envi-ronmental extremists and their overzealous regulations, which were causing legitimate businessmen like Arthur Mack—a job creator!—to have to defend themselves in court for the simple crime of wanting to help American businesses grow. Arthur was a good capitalist who should be celebrated rather than incar-cerated, one of his attorneys told a CNBC anchor, who nodded seriously before asking, "But why the witch hunt?"

"Arthur Mack loves America," said his blue-suited attorney

with the clerical fringe of hair around his shiny dome. "Arthur Mack was investing in America, in job creating, in energy independence, in gas and oil and our carbon fuel future. He is being punished for not being green. This is pure eco-Nazi monkey-wrenching."

It was a surprising strategy, grandstanding in lieu of a reasoned legal defense, but it seemed to be confusing the usual media outlets. None of the reporters had the will or inclination to actually try to understand the exact nature of Arthur's alleged fraud, and so they were resorting to bogus, balanced coverage, mentioning in every story both the indictments and fraud charges *and* the brazenly ridiculous defense. The New York media were caught in a bipolar frenzy: "What do the whales want? And is Arthur Mack the victim of an environmentalist conspiracy?"

AS GEMMA PACKED UP THE kids' rooms, their plush toys and Legos and pop-up books divided into "keep," "put into storage," or "trash"—she had explained that they couldn't bring it all back to the city because they would be sharing a room in the new apartment, farther east, much farther, on First Avenue, in fact—she felt guilty for what the girls were losing in the here and now, and in the future. They would be regular people. And, Gemma had to admit, considering what the world had become, regular had come to seem horrible.

When they woke up the next morning, the girls wanted to go online to see about the whales. A half-dozen had washed up so far. The story was leading the TV news, and in daylight aerial-drone shots, the huge gray whales looked like giant bloated worms on the sand. A marine biologist on CNN was talking about how the powerful low-frequency sonar pings used by the

U.S. Navy, the loudest sounds ever made underwater, could cause severe hemorrhaging in the animals, making them sick and driving them ashore.

"They are killing themselves?" the anchor asked.

"They are asking for help," the marine biologist responded.

On another network was a Texas preacher, Pastor Roger, who declared that the whales were a sign from God that the government was overregulating the offshore drilling industry. "He is sending us a message: Drill, baby, drill."

Gemma urged the girls to eat breakfast and get to work sorting their stuff. She wanted to be on the road back to the city by this evening and she did not want the girls catching an image of their father in the event the network needed to fill time with additional coverage of his case. Gemma had learned to avoid all their friends, all her daughters' friends' parents, virtually everyone they knew, but what was hardest to control was the media's hounding, their staking-out of their apartment building and the girls' school. They moved to a hotel downtown for a few days until the original coverage ebbed.

Gemma had always prided herself on being street-smart. She made her way from Santa Monica High School to the music department at ICM—okay, she handled Contemporary Classical, not exactly a profit center for the agency, but still, very impressive for a girl who had never gone to college. Her weakness was always Continental men, and since her arrival in Manhattan at twenty-three, she had gone through a succession of Jean-Claudes and Antonios and Juan-Carloses until she met Arthur, a dude's dude. He, too, had come east, from Newport Beach to Manhattan, where he claimed to be an energies trader at Merrill Lynch, though it turned out he was a retail broker at a local Merrill branch. He had blond hair, a dozen or so freckles on each cheek, thin lips (perpetually grinning, it seemed), and gapped teeth. He had a knack, Gemma noticed shortly after their first meeting at a friend's summer share, of fitting in with any crowd. No, that wasn't it, he didn't fit in so much as come forward as such a winning example of a type, the unflappable banker bro with surfer's diction and a knack for the winning anecdote, the funny riff, the back-slapping, shit-eating-grinned delight he took in just being able to say a word like "tranche," which he would repeat over and over again to himself, a symptom, Gemma now believed, of a kind of mild autism.

Oh, but he had always been a fine-looking man, with his pleasingly thick dirty-blond hair, rectangular head, wide forehead, thick brows, prominent cheekbones, and the self-confidence of having been a terrific three-sport athlete (volleyball, tennis, and surfing) in high school. Women took one look at him and never questioned why Gemma was with him.

But she knew, she had known all along: he was a total idiot. Gemma cursed her own superficiality for ever having fallen for the whole package. She poured herself a glass of 2005 Domaine Armand Rousseau—the cellar was going to be sold or seized anyway, so she might as well drink its best bottles.

She sipped her wine and listened to her daughters upstairs. She hated Arthur precisely for the fact that she was now joined for life with him, because of the girls. Now, as Gemma considered the hurried packing they had to do, the emptying of the house before it could be leased, so that the mortgage could be serviced lest the bank foreclosed, she felt a kind of fatigue and exhaustion at the work ahead of her. She stood up, wineglass in one hand, and with her other swept a dozen books from an open-sided built-in bookcase onto the floor, where they fell with a slapping sound.

"Mom? What was that?"

"Nothing. Books."

The girls, she had to keep her shit together for the girls.

We wanna see the whales. We wanna see the whales. Gemma had been listening to this chorus from her daughters for three days. The best technology that reality television, network journalism, and the marine mammal rescue industry could afford had been unable to return the half-dozen gray whales to the Atlantic. The good news was their ascendance as media stars gradually drove her husband's mug shot off the news. Now it was all about *Whale Watch,* as the entertainment industrial complex converged on East Hampton with anchormen and reality television environmentalists—craggy-faced, bearded, in slickers and ponchos, studying tidal programs on their laptops and barking into handheld radios—why did they even need radios? Cell coverage out here was excellent. A half-dozen beached whales, which should have diverted the nation's attentions from the usual television frivolities to refocus on something real, were instead becoming fuel for *more* frivolity as shows sprang up on every network and cable news station with titles like *Long Island Aquacalypse, The Whalocaust,* and *Real Whales of East Hampton.* The Coast Guard's solution to getting the whales back into the ocean had been to let the private sector work its magic by auctioning the media rights and allowing the debeaching to become a reality program. It was brilliant: let the free market free the whales. Fox had won the bidding, paying millions to the Coast Guard and the township of East Hampton and immediately installing construction barriers around the precious telegenic mammals to block competing networks and paying the FAA to close the airspace above the beach to rival news drones. The oceanographers, aquatic veterinarians, and marine animal rescue team members who were working on freeing the whales were required to sign release forms. If they resisted, they were offered $500 a day. If they further resisted, they were ordered off the beach and replaced with willing, screened oceanographers and veterinarians who were better-looking anyway, more racially diverse, and had already disclosed in casting meetings their various personal, and potentially dramatic, problems, ranging from sex addiction to alcoholism to bipolar disorder.

The whales, meanwhile, were dying. A beached whale could survive seventy-two hours in the best of circumstances, its lungs slowly crushed by gravity. Even with hoses spraying salt water, steady applications by increasingly intoxicated marine rescue team members of a saline and kelp blend, and krill fired into their perpetually grinning mouths, the whales seemed to be worsening. For the half hour a day that Fox opened the airspace to rival news drones—it was viewed as good promotion—the crews were ordered to operate with apparent professionalism, though more than one anchorman wondered why the digging of the channels from the high tide to the whales was taking so long. And the day that a bulldozer's plow gouged a two-yard chunk of flesh from a stranded whale's tail stock there was no media access at all as the veterinarians sought to stanch the blood and fight off the hordes of seagulls that descended to feast on the exposed meat.

There were hundreds of reporters killing days in their satellite vans or drinking at the Beach House, and in their frustration they were door-stopping local residents to ask them what they thought of Whalemageddon. Gemma's intercom had been buzzing steadily with reporters asking to speak with "a resident," none of the reporters actually realizing that she was a principal in the last story they had cared about. When she told them to stop buzzing and that she wasn't interested in talking about the whales, they stumbled back down her driveway and on to the next house. Still, she couldn't make her daily five-mile run down the beach and was reduced to running on the treadmill in the basement fitness room. The neighborhood had gone to the whales.

The broker, an attractive brunette in a pressed white blouse and gray slacks, told Gemma she could get $20,000 a month year round, or $60,000 a month between Memorial Day and Labor Day.

"Why?" Gemma asked. "The weather doesn't work anymore. What difference does it make when you rent it?"

It had hit eighty degrees one day last January. And it had snowed before Labor Day.

The broker nodded. Gemma suspected the broker knew who she was but was too polite to mention it.

"Tradition," the broker said and shrugged.

"I just want to rent it. Now. I don't want to wait."

"We'll send our guys out here to photograph it today."

The broker gave a smile that Gemma detested for the sympathy she perceived. Or was this the usual default smile of a woman who worked in a business where pleasing buyers and sellers started with a vacant grin?

Franny and Ginny had become bogged down sorting through their old toys. And these were only the second-tier toys, the stuff that had not been loved enough to make it back to the city. How long would it take them to sort through the city toys? Gemma had been tempted to toss every photo of Arthur into the plastic garbage bags but decided, for her daughters' sake, that she had to save a few. She went through the bedrooms, tossing out old magazines, boxing up books, and trying to figure out what to do with the various driftwood and seashell tchotchkes that inhabited coffee tables and bookshelves. She picked up a carton filled with seashells and coral bits and conch and took it out on the deck to the wooden railing that lined the pool and cast the marine detritus back onto the beach.

She walked over to the pool and opened the doors to the slatted wooden chests where the pool equipment and aquatic toys were kept, the masks, snorkels, goggles, noodles, and flippers that at the end of a summer day were strewn all over the deck. She began to gather the rubber gear, some of it still sandy, but then dropped it. Whoever rented the place could use all this stuff as well.

She walked back to the edge of the deck, which had been built years ago, in contravention of local ordinances, over the sea-grassy dunes. The cloud cover was thick above her, giving way at the horizon, where a sliver of golden light and blue sea extended in a long strip as far as she could see in both directions. The appearance of that strip of light to the east was momentarily disorienting, making Gemma feel as if it were early morning instead of midafternoon.

A few hundred seagulls standing at attention on the beach, facing the whales, were patiently awaiting the dying that they sniffed in the breeze. What was worse—humans feasting on the spectacle or seagulls hoping for an actual feast?

She would leave tonight if she could.

CHAPTER 3

N THIS CLIMACTIC AGE OF American capitalism, the end-game, I suspect, where the forces of profit and avarice are putting the final squeeze on all of us and we find ourselves subsiding in a denuded wasteland of McMansions, succumbing to antibiotic-resistant strains of mutated microbes or shriveling as our multiplying tumors are excised from our bodies and watching our final generation of obese, attention-deficit-disordered children grow up functionally illiterate and capable only of sliding their thick fingers across touch screens until finally the Chinese think of a product that all this American flesh can be made into—sofas, perhaps, an appropriate use for couch potatoes—I find myself still plying my trade despite all evidence to the contrary.

Getting through full days of this shit—watching the world end fucking sucks—requires some of the strongest weed ever grown. My marijuana provided now by the same companies that formerly retailed cigarettes—Atria, R. J Reynolds, Liggett—and that have driven the mom-and-pop medical marijuana shops out of business.

This is what it's come to. In my early middle age, I've become a more grown-up version of the stoner I was at sixteen, only now I can afford better weed and munchies. But the rest of it, my life, if you actually followed the path of my day, like one of those *Family Circus* cartoons where a dotted line traces the activities of the young rascal of an afternoon, would make Mr. Farnsworth and Mrs. Shirley, two high school teachers who foretold my adult fecklessness, feel smug.

For my journey through my day lacks a specific vigor. I do the minimum. I try to prepare the children for school, pack their lunches, even drive them on late mornings or when they can't be compelled to walk, contributing, in this way and many others, to the carbon-emissions nightmare we have careened toward in our SUVs—I still drive a hybrid, grandfathered in from when hybrids and electric cars were still legal—and, for the most privileged among us, private jets. I am the adequate father of Ronin and Jinx, the boy thirteen and the girl ten; ex-husband of Anya, former wife of fourteen years. I knew having children was an awful idea; it invests you. Suddenly, the malignant activities of man, our tireless turning-to-shit of everything around us, of ourselves, even, all makes us anxious because of them. Our kids will have to live in all this shit, shit that we have all made. We suck.

So, however long it takes to get from here to Armageddon, until we are more tumor than human, until our Earth is more landfill than land, until our seas are more plastic bags than H_2O, I have to keep muddling through, providing for a family; making sure my children are clothed, fed, vaccinated; getting pipes snaked and modems rebooted and cats defleaed.

Or, at least I did when there were still cats.

Remember cats? They were cute.

WHILE I'M WALKING TO MY office, down the narrow, putatively charming streets, Iliff, Albright, Bashford, lined with two-story Cape Cod–style houses, the bulk of these monstrosities too big for the lots, crowding out the vestigial front yards that are too small for any children to play catch on, much more mount a touch football game, if any children can be induced to look up from PlayStation 7 or X^3-Box long enough to consider an actual game involving sticks and balls instead of paddles and joysticks, I see jogging past me a woman, attractive, freckled face, narrow reddish neck, tanned clavicle, Lycra T-shirt. She wears headphones, of course, and sunglasses, and runs on her heels, her skintight jodphur-like trousers making swishing noises as she passes. And behind her trails a pointy-snouted dog, sharp-eared, high curled tail, tongue hanging from a mouthful of glistening teeth. No collar. Gray and rust coat. The canine regards me warily as it trots past. It takes me a few seconds but . . . that's no dog.

That's a coyote. In high morning, a full six hours past its bedtime. And this nasty creature is padding along, stalking, apparently, a jogger.

What did I say? About end times?

"Hey, lady," I shout. "Miss! HEY!"

Her headphones drown me out.

The two of them, jogger and coyote, are moving too fast. I hesitate to give chase. But I turn, trot after them, waving my hands, the coyote turning to watch me for a moment, as if to confirm, yes, a human is chasing me. Ah, the hunter is now the hunted! The coyote's eyes are green-brown, pupils slit and appraising, also inquisitive, as if—is this guy, this man, this biped, serious?

He yips. High-pitched, followed by a long, drawn-out growl that sounds almost thoughtful.

Who does this mutt think he is talking to? I retain the pride in being of the species *Homo sapiens*, still ruler of this planet. The coyotes are inheriting the Earth, of course, up to twenty pups a litter, vast tracts of foreclosed homes to thrive in and around, their only natural predator, the mountain lion, having been driven to extinction. And for years they've been growing fat on domesticated cats, who themselves are in danger of extinction. They've moved up the food chain and lately have been increasingly attacking humans. But can't you, coyote, wait just a decade or two? Then all this will be yours.

Then from behind me I hear clicking noises, paws and claws on concrete, and I turn and see trotting on the road behind me another pair of coyotes. And making fast progress beside me on the lawn above a white retaining wall is another. They all run in the same tongue-dangling-from-mouth manner, and they look past me, as if they aren't interested in me at all, as if they are just having a little trot, a midmorning constitutional.

Yet we are—I am—being hunted. Did coyotes begin hunting humans in broad daylight when they ran out of cats?

When I turn back to the jogger, the coyote in front of me is gone and I see the jogger's shapely posterior just a few strides ahead of me. I seem to have accelerated.

I can pass the woman, leave her to her fate, but instead I decide to stop her and warn her of the situation. Perhaps we can trot to my house, or to my car, drive to have coffee, laugh about our moment in the food chain.

But when I reach out to touch her arm, she jumps and slows down, removing her headphone from one ear.

"Coyotes," I say and jerk my thumb over my shoulder.

She looks over her shoulder. "What are you talking about?"

I look back again.

The animals have vanished.

I suddenly see the situation from her point of view: bedraggled, somewhat hairy and wild-looking pedestrian comes out of nowhere and accosts her, claiming a nocturnal animal is stalking her at eleven a.m.

"Don't you dare touch me," she says, "or I'll Mace your face."

Her right hand comes up with a pepper-spray bottle, which she fires at my head.

I gag, cough, and sprint forward just to get out of the cloud of gas. "You said 'OR,'" I gasp. "You said 'OR I'll Mace you.' And I didn't touch—"

"Fuck you, subprime," she shouts and runs ahead.

My face hurts, the inside of my nostrils, my throat, my esophagus, my larynx, my mouth, my tongue, everything is stinging, burning as if I have been submerged in Tabasco. And the more I breathe, the more I burn.

I lie down on the grassy berm between the curb and the sidewalk, trying to take shallow breaths, trying not to breathe at all, waiting for the pain to subside.

But it never really does.

IN MY OFFICE THERE IS a metallic desk covered with paper that is itself coated with a layer of soot, the sediment left by the thick clouds of particulate smog that back up against our mountains, turning the sky its orange-brown, the leaves gray, even giving my snot a black tinge. The soot is piled so thick where the desk meets the wall that it has made a small filth dune. My corner office faces east and north, there is a cocktail sign for the bar downstairs on the outside where those two walls meet, a red neon cursive that blinks on at dusk. I have a metallic bookcase and a metallic chair with a rust-colored seat, all of this furniture the surplus of a local tool-and-die company bought by the Chinese decades ago.

I am surrounded by self-help professionals. There is a life coach next door, a blond woman of indeterminate age with an impressive bust who makes her visitors take off their shoes and leave them beneath a stool outside her office. There is an immense black woman next door to her who drives a dune buggy and practices some sort of aromatherapy. There is a woman who wears sandals and works in an office with a sign on the door that says "Creative Success Strategies." I'm not sure what any of these people actually do, but there's apparently a huge business in seeking to assuage the bad feelings of the many.

I sometimes feel like stopping their clients and telling them that they feel bad because things are actually getting shittier. "It's not you. It's the whole world." But I just walk past them to my office, where I drop my backpack and then go out to the men's room to wash more pepper spray off my face.

I have a career. Or had one. I am something of a fluke in that I make a living from writing: list articles, stories for longform fetishists, books every so often. I was fortunate in that I started when journalism was a vast and thriving field: I was a writer for *Time* and then *Sports Illustrated*, secured contracts at profligate start-ups and the relaunched *Bloomberg Businessweek*. I turned one of my early articles into a popular book, *What You Wish For*, about a small town in Pennsylvania that became environmentally devastated, but wealthy, through fracking, and was then destroyed by petty infighting and alcoholism, like a village of drunken lottery winners. I've done nothing of comparable quality or success since, but editors and content curators still recognize my name. I'm a hack, but at least hackery supports my family, or has supported us. Amid the great prairie fire of media failure, I have thrived. Though I owe everyone stories. I am perpetually behind, and falling further.

Lawsuits were the best thing ever to happen to my career. No magazine wants to fire a writer who is a codefendant in a multimillion-dollar libel suit. So the great empire of Bloomberg and I are still in business, only because their lawyers don't want to risk turning me against the company. I remain on the draw, a modest sum sloshing into my bank account every month as my latest lawsuit trudges its way through the courts.

My editor at Bloomberg calls, a smart man, Rajiv, who is second in command.

"Larry Ellison," he says.

This is what editors do. They call me up and say a name.

I sometimes say one back.

"Sean Parker."

He seems to think about this and then says:

"Andrew Mason."

I don't know who that is, so I Google him. I quickly come up with a reply.

"Reed Hastings."

That seems to have satisfied him.

"Let me think about that and get back to you."

I can picture him on the third floor of the Bloomberg building, sitting behind his terminal, which I am sure he doesn't know how to operate.

I decide to have a little fun with him and ask for a bond quote, which, if he actually knew how to use the terminal, would be easy.

"Hey," I say to Rajiv, "can you tell me what GE '28 five and halfs are trading at?"

"Fuck you," he says. "Hey, stop getting sued, okay?"

He hangs up.

I am about to open up an e-mail from Bloomberg's lawyer, who recently, and correctly, deduced that the story on the Texas mega-preacher Pastor Roger, whose chapel is a converted football stadium, was so poorly reported that to call it a fabrication would be giving me too much credit. I had indeed made a key error in claiming that Pastor Roger participated in a college danceathon in support of Planned Parenthood while he was at Oral Roberts. But there was so much else wrong with my story, the preacher's age, wife's name, number of children, grad school, and so forth, that it would be hard for him to claim malice or libelous intent. Because I got EVERYTHING wrong. The lawyer, Ed Minskoff, was delighted when he discovered just how badly I had fucked up.

"Stupidity *is* a defense," he said in a conference call that included many of Bloomberg's top brass.

"You just have to be you" was how Rajiv paraphrased the defense strategy, should I be called to testify.

The lawyer sends out weekly updates as to the progress of the case. Pastor Roger, who among other things scoffed at the notion of global warming and climate change and government regulation to ensure clean drinking water and *E. coli*–free produce, was on television just yesterday claiming again that there was still so much space in the United States that every family in America could have a five-bedroom home with a three-car garage and a backyard and that wouldn't even fill up Texas! In his sermons he insists that God gave us oil and gas and land and grain, the animals, the plants, "the rocks, the dust, the oceans, the sky, it's all ours! And that doesn't mean just that part of the Earth the federal government says is our 'dominion,' that means ALL of the Earth."

And I had made the mistake of saying he had once raised money for Planned Parenthood.

Pastor Roger was demanding $25 million and an apology on the cover of *Bloomberg Businessweek*.

I had expected Ed Minskoff to be more stern with me, but then I realized that not only were my lawsuits keeping me employed, they were also keeping Ed Minskoff employed.

As I light up my first joint of the day, an Altria Strawberry Cough, I think that by now even those editors most disposed to give me a break must be tiring of my lousy performance. Surely, this has to be coming to an end. Then what will I do?

Thank God for my lawsuits.

"THIS IS MARK NAKAMURA, VICE principal here at the Subway Fresh Take Paul Revere Charter Middle School, can you call us back as soon as you get this?"

Ronin was called into the vice principal's office, I am told when I call back. There has been an incident.

"Is he okay? What kind of incident?" I ask.

I am too high to deal with this. Shit.

"Can you or his mother come and pick him up?" Mark Nakamura says. "He's physically intact."

"What does that mean? Is something wrong?"

"We'll discuss it with you or Ronin's mother when you get here. Sign in at the C Building, please."

I call Anya, but she doesn't pick up. She never does. She must be at yoga. I have to trot home, still coughing up bits of my pepper-spiced lung as I go, the bad parts, I hope.

Sunset Boulevard from PCH to the 405 has been closed for three years, the outside lanes having finally become more pothole than road and collapsing into actual sinkholes for long stretches. Since the privatization of the Los Angeles County Department of Public Works, pothole repair has completely ceased; the department's resources are now focused entirely on the building of more profitable elevated toll roads connecting Beverly Hills and Malibu to the private aviation terminals at Santa Monica Airport and LAX.

So I sit in traffic in the thick haze of marine smog. The oil rigs offshore—the scandal over their having been drilled one mile closer to the beach than the oil companies had promised had passed in one news cycle—stretch to the horizon like an invading army of black beetles.

At the C Building I sign in, receiving a coupon good for one dollar off on a foot-long sub, and am directed to Vice Principal Nakamura's office, outside of which I see my son sitting with his backpack on his thighs. Ronin has thin brown hair that has grown to shoulder length, a semicircular forehead, thin, surprisingly arched eyebrows, and dark brown eyes. He also has my ex-wife's nose, slender, with large nostrils, her pronounced chin and long neck, and my thick lower lip. He was a cute boy, and still is, though in his current preferred outfit of painter's cap, noise-reduction headphones, black T-shirt, black pegged denims, and high-top skate shoes, he looks more like a member of a struggling boy band working the drive-thru window to pay for his hip-hop dance lessons.

Behind him is a cartoon of Paul Revere riding with a sandwich in each hand above a caption reading: "Two if by land." (Does this even make sense? I am so stoned I am having trouble following the logic of it. Two if by land, that was the signal from the Old North Church; it had nothing to do with Paul Revere, or did it? I can't remember.)

Ronin's eyes are red. He has been crying.

"What's going on, Rone?"

Before he can answer, Vice Principal Nakamura walks around his desk and out the door to greet me.

"You're Mr. Schwab? I'm going to have Dean of Student Affairs Ramos sit in."

"Sit in on what?"

"We're going to go over the incident."

I take a seat facing Vice Principal Nakamura. Behind him is a filing cabinet upon which sits a glass plaque on a black base: "Los Angeles Area 5 Administrator of the Year." Vice Principal Nakamura gets up and closes the door. I catch a last glimpse of Ronin, his right leg pumping his backpack up and down.

"We'll begin. Ms. Ramos will join shortly."

My heart rate has climbed and I have a terribly dry mouth. I need a breath mint, or a glass of water. I feel that if called upon to speak, I will be unable to part my tongue from the roof of my mouth.

If I understand Vice Principal Nakamura (and suddenly I am not sure I understand anything), Ronin is being accused of sexual harassment. A teacher, Ms.——

There is a knock at the door and in walks Ms. Ramos, an Asian woman with a rigid perm and a large mole next to her nose.

(It is a very large mole, so large as to be verging on the freakish. It's barely smaller than a dime. Or is that not so big at all? Are many moles actually that big and I'm just focusing on this one because it is the only mole in the room? I have to stop looking at Ms. Ramos's mole.)

Ms. Maddoxx observed Ronin inappropriately touching another student.

(I am going to do it, I am going to open my mouth, I am going to unstick my tongue from my palate. There. I've done it. It sounded like old wallpaper being peeled from stucco.)

"Inappropriately? How?" I ask. "He's thirteen."

(Did I play the age card too early? I need to focus.)

"The contact was observed by a teacher. It involved, it was, a hand, the . . . uh"—Vice Principal Nakamura looks down at his notes—"the right hand was placed on the buttocks of a female student."

Ms. Ramos's mole quivers, and then she speaks. "It was a surreptitious fondling of the buttocks. A predatory act—"

"Whoa, whoa," I say. I need to slow this whole thing down. Is this really happening? "Predatory? Ronin is thirteen."

(Shit, I just said that again.)

Vice Principal Nakamura nods. "We are aware of our students' ages and the parameters of age-appropriate behavior."

"And this," says Ms. Ramos, "is not appropriate at any age."

"Is the girl that upset?" I ask. "Who was it?"

"We can't tell you the student's name. Her response is not germane. Her parents have been informed. At this point, she is completely removed from this incident and will no longer be apprised of any action taken against Ronin."

"Action? What action?" I ask.

"Sexual harassment will not be tolerated in our school. The Subway Fresh Take Paul Revere Middle School code of student conduct makes that very clear."

(I am about to say it again: He's thirteen. But I stop myself.)

"Look, did he know the girl? I mean, kids do this stuff. They grab ass. We all did it."

Vice Principal Nakamura and Ms. Ramos glance at each other in such a way that I can tell they never played grab-ass.

"We've suspended Ronin for two days," Vice Principal Nakamura says. "He will spend lunches in Concentration. And he is required to attend a Youth Sexual Conduct and Guidance seminar once a week. It meets in the library after school on Tuesdays. We have also told him that until further notice he is not to have any out-of-class one-on-one contact with any female student. At least until the conclusion of the seminar. This was my recommendation, and Ms. Ramos agrees with me."

"What's Concentration?" I ask.

"It's a room that is staffed during lunch where a student may think about his actions."

"You actually call it 'Concentration'? Is it surrounded by an electrified barbed-wire fence?"

They don't appreciate my comment.

"No contact?" I ask. "What does that mean. He can't talk to a girl?"

"Oh, he can talk to a female, just not out of class or in a one-on-one situation."

I purse my lips. "But it seems as if . . . as if what is needed here is a good talking-to. An explanation: You can't, you know, grab ass."

"Mr. Schwab. I don't think 'grab *a-word* is a useful teaching expression."

"But a ban? On talking to girls? This just seems like an awful lot of punishment."

"This is serious, Mr. Schwab. We have a legal responsibility here, as do you."

Ah, I think, *that's what this is about. Nobody wants a lawsuit.*

"Please, talk to your son, have a serious talk about this, about sexuality, perhaps, based on his curiosity in the opposite sex. Perhaps it is time to have the talk about contraception."

"If he's not allowed to even talk to a girl, I don't think Ronin is going to be getting to first base, forget about scoring."

There is a long silence.

Of course they don't consider the baseball scoring system to be an appropriate method for describing teen sexual behavior.

IN THE CAR ON THE way home, as we drive down San Vincente, past the artificial palm trees that now line the median island, I ask Ronin for his version of events.

He is seated in the passenger seat, his backpack at his feet. "I don't want to talk about it. Dad, it's embarrassing." His voice is on the precipice of changing, it slips occasionally, dropping an octave or two, before scrambling back up to his boyish tenor.

"I've heard the school's version of events, and I need to hear yours."

"What did they say?"

"That you . . . that you grabbed another student."

"'Grabbed'?"

"I don't think they used that word. They said 'inappropriate touching.'"

"Whatever," he says, his voice dropping, then rising. "That is so retarded."

"Was there any touching?"

"I pinched Ashley McDaniels's butt. Like, once. Hard. She liked it."

"How do you know she liked it?"

"She smiled. She smiled when I did it yesterday, and then we walked together to English."

"Did you ask her if she liked it?"

"No, that would be embarrassing."

"But it's not embarrassing to pinch her butt?"

"No, because she smiled at me afterward. But you can't go, like, 'Do you like when I pinch your butt?' That would be weird."

He made sense. In these matters, between a man and a woman, or a boy and a girl, certain things are best left unsaid.

"Okay, but you understand why Vice Principal Nakamura is sending you to Concentration and to that special after-school thing."

"He said I have to go to Freaks?"

"No, it's this after-school program where you are going to talk about, you know, growing up and stuff."

"That's Freaks. And I'm NOT GOING TO FREAKS."

MY EX-WIFE IS ANGRIER WITH the school than with me. She lives a few miles away in a rented house overlooking a canyon where she is waiting when I drop Ronin off and explain the reasons for his suspension. She wants to hire a lawyer, she wants to sue the school, she believes our son is being defamed and the school is overreacting. All of which may be true, but I'm not sure we can make much of a case.

"He pinched a girl's butt?" she says. "So what? He's a boy. Boys and girls are supposed to play with each other in this way. It's normal."

"They disagree. This is the new normal."

She studies me. "Have you had a puff?"

I shake my head. "I was pepper-sprayed."

She is about to go down this conversational path but then stops herself, staying on subject. "They can't do this."

My ex-wife has short black hair with fishhook-shaped, skull-hugging curls that hang over her ears, a narrow forehead, the long, slender nose. She has a pleasingly ovoid face, perfectly symmetrical; babies smile when they look at her. Her skin is surprisingly clear and largely unwrinkled, the first infinitesimally small canyons in the flesh now radiating from her narrow, almost Asian-shaped blue eyes.

Anya is still in her yoga togs: tight leggings, sports bra. When we met we were the same height, but while I have spent the last fifteen years slouching, she has been stretching, for yoga, for Pilates, for bar method, for capoeira, for parkour, for yoga-

Pilates, for bar-yoga, for parkoeira. The women in her family are all long and slender, and Anya accentuates that with her predisposition to a bland, tasteless diet of high-fiber cereals and breads and high-antioxidant fruits and vegetables. Whenever a new food is found to have wondrous antiaging or anticancer benefits, it will turn out that Anya has been eating it by the bushel her whole life.

I like to eat steak.

If when we met it was plausible that a woman like her might entertain a man like me—she was better-looking, a model actually, but in my prime I had a certain rogueish, Keanu Reeves charm. Now we would be walking proof that men and women don't always marry commensurately attractive partners.

"Did you pinch a girl's butt?" Anya asks Ronin. "Without her asking?"

"Who asks 'Will you pinch my butt?'? God, this is so embarrassing."

"Who is she? Let's talk to her parents," Anya suggests.

Ronin runs to his room. "NO!"

"We can't talk to her parents. We're not even supposed to know who it is. He has to do some special classes, some after-school thing where they talk about sexuality."

"Because of this?"

I nod.

Anya says, "Ronin shouldn't be singled out because of this incident. That's wrong."

There is so much going wrong I'm not sure this is where we should be taking a stand.

As I'm driving back down to my house, Rajiv calls me from Bloomberg.

"It's awfully late to still be at your terminal," I say.

"Arthur Mack," he says.

Are we playing this game again?

"Evan Spiegel," I say.

"No, I mean can you do Arthur Mack? He's already indicted. Richie, not even you can get sued by a guilty man. Here, wait."

A moment of silence as he attends to something.

"I just sent you Ms. Mack's mother's address. That's where she's staying. In Santa Monica, near you."

Back home, I light up a Strawberry Cough spliff and Google photos of Gemma Mack. Gemma and Arthur at a museum fundraiser, Gemma and Arthur at a party in the Hamptons, Gemma and Arthur at a hospital benefit. She never smiles; instead, she stares blankly at the camera as if she just wants the shot to be over. Arthur grins widely, as though he has just been told a hilarious joke; he is never looking at the camera. There is something hyena-like about his expression, as if he is gloating through the computer screen about his exploits in capitalism and cuckoldry.

There is something familiar about Gemma, and not because she's been in the news lately. That stern expression, the pretty freckled features, the blond highlights—she's the coyote woman!

I still feel her sting.

I send a note to Gemma Mack, reintroducing myself, explaining who I am and what I am working on. Can we meet, I ask, this time unarmed?

IT WAS HARD NOW TO ascertain what the developer's vision might have been. Sargam doubted he had any aesthetic vision at all, but what he did have was an appetite. There had been at least six hundred houses with fifty-foot frontages on each, in three styles—the largest five bedrooms and 3,600 square feet, the smallest three bedrooms and 2,800 square feet—with corresponding price points. Yet with this sprawling ambition, he, or she, had not bothered to imagine the need for a store, a park, a library, a bench, a gas station, a school, or a tree. Who would live here?

There were a few takers, lured by unkept promises of trees and schools, but sold because of complicated and usurious financing that was ultimately judged to be the fault of the borrower. If those subprimes had been so witless as to be unable to read a damn contract, then whose fault was that? Not the banks'. Blaming the banks would be like blaming the weather. Sure, they were greedy and ruthlessly profit-driven and served no other master but shareholder returns, but that's what they were *supposed* to be. Banks acting any other way would be like rain falling upward.

There had been, for a few precious months before the defaults and the foreclosures and the repossessions, the first stirrings of what might be called a community: Mrs. Villablanca walking her dog and waving to her nearest neighbor, Mr. Gonzalez, who lived four yet-to-be-sold houses away. It seemed that it was only a matter of time before those houses in between filled in and a little town would flourish. There would be block parties, families sitting around, having tamales and *carne asada*. A few residents even planted trees, stunted, barren ficuses and acacias, forlorn-looking in the dry, sandy dirt next to the concrete foundations.

Long before there were developments and highway systems, those hardy, misguided pioneers who wandered through this territory on spindly horses choking on chalky sand would have shuddered at the thought of even bedding down here, miles from water, miles from shelter, miles from shade. Yet here they were, the first few dozen of what the developer promised would be a community of many thousands, hooked up to the grid, stealing aquifer water from farmers upstate. There would be a school bus coming through every morning to pick up little Juan and Maria and deliver them to a fine K-through-12 just sixty miles away. It was a version, however dry and withered and sand-choked, of the American dream.

SARGAM, OF COURSE, HAD ARRIVED long after the Villablancas and Gonzalezes had moved out, loading what they could into their listing minivans and pickup trucks and making their way south and east, to try their luck in Arizona or New Mexico or Texas. They were probably picking fruit, Sargam imagined, and maybe they were even thinking of their time in Valence as the finest of their lives, when they almost had a home in an almost-community. That may well have been the last time when almost was good enough, when almost middle class, almost happy, almost satisfied, and getting almost enough sleep and almost having the car you wanted and the spouse you dreamed of was enough to get you an almost decent life. That era had closed. Now there were only those who had everything, and the rest of us who had nothing.

Sargam came to Valence on a battered white Yamaha with clanking saddle cases and a creaky seat. The bike was coated in dust and leaking oil from the crankcase and fluid from the rear brake lines. Sargam had coasted down the off-ramp from the highway on fumes and parked in the first driveway she saw, a cracked, paved spit that fronted a boarded-up three-bedroom. She slipped off her helmet, shook her black hair loose, and studied the row of similarly abandoned houses; she knew she wasn't alone. She heard a dog barking. Heard a hammer banging a nail. Could sense in the too quiet that others had paused mid-task and were watching her.

She leaned her bike on its kickstand and slipped a water bottle from one of its cases. Took a drink, poured water over her face, and whipped her hair sideways to see from the corner of her eye a little girl peering at her from around the corner of the next house.

When she turned to look directly, the girl was gone.

Sargam had been to a hundred abandoned exurbs like this. Most of them had become the refuge of meth cookers, krokodil mixers, their customers, and those who didn't mind being in their company: smugglers, illegals, fugitives, subprimes who had given up. But other exurbs became inhabited by those who wanted communities, subprimes who didn't have the credit score required to pass a job screening, to rent a proper apartment, subprimes whose bad credit had driven them out of the world and who now were subsisting on the fringes of the economy, on cash and barter, on propane tanks, illegal solar rigs, wood fires, purified water, and canned food. There was a distinctive pattern of habitation: one house was kept up while the surrounding ones were gradually stripped, the wood to be burned for fuel, the fittings sold as scrap.

"If you're looking for crank, keep riding," she heard a voice behind her.

She turned to see a man in dusty black leather high-top sneakers, jeans, a flannel shirt open over a hairless chest and flat stomach. He wore a baseball cap with a UPS patch. He had a stubbled face, thin lips, a pronounced upper-lip apron, and a long nose. His eyes had a surprised, almost humorous quality, and as he gave his warning, he managed to be welcoming.

Sargam shook her head. "Never tried it, never want to."

The man scratched the bottom of the right side of his chin. "And you won't here. We're trying to keep it civil. If you want to stay a while, why don't you ride your bike down off of Bienvenida—that's what they named this street—and find a squat off the main drag. It's quiet here, and we aim to keep it quiet."

A few more residents had emerged, hands held over eyes to block the sun. They studied Sargam with expressions verging from hostility to warmth to curiosity to lust, the range she elicited everywhere she went.

"Where you from?"

She lunged her bike off its kickstand and backed it down the driveway, bracing her slight weight against the heavy machine.

"Nowhere. Everywhere. I'm riding around," Sargam said. "I'm trying to see what I can see."

"And what are you seeing?"

"I'll tell you when I see it."

She pushed her bike down the street, the small crowd parting for her. Sargam sensed that the individuals cohered into a few families, the men and boys linked to the women and girls. She liked that idea of families settling in a place that, at some point— if anyone had thought things through beyond slapping up drywall and getting signatures on loan documents—was intended for families. Or was meant to tempt families.

"There's a few houses unlocked on Chapala. Second street down," the man called.

SARGAM PUSHED OPEN THE FRONT door; it gave silently on its still-oiled hinges into an entrance with an alcove on which still sat an opened can of eggshell-white paint with dried drippings running down its sides. The interior had been this optimistic white, but previous squatters had left their impressions in pencil, paint, and urine stains on the walls. "Subprime and Proud," read one typical graffito; "National Debt Holiday NOW," read another; and "I Want A Woman With A Juicy Box" read yet another. To the right of the living room was a kitchen with a center island stripped of its stone, and counters with cavities where appliances belonged. A row of double-glass doors opened onto a backyard of bare dirt—no one had bothered to plant anything back there.

Sargam guessed the house had never been lived in by an owner, just squatted in by successive subprimes looking for a place to crash. She preferred this to houses that still bore traces of actual owner-occupiers: stickers pasted by kids onto closet doors, a basketball rim over the garage, recipes tacked up inside cabinet doors. In those former homes she felt the void, all the emotions the home once had held gone like vanished spirits, leaving only the looted soulless shelter.

She rolled her bike up over the threshold and into the living room, flipping open the saddle cases. The house did not smell too bad; some faint pissy odor was detectable but she had experienced worse. She knew better than to look in the bathrooms. She packed a spade she used to dig a latrine trench wherever she stopped. She guessed the living room was the safest spot to camp, enjoying, as it did, good visibility of the backyard and the front door.

The pressing need was water. She guessed there had to be a water source, otherwise this community of subprimes would not have settled in. She did a quick scan of the yard and house for fuel but failed to find any and removed a can of Sterno from her the bike box, unscrewed the top, and lit it, then opened a can of vegetarian chili. She would eat first and then go looking for water. She still had two liters left.

There was a knock at the door.

"Come in."

It was the man in the UPS cap. "I never properly introduced myself."

He removed his cap, stringy brown hair falling over his craggy, stern face. "Darren."

She stood up, leaving her spoon in the chili can. "I'm Sargam."

"We're all subprimes here, but we're honest. No drugs. Trying to keep out the criminals and keep the good folks safe."

"I can appreciate that. How long you been here?"

"Four months. We have it pretty good. There's water, that's what I came to tell you about, an aquifer well down the end of Yucca. You need a bucket or a pot or something to haul it out. But it's good water, clean."

Sargam thanked him.

"How long you plan on staying?"

"I don't stay anywhere too long."

"Are you looking for something? You're not the law, are you? Or working for a credit agency?"

Sargam shook her head.

"You don't look like it, but I had to check."

"Like I said, I'm just riding," Sargam said. "Looking to see how we're all getting by."

"If you like, if you're not too tired from the road, we have a couple folks here who can deejay a little, they've got their turntables, some records, and we've got a kid who's pretty good with the drums and another who can pick a little on the guitar. Tonight's a dance. We only do it once in a while, lest the noise attracts too much attention. You never know when the banks or the owners or whoever holds the note might wake up and run us all off."

SHE WASHED UP WITH WATER from the aquifer and then napped for a few minutes before a rooster crowing woke her up, and then she heard the music. At first, Sargam listened for the rumble of a generator, but then she realized they must be running outlaw power—solar energy, which big oil had gotten banned through the National Energy Independence Act. Someone had managed to haul in a bunch of old house and R&B albums, some artists Sargam recognized: Massive Attack, Tricky, and one of her favorite old-school jams, the Sam Cooke classic "Bring It on Home to Me."

She followed Sam's plaintive voice to a crowd gathered on a driveway that served as a dance floor. The turntables were set up in a garage, the door swung open, the power cables snaking down from out-of-sight panels. There were two aluminum cone lights clipped to each bottom corner of the opened garage. The light cast stark, jerky shadows far larger than the dancers, who were clapping and stomping their feet.

Darren saw Sargam and approached her, handing her a cup, which she sniffed. It was beer, a little warm.

"Homebrew," Darren shouted over the music. "Strong."

She sipped.

The DJ, a biracial man in his twenties, pale skin but with kinky hair, nodded into his headphones as he faded out the R&B track and kicked in Primal Scream's "Come Together," the crowd waving their hands in the air. Most of those dancing were in their twenties and thirties, while around the edges stood a few middle-aged and older folks, smiling, chatting, a few passing hand-rolled cigarettes back and forth. There were kids snaking their way through the dance floor, until a few of the younger, prettier women began shaking their skirts at the children to make way for the real boogying.

Sargam was intentionally ignoring the studied looks she was getting, the whispers. How many young, pretty women just show up on motorcycles in subprime squats? Not many, Sargam knew, but she was used to explaining herself and allaying suspicions. And she was careful to keep her eyes off any of the attached men.

But this Ryanville was different from the others she had passed through. Here they seemed to have created some order in their lives, organized enough to have a little party, and tough enough to keep out the tweakers who could be relied on to ruin such affairs.

"You wanna dance?" Darren asked.

"Not yet," Sargam said. "How many of you live here?"

"About a hundred," he said and explained that the core was a group of about a dozen families with children. After running off the meth heads who had been there when they came, they figured out where the aquifer was capped and drilled a tap into the valve pipes at the end of Yucca. As more subprimes arrived, the first families made up the rules: no hard drugs, no criminals. Nobody wanted the law to come sniffing around, and so far, there had not been any incidents.

"The closest supermarket is forty-five minutes away and we make two runs a week. But we're also growing beets, carrots, radishes, onions. With water anything is possible. We have a few goats. You probably heard the chickens. Hard to keep the coyotes off them."

Later, there was a bonfire in the backyard while a Latino man strummed his guitar and sang quietly in English. He wore a leather vest over a white T-shirt, faded jeans, and white high-top sneakers. His lidded, black-olive-colored eyes gave him a sleepy look, and even when he sang, he seemed weary as he enunciated the lyrics.

I got a letter from the government the other day
I opened it. It said they were suckers
You think a free man would give a damn
About their taxes or whatever?

I got a letter from the creditor the other day
I opened it. It said they were rerating me
You think a broke man would give a damn
About their FICO or whatever?

I got a letter from the banker the other day
I opened it. It said they were repossessing me
You think a subprime man would give a damn
About their underwater or whatever?

I got a letter from the student loan the other day
I opened it. It said they would take my pay
You think an unemployed man gives a damn
About their garnishing or whatever?

I got a letter from you the other day
I opened it. It asked if I was free
You think I have anything holding me?
About two seconds flat and I was gone to you

The group gathered around the fire, sitting on broken-down lawn chairs, benches fashioned from salvage wood, and wool blankets spread on the dirt. The temperature had dropped and Sargam found herself pulling her leather jacket tight around her. The group had been singing along and hooting but now the guitar player was singing a softer song, in Spanish. A pack of dogs had gathered at the flickering edge of the light, watching the fire.

Darren found his way to where Sargam was standing. He had in his arms a blanket that he shook open and spread out.

She felt the hot air of the fire against her face. She looked at the happy people, all the faces made soft orange by the light, the easy smiles, the gentle nodding to the music. Why couldn't every one of these abandoned developments find this sort of low buzz of contentment?

It was not perfect, she knew. Darren had filled her in. The kids didn't have a school. The men were struggling to pay for the gas that took them to those few menial jobs they could get. They would run out of wood. They would run out of propane. They would never run out of coyotes, dust, heat, sun, and cracked lips; everyone stank of sweat, and you couldn't keep yourself clean. But they were free here in a way they had never been back in their foreclosed homes, or in underpass Ryanvilles, or driving slow and scared down darkened highways.

Each of them had once been nominally the owner of a house or a condominium, and each had lost their job, their home, and had to set out on the road.

"It wasn't working for us anymore," Darren said, "any more than it was working for whoever had once lived here and then had to leave. You know those abandoned Hopi cities? Or the Indian towns along the Gila River? The folks who lived there just . . . they got out. Like we did. There's no reason to stay anywhere anymore. We don't own nothing but ourselves."

A few children had fallen asleep in the glow of the fire. Someone had laid a blanket over them.

"It's hard on the children, not going to a real school, but their parents didn't have a choice. You lose your home. You can wait around for the warrant, which you can't pay, and then you end up in debtors' prison—and how is that good for children? No, you have to run."

She drowsed until the fire was embers, and then roused herself, leaving Darren asleep on the blanket.

SARGAM SLEPT IN A SLEEPING bag in her abandoned house. The next morning, she made instant coffee in a tin cup over a Sterno can, and then went out to see the settlement already abuzz with activity. There were two dozen folks working in the vegetable plots, a boy tossing feed corn to chickens from a sack slung over his shoulder, a few men pouring water from clear plastic drums into black plastic tubing. Sargam could see an improvised, rudimentary irrigation system, water spouting from black tubing pricked with holes. There were funnel-shaped valves every twenty-five yards along the tube, and the men walked down the tube, pouring from the drums. It was hot, sticky work, and had to be done before ten a.m. or you could get heatstroke in the furnace of the midday sun. By midmorning most everyone was indoors or in shade, the harsh, probing heat putting a hush on the community so that if you were just passing by, you might not guess there were over a hundred people scratching out a living from the earth and odd jobs.

Midafternoon, a black woman walked down Yucca, banging a pot with a wooden spoon, and slowly, and not without groans, a crew of children followed her to a stucco house at the end of the road, where they took seats on the floor or the back step. Using a whiteboard she had scavenged, she gave them some elementary lessons in mathematics and English, the children every bit as bored and resentful as if they were in the best of classrooms.

Sargam, wearing desert boots, jeans, and a T-shirt, wandered through the community, lending a hand in the fields, bending down to pull up radishes and beets while the women asked her where she was from, if she had a man or children.

Lest the women take her reluctance to answer these questions as standoffishness, Sargam explained as best she could. She didn't know her parents. She had never learned her given name. She had run away from her foster parents as soon as she reached puberty. She'd done plenty she wasn't proud of since then. She'd lied. She'd robbed. She'd stolen. She didn't tell them but they could figure out for themselves that she had lain with men for money.

It had been fifteen years since she left that foster home.

"That bike you rode in on," one of them said. "Pretty bike. Where did you get it?"

"Stole it from a dude. A bad man. That was two thousand miles and three states ago."

The women laughed. Sara, a blonde with a ridged forehead and a broad nose, stood up, wiped her arm across her brow, and asked, "How old are you?"

"I don't know my birthday. Thirty?" Sargam said. "I'm such a mutt. I've never seen an older version of me. Nothing to compare me to."

The work was harder than any Sargam had done, and after an hour her upper back and shoulders were sore and she was grateful when the woman said that was enough for today.

"How come the men don't do any fieldwork?" Sargam asked.

"Oh, they do," said Sara. "Most of them were up on a job in Standard. Construction. We need all the currency we can get. We pool what we have and somehow it's enough, but there's nothing put away. And the kids would like new sneakers. A new soccer ball. That's the part of this that still breaks my heart. My own daughters are growing up out here. How are we gonna get a Christmas tree? Forget the gifts under it."

"I never had a tree," Sargam said. "I turned out okay."

Sara smiled. "With all due respect, you're a tough girl. I suppose our kids are gonna come up as hard people. You know, you want your kids to have a gentle childhood, but that won't serve them nowadays, will it?"

"I haven't seen much that I would call gentle since I've been on the road." Sargam swung her hip out and knocked Sara a little sideways. "And who you calling tough?"

THAT NIGHT THERE WERE FIRES set in split oil drums with wire grills laid across them, potatoes, carrots, and squash roasting alongside six plump chickens. Sara had set out pots of lentils and pots of rice. The tired men and women and the eager children all waited their turn in line. They received one piece of chicken each, but as much vegetables, lentils, and rice as they could eat, and all the hot sauce they could want to spike it all with. From plastic cups they drank iced tea. They sat around eating on the blankets, benches, and lawn chairs, the fatigue from their day showing in their faces. After dinner, a few of them summoned the energy to join the kids in a pickup soccer game in the fading desert light.

Darren came over. He'd been on the work site all day, and he still had a thick leather work belt with his tools hanging low on his skinny hips. He set down his plastic plate, worked the belt free, and then took a seat next to Sargam.

"You're still here." He smiled.

He took a forkful of rice and lentils and chewed slowly. "Most folks, a day picking will drive them off."

"I could see why," Sargam said. "It *is* an honest day's work."

"But you can't beat the pay," Darren said, holding up his plate.

"Or the company."

Sargam could swear she saw Darren blush a shade at this before he turned away.

"Do you think this can last?" Sargam asked. "I've been riding around, and this is the first place I've come to where it seems to be working."

"What?"

"This communal sort of life, share and share alike. It's a place built on fairness."

"That's all we have. They took everything else. But they couldn't take a man's sense of what's right."

"In another time they would call this—"

"Socialism," Darren said. "I know. *Shhhh*. But I like 'fairness.' That's a better word. You tell these folks here that we are practicing socialism, hell, they might pack up and leave."

Sargam surveyed the plowed land, the grooved earth extending clear to the farthest reaches of the development, running between the houses and right up to the streets. "But the land, you can't stay here forever. Someone will want to restake their claim."

"I know. If we can make it ten years we could make a case for adverse possession, but what are the odds of that? We'll get run off. But who knows? There's no market for these houses. Look at those old mining ghost towns. Nobody ever came back to claim those houses."

Darren cleared his plate. One of the girls playing soccer scored a goal and the field erupted in cheers. An older boy ran down to retrieve the ball from between some squash plants, and somewhere in the distance a coyote howled, and then a dog from nearby barked an answer. A few men and women were hauling the pots of lentils and rice down toward a chicken pen, trailed by three hungry dogs. The sun sunk in an egg-yolk disc, and in those last moments before sliding down into the horizon, it sprayed orange and purple all across the sky and everyone's face glowed a pinkish hue so that they all looked ruddy and healthy.

A man in blue dungaree overalls tossed logs into the same pit as yesterday, and set to work making a fire.

"Can't see why anybody would ever leave," Sargam said.

DARREN CAME TO HER IN the night, after Sargam had spread out her sleeping bag and changed into the tank top and sweatpants she slept in. He gave a cautious knock at the door, two taps, and at first Sargam thought it might be a raccoon digging in the dirt, casting pebbles against the door. When he knocked again, she stood up, slipped on her jacket, and called out.

"It's me, Darren," he said.

She walked over on bare feet and opened the door. He had a flashlight, which he shined down toward the floor.

"Hey there," Sargam said.

"I was trying to think of a reason why I had to come and check on you, but I couldn't think of any."

Sargam waved him in.

"How about just saying you wanted to see me?"

His pale skin was ghostly in the dark, and yellow up his arm in the peripheral light cast by his flashlight.

She was dark, her amber skin and black hair obscured in shadow so that he couldn't see where she ended and the rest of the world began.

Her white tank top was the clearest indicator of where she was. But Darren, unable to see Sargam's face, was having difficulty picking up any visual cues as to how welcome he really was.

"So, you're okay?" he said.

"Now, Darren, don't go all wishy-washy on me now. You had the moxie to come knocking on my door."

She pulled him toward her and kissed him. They both smelled of hard work, and neither had washed, so the mutual stench was hardly off-putting. They hugged each other for a moment, as if trying to catch up with the surprising suddenness of their kiss.

Darren shined the flashlight around the living room.

Sargam had cleaned out the place, tossing the empty cans, cigarette butts, and plastic water bottles into a garbage bag that she had discarded in one of the bathrooms. With a borrowed broom she had swept out the living room and even drilled a U-bolt lock into one of the cabinets to secure her pack while she was out. She had laid some newspaper under her bike to sop the fluids and was planning on replacing the oil-pan gasket to stop the oil leak. The room had the pleasant, slightly sweet smell of bike oil and metal mixed with some desert rosemary coming in through the open window.

"How's the bike?" Darren asked, as if worried that she might leave as soon as she had done her repairs.

"I could get it done in a day or two, if I wanted. But I've met some interesting folks and thought I might stick around."

"Anyone in particular?"

"This one really hot guy, a socialist."

"How could you ever fall for one of them?"

They kissed again and made their way to Sargam's bedroll.

It had been a few months since Sargam had been with a man, and it took some getting used to—the shape and length of his body. He was long and bony, skinny-legged and flat-stomached, with a few sparse blond chest hairs. He was delicate in the beginning as they kissed, but then became rough and insistent with his lips and tongue in a way that she liked. It became clear they were going to make love, their urgency as they kissed and grabbed each other, her hands pulling down his jeans, his reaching inside her sweats. When their pants were off, she guided his penis so the head was against her vulva, but did not guide further. She wanted him to have to work his way in. She was wet and open and he slid inside in stages and she gasped at his length, pushed back against him and she came just after he did, shaking in small shivers as she caught her breath.

Later, as they lay together, the coyotes were howling again, an impatient chorus that seemed uncomfortably close, as if they were just out of sight, behind the wall, an arm's length away. When Sargam sat up in the night, listening, she checked beside her for Darren, but he was gone. By then the coyotes had quieted, but there wasn't silence, for they were so near Sargam thought she could hear their short, quick breaths.

CHAPTER 4

PASTOR ROGER WAS DEADLY OUT to about eighteen feet, but beyond that his prayers went unanswered as he clanked everything off the front of the rim. At eight a.m., every day save Sunday, he played his three-on-three basketball game, dribbling and shooting on the actual court where the San Antonio Spurs had won multiple NBA titles. He had had that very court ripped up, plank by plank, and relaid here in the office compound of his mega-church, which at one point had been the home stadium of the Dallas Cowboys. His body man, a former Los Angeles Jaguars fullback, Devin Dudley, and security man and former Texas State small forward, Gerald Nutley, were his teammates and they regularly thrashed their opposition, primarily because nobody was willing to hard-foul Pastor Roger during his infrequent drives to the hoop.

Pastor Roger was a shoot-first, pass-never point guard whose teammates had better be good rebounders and defenders, because that was the only way they would ever get the ball. When Anderson Cooper from *60 Minutes* asked him about his style of play, Pastor Roger described himself as a facilitator, a player who sacrificed his own numbers so that his teammates might thrive. And he truly believed what he was saying, despite all evidence to the contrary.

Yet the image of the humble pastor playing his daily basketball game had stuck and scored very highly in his director of communications' eight-tier pyramid of relatability, which the pastor and his DOC studied daily in search of ways to make Pastor Roger more famous, and to secure for him more radiostation clears, congregants, and tithings.

The pastor swished his last shot, an unguarded fifteen-footer, shook the hands of his opponents, and came to the glassed-in room facing the court, where waiting for him in a plush chair was Arthur Mack, whose bail Pastor Roger himself had put up. His own attorneys had pledged to ensure that the controversial "financial advisor" was not a flight risk and agreed to pay for the tracking anklet now clasped to Arthur's leg.

Pastor Roger sat down and wiped his face with a small white towel. His body man handed him a bottle of water, which he sipped as he settled his breathing.

"Arthur, do you know why I have vouched for you? Invited you to an audience with me?"

Arthur had been wondering about this very fact for the entire flight down. The pastor's private jet had all the usual perks of lavish travel—burnished hardwood paneled cabin, the wide, spacious seats, the catered spread of almost edible sandwiches—save one: the liquor. There was nothing to drink on the plane but decaffeinated Coca-Cola and bottled water. Denied the distraction of 7-and-7s, as the plane banked between columns of smoke cast from prairie burning throughout the firebelt of Missouri,

Arkansas, Oklahoma, and Texas, Arthur had wrestled with the notion of why Pastor Roger would send a jet for him and ultimately concluded that no matter what the pastor had in store for him, it was better than Rikers Island or the Turtle Bay apartment where he had been hiding out since he made bail. It was owned by his mistress's father, an Iranian Jew of considerable girth who suspected that Arthur still had millions stashed away and regularly demanded the return of his half-million-dollar investment, which Arthur had in fact lost along with every other dollar of dumb money in his care. His mistress, a pretty, hirsute brunette who spent most of her hours in various depilation and epilation procedures, had remained loyal to Arthur, turning up at the courthouse every day he had to appear and even visiting him at the Downtown Detention Center when he was locked up there.

Yet he had grown tired of her loyalty, and restless in his new life of house arrest, so that when Pastor Roger called, offering to pull strings and arrange for his visit to Texas, he leaped at the chance. Apparently, Arthur had become something of a folk hero down there as an alleged victim of regulatory overreach.

"Son, when it gets to the point an American can't build a profitable business without the federal government coming in and tearing it down, well, that's the point at which we may need to revisit the Constitution and remind our countrymen of our inalienable rights."

Arthur was slow to accept the notion that he was the victim of overregulation, rather than the perpetrator of a fraud, as that had not previously seemed a promising legal strategy, but as a potential for a new line of work, that of Free Market Hero and Regulator Fighter, he was coming to embrace the concept, though he was having trouble with the details.

Pastor Roger, having rehydrated from his basketball game,

was telling Arthur that he first had to repent for his sins. He had strayed from his marriage—was he in touch with his wife? would she be open to coming to Dallas for a reconciliation service performed by Pastor Roger?—and had abandoned his children—could they come down? Pastor Roger would love to have them onstage during a sermon. His redemptions always started in the home, with family.

"We've all sinned. That's the meaning of being born again. We come to Jesus, we repent, and we move on. No harm, no foul," said Pastor Roger. His voice, a soft twang, gentle, prone to cracking and sometimes on the verge of tears. It was a voice famous throughout the nation, from his radio shows and televised sermons and his numerous appearances alongside politicians, celebrities, and troubled reality-TV stars. He had been on Oprah's couch so many times he was rumored to be her successor. He had published twenty-seven best-selling books, each with his blue eyes and aspirin-white teeth gleaming on the cover. Yet Arthur, not an avid media devotee, knew only that Pastor Roger was famous, and rich, and powerful.

Pastor Roger sized up the material the Lord had given him. Arthur Mack was a handsome man, with good carriage and fine Caucasian features, but he lacked a certain cunning around the eyes. He was not, Pastor Roger quickly assessed, a complex thinker.

"Do you know where your wife and children are?" Pastor Roger asked.

"Sure. Um, I think so."

"Do you understand what you are being given here?"

"Yeah, I, um . . . what are you giving me again?"

"Redemption!"

"Right, yeah, redemption."

He had been driven in from the jet in a black Escalade V24

Turbo—the lowest-gas-mileage passenger vehicle currently sold in the United States—and escorted into the Freedom Prairie Church, where he was met by a man with white hair and a black suit, Steven Shopper, director of communications for the FPC. Shopper led him around the church's vast nave, the Dallas Cowboys' former field covered with planks and carpeted and filled with seats that rose to where the stands had been. There were four waterfalls gurgling over large, brown rock formations built into the stands down to where the sidelines once were. The old stadium benches had been removed and replaced with chairs angled toward the pulpit and its 150-foot-wide screen so that the 78,000 who gathered here three times every Sunday and once on Mondays and Saturdays could watch Pastor Roger give his tearful sermons. There was now actually more advertising signage than there had been when it was a football stadium. Chick-fil-A and Taco Bell, Dell-Hewlett and Pepper Industries signs were everywhere. The great Freedom Prairie Church was empty, save for a few technicians on the distant stage who had gathered to look at a tablet. Arthur was led to the edge of the nave, to where the fifty-yard-line seats once were, and then through the old tunnel, past where the concessionaires had sold nachos and churros, where congregants now could buy Jesus Man action figures and Jesus Freak T-shirts, mugs, caps, key chains, beverage cozies, and iPhone cases; and down the elevator to Pastor Roger's office complex and family area, where he was ushered into a glassed-in room where he was to wait while the pastor played his daily three-on-three.

Pastor Roger was surprisingly fit for a man in his fifties, looking like a cross between Andrew Jackson and one of the Jonas Brothers, that long, stern American face softened by a curly poof of dyed-black hair and skin peeled to a curry-powder taupe.

Arthur asked him, "So, what about my defense?"

"Get some rest," Pastor Roger said. "We have guest rooms off the vestry. And then we'll get you down to the studio and have you come on the show. Today! We're gonna talk about your case and how vital to God's will and American energy independence the trading in carbon credits really is. What you were doing was the Lord's work, only the markets turned against you, and then the regulators stabbed you in the back, isn't that right, son?"

Arthur mouthed the words "God's work" and stood.

"Now get some rest, have a healthy breakfast. We serve six kinds of bacon, you know."

Steve Shopper reappeared and said he would be helping Arthur to settle in and get comfortable, and also guide Arthur through the messaging.

"We love this story," said Steve Shopper as he led Arthur into the hall. "There's been a rush to judgment, an unwillingness to understand that if what you were doing was wrong, then what Sam Walton and Henry Ford and T. Boone Pickens did was also wrong. The teachings of Ayn Rand are clear: you make your own dollar, damnit and damn the rest. You know what your mistake was? Trying to make that red-blooded American dollar in that un-American New York City. Yankee lawyers don't understand that the carbon credit derivative business is the underpinning of our energy independence."

Arthur nodded. They were walking past the vast support struts of the old stadium, the morning sun blasting through the glassed-in walls and the huge stained-glass effigies of Jesus Christ and Pastor Roger. The old mezzanine floor had been carpeted a plush green, and the walls painted rust and orange and sienna, and from the ceiling, which was terraced upward beneath the upper decks, hung gold and silver and blue banners, like little pennants with fleurs-de-lis embroidered all over them.

Steve Shopper showed Arthur into a room where he was immediately assaulted by the artificial cold. There were three overstuffed leather sofas surrounding a shiny varnished oak table. On the wall were framed oil paintings of Pastor Roger on horseback, stalking through brush holding a rifle, and at the wheel of a large SUV, flanked by Thomas Jefferson and George Washington.

Through a large passage was a dining room with seating for twelve, and off this room was a hallway to a bedroom and bathroom.

"There's a kitchen behind the dining room. Are you hungry? Just pick up the phone and a chef will bring up some bacon."

"Doesn't the pastor need this room?"

"Oh, this is a guest room. There are twenty-five like it. For special guests to his sermons."

Arthur sat down on one of the sofas. "It's freezing in here."

"Isn't it wonderful!" Steve Shopper smiled. "You'll get some rest, a short nap, and we'll go over your talking points."

It was too cold to lie down. Arthur got up and walked around the room and made his way down the hall to the bedroom. There was a single bed with a folded-over sheet and a thin blanket. He would have loved a drink, but he knew without asking that there probably wasn't a beer to be had in the whole complex. He arranged himself on the bed, pulling the thin blanket over him.

Arthur Mack was cold, and uncomfortable, and unsure of why exactly he was here, but he recognized opportunity, just as he had those years ago when he started his hedge fund. But what he felt, more powerfully than he had ever felt before, was a strange sense that he had at last found his flock, that these were folks who understood him, who really appreciated him. They get me, he thought, they really, really get me.

PASTOR ROGER WAS SPEAKING INTO a microphone and facing a camera in a darkened TV studio, one of a half-dozen in the bowels of the stadium where he did postproduction on his own sermons, or could appear as a guest on any of a series of KIK-TV or Fox News shows. He had grown up in television. His grandfather was a televangelist preaching mainstream Southern Baptist Conference liturgy who'd had the brainstorm of buying his own television stations in several Texas markets, the better to spread his own Sunday message. As a child, Pastor Roger picked up the technical aspects of putting on a Sunday devotional service, learning how to adjust the lighting around the platform, as his grandfather called the area around the pulpit. Working behind the scenes suited the shy, soft-spoken boy. By the time he was seventeen, he was producing his grandfather's show and had a network executive's understanding of television markets—time slots, lead-ins, and cost-per-ratings points. Pastor Billy vigorously preached the message every Sunday until he was eighty-six, when he wound up in a Dallas hospital and turned to young Roger and urged him to take the platform.

Pastor Roger, already in his late twenties, a dropout who had completed a year and a half at Oral Roberts, had never spoken in public, yet that first Sunday as he did the noon service he felt the power of God speaking through him. He carried on his grandfather's message of stern self-reliance but found himself adding to it huge dollops of American exceptionalism, free-market glorification, and Ayn Rand objectivism. He had always loved America, of course, but he was surprised by the virulence of his words, his assertion of the market as the hand of God, and of government regulation as the devil's claw. He combined this with a promise to his congregants that if they believed in God, and if they continued to congregate in the Church of Texas, as it was then called, that they too would be made wealthy by the free market. God wants us all to be rich, he assured his flock every Sunday. God wants us to have a big life, a gigantic life, a ten-thousand-square-foot-mansion-and-a-rib-eye-every-night kind of life. Do you know who is blocking that connection to God?

And the congregants would cry out: Big Government. The Regulators. The Environmentalists. The Progressives. The Takers.

He had surprised himself by his hatred of all those who stood in the way of progress, who disputed that God had given man dominion over all the fish of the sea and birds of the air, over all the livestock, over all the Earth. All of it, Pastor Roger would pound the pulpit, all of it. Every rock. Every tree. Every drop. It is ours to use! Those who would deny us that dominion? They are the enemies of God.

It was a powerful message. His grandfather never took the platform again.

HE HIMSELF WAS NOT WEALTHY. But his Church had prospered. There were the television stations, the books, the stadium-cum-church, purchased from the city of Irvine for $180 million and refurbished for another $150 million. There were the action figures and religious trinkets and devotional bathmats and bracelets and hoodies and even panties. He was the CEO of a multibillion-dollar nonprofit corporation, giving counsel to the wealthiest and most powerful of American business and political leaders, who came to Pastor Roger when they had their occa-sional doubts about their policies or strategies. The climate, they sometimes observed, *did* seem a little, you know, *off-kilter*, like too cold in the summer, hot in the winter, all these fires. Miami flooding, New York City flooding, Santa Monica flooding. And those whales! What the heck did the pastor make of that?

His job was to reassure them. This is God's will. The Earth, and all its resources, are but tools for men.

In his darkened studio a CNN host was asking what he made of Whalemageddon, those dozen or so whales on an East Hampton beach?

"The great beasts are serving man," Pastor Roger intoned, "are giving themselves over to us so that we may better exploit the resources of the sea."

"Moving on," a blond anchorette jumped in, "we hear that you are working with Arthur Mack? He flew down yesterday to seek your counsel?"

"I'm personally involved in the Arthur Mack case. I spoke with the district attorney up there in New York and told him that I would vouch for Mr. Mack and that I was offering him spiritual guidance. He is a lost soul. And he has sinned against his family. But let's separate his failings as a family man from his career as an entrepreneur and pioneer in the carbon credit derivative swap business."

"He is accused of defrauding his investors."

"Every entrepreneur I know has made a few mistakes," Pastor Roger said. "I am working to reconcile Mr. Mack with his family. To reconnect him with his faith so that he might be reborn. We owe our businessmen second chances."

"Indeed. All the ladies in the studio are gaga over Mr. Mack."

PASTOR ROGER STILL WROTE HIS sermons in a low-ceilinged office above his garage. He lived in a humble, five-thousand-square-foot house in Southlake, Texas, his home a fifth the size of the neighboring houses, both of which he also owned. He retired back to Southlake in the middle of most weekdays to write his sermons and it was here that Arthur Mack was summoned after his fitful sleep. There were two older ladies seated on a sofa, both dressed in skirt-and-jacket suits with gold brooches on their chests. They seemed to be sisters; both had the same widow's peak and brown-going-gray hair. They nodded simultaneously when they were introduced to Arthur Mack.

"This is Dottie and Dorrie Pepper," Pastor Roger said.

Arthur greeted them. He associated their names with a large privately held energy concern. Among the businesses they owned: Pepper Carbon, Sunrise Energy, Pepper Petroleum, Potash Corp., Pepper Equipment, Olmstead Petroleum, Birch Towels, Burlington Fabrics, Pepper Minerals, Swanson Foods, Barker Fibers, Columbia Coal & Energy, HG Extraction, Pepper Extraction, Pepper Bank, and Ortho Chemicals.

"We see the world much as you do," Dorrie said. "We believe that entrepreneurs and job creators, such as yourself, and ourselves, should be unencumbered by the deviltry of regulation."

"We see you as another John Brown," said Pastor Roger.

"The singer?" asked Arthur Mack, confused at why Pastor Roger was equating him with a black soul vocalist.

"The abolitionist," Pastor Roger said. "You must stand up for the cause of liberty, freedom, freedom to trade, to invest, just as John Brown sought freedom for slaves to trade and invest. The history of mankind is the long journey to the free market. The arc of history bends toward free trade. The market is the expression of God, the invisible hand is his hand, God's hand, directing our affairs. To exclude any man from that market is to keep him in bondage."

"Amen," said both women.

Arthur had taken a seat in a wooden chair next to Pastor Roger's desk. The pastor sat facing him, leaning forward. "Pray with us," he urged Arthur.

The pastor was already on his knees, his eyes closed. Cautiously, Arthur got down on his knees as well. The pastor's hands were offered, palms upward, and Arthur looked down at them, unsure, before extending his own hands, palms down, and joining them to Pastor Roger's. The two sisters walked over and kneeled, laying their hands atop Arthur's.

"Are you twins?" Arthur asked.

"Ssshh."

"Our Father, dear Lord Jesus Christ, provide us with the strength so that Arthur might fight the forces of repression and regulation and socialism and progressivism who would seek to usurp God's will by cutting off the invisible hand. He will need strength as he goes forth, to stand up to the evil of regulation, to those who would ask that men submit to a power other than their maker. Our Father, make Arthur Mack pure so that he may be fortified in this crusade, bring him together with his family, with his children, with his wife, so that he may live in God's blessed holy union."

Arthur opened his eyes and studied the pastor. He was trembling slightly as he prayed, mouthing the words through thin, pink lips and orange skin.

"We pray now for clarity of purpose, so that Arthur may hold his vision steady and focus on the needs and successes of his fellow entrepreneurs. We pray for wisdom to guide others to abundance, and that the abundance will surround us and be available for the taking, and that we may be shameless and unapologetic upon its receipt, for we deserve abundance. We pray to carry forth these convictions during the battle of business and communications and media. For all of these things we pray, for Arthur Mack is an entrepreneur, that holiest of God's warriors."

Pastor Roger rose and gazed into Arthur Mack's eyes. He stared for an uncomfortably long time and then sat back in his wooden desk chair.

"Arthur, do you understand why you are here?" asked Dottie Pepper.

"Because I'm like James Brown?"

"*John* Brown."

"Right, John Brown."

"Because we patriots, entrepreneurs, good men and women, want nothing less than energy independence for our nation. We believe fiercely in the free market, as you do too, and we don't believe a man should be persecuted for seeking to create jobs, bestow abundance, and enrich his fellow capitalists. That's what you were doing, correct?"

"I was trading C3DS3s."

"Yes, you were, a righteous expression of the invisible hand."

"Though I didn't invest so well. I got in a little over my—"

"Arthur, Arthur, we take the long view here. Perhaps the invisible hand had not yet pointed to you, there is nothing illegal about that."

"That's what I thought. I was going to make it all back."

"Sure you were, Arthur, that's why we can't have the courts and the media and the regulators and those heathen bands of Eskimos up in Alaska getting their fur knickers in a twist over your case, your investments, because these instruments are important, they allow great men and great companies to take greater risks, risks that must be taken if America is going to continue to prosper. So you need to go back to New York, recommit to your wife, your children, and then we will do all we can to rehabilitate you and get your case dismissed. And that starts with you coming to the platform on Sunday and turning your will and your life over to the care of Jesus Christ our Savior."

"And you'll get me off?"

Pastor Roger put his hands together in prayer. "With God's will, yes."

ARTHUR MACK WATCHED PASTOR ROGER'S sermon from a seat near the platform. The choir started up and the Grammy-award-winning recording artist Faith Hill came onstage and sang "It's All God" as 72,000 congregants stood and began swaying. The acres of LED signage were now scrolling brands and logos and advertisements for upcoming television shows and new mobile phone models and two-for-one Bacon Tuesdays at Ruby Tuesdays. Pastor Roger thanked his sponsors and then welcomed Arthur to the Freedom Prairie Church, telling his flock that Arthur Mack was a new congregant and to give him a warm Freedom Prairie welcome. "He's an entrepreneur, doing God's will, and was on his way to discovering God's vision for him when the regulators and the progressives—and the liberal media—decided they needed to take him down a few notches."

There was a chorus of boos at the mention of the usual sus-pects, and then cheers when Arthur stood up and waved. Those seated around Arthur back-slapped him and gave him hugs, assuring him that he had come to the right place. Pastor Roger welcomed another singer to the stage, and the great host stood up to sway to the singing of "Come Just As You Are," and when the great host swayed with the gospel singers, Arthur swayed as well, and when the baskets were passed down the rows, he even would have given, had he any money to give. When the sermon was over, the songs sung, and the money tithed, Arthur realized he didn't know where to go. He sat for a while as the congregants drifted out, huge smiles on their faces as they exchanged encompassing hugs.

After the vast stadium was draining of congregants on their way to pick up their children at Captain's Club ("brought to you by Pepper Extraction"), the 15,000-capacity facility for those believers under thirteen, Steve Shopper came out from behind the platform, where roadies were wrapping cables and wires and putting microphones in boxes.

"Mr. Mack, how did you enjoy our service?"

"Quite a show," said Arthur.

"Ms. Faith Hill!" Steve Shopper said. "Herself. Few entertainers turn down the pastor."

Arthur shrugged.

"We have a car waiting, to get you to a flight to Los Angeles. Your wife and lovely daughters, we understand, are now in L.A."

"That's where she's from."

"Rebuild the trust in your marriage, Arthur. That is Pastor Roger's fondest wish for you. Seize your beautiful life. You met the Peppers, they are among the many godly entrepreneurs who are interested in your case and know that you did nothing wrong. Now go forth and seize that big life."

THEY HAD BOOKED ARTHUR INTO Upright Class for the flight to L.A., a cushioned backseat and two armrests but no actual seat. They did not even offer drinks in Upright, which meant Arthur still had not had that cocktail he'd been craving since leaving New York.

Somehow, his abysmal trading landed him a place in Freedom Prairie Church and the attention of the most powerful pastor and some of the wealthiest conservatives in America. He wasn't sure why they were so interested in his trading of C3DS3s, but even he could follow the logic of Pastor Roger believing fiercely in the free market, and his supporters in the oil, gas, and fracking industries all believing fervently in their rights to pollute, and their rights to trade those rights to pollute, so as to reduce their costs and liabilities. The Arthur Macks of the world, in their worldview, were as instrumental to the process of exploitation of our God-given resources as were the boreholes and fracture pumps above a great field of shale.

Now, Arthur thought, if he could just get a goddamn drink, then he might have a shot at figuring out a way to exploit all this to his own advantage. After all, who was better at working complicated angles and figuring out this kind of super-complicated stuff and then profiting from it than Arthur Mack, his one recent six-year-long series of setbacks notwithstanding?

CHAPTER 5

TOLD YOU THAT ARTHUR MACK was a dodgy fellow," said Gemma's mother, Doreen, as she salt-and-peppered a pot roast before setting it into a Dutch oven filled with onions, carrots, and potatoes.

"Okay, Mom," Gemma said.

"Oh, he was easy on the eyes, and handsome enough in his kind of sleazy, car-salesman way, but I told you: Don't trust him."

Doreen took a drag on her Menthol 100 and set the pot in the preheated oven. It was an old GE range with four coiled electric burners on top, a broken analog clock set between the Bakelite knobs, and the enamel chipped off from so many years of gravy stains removed with steel wool. The bottle of J&B was already on the counter, the glass waiting by the sink. From a plastic tray in the freezer she removed a handful of half-moon ice slivers and tossed them into the glass. The whiskey pouring over it made a reassuring crackle, and then Doreen turned to her daughter.

"Goodness, that was rude of me. You want one, darling? Have a drink with me."

"I'll fix one myself."

Gemma retraced her mother's steps and soon the two were drinking in the tiny tiled kitchen, one window facing west, the other north over a two-basin sink—and no appliance dating from after Reagan's second term.

"Here's to your escape," Doreen said, raising her glass.

"It's not an escape, it's a . . . break," Gemma said. "Mom, I've been reluctant to ask, but, could you not smoke in the house when the girls are here?"

A clenched look came over Doreen's face, her eyes narrowing behind her glasses, her lips pursing, but just as quickly it vanished and she nodded. "Okay, okay, for the girls."

"But you can finish that one," Gemma said.

"I intend to."

GEMMA WAS BACK IN HER adolescent bedroom, the same narrow single bed, wheezy piano, and tall, dark oak hutch that Gemma always thought looked like it belonged in a kitchen rather than a bedroom. The carpet had been changed, thank heaven, and her old clothes had been thrown away or boxed up in the garage, but there were still a few vestiges of her teenage self. The bottom half of a Duran Duran sticker and the remains of a Tecate bumper sticker were still on the inside of the closet door, along with a taped-up school photo of her best friend, Holly Duba. The view out the window, through the upward-thrusting branches of a pomegranate tree, was reassuring. Even the feel of the mattress was right, the smell of the sheets and pillowcase familiar in the way that only home can be.

The girls were sleeping in her brother's old bedroom, sharing his queen-size bed. They were excited by this change in routine, their leaving school in the middle of the term, the flight to L.A. to visit Gammer, but they were discomfited by undiscussed issues. Did their father know they were going to Santa Monica? And where exactly was Dad? And why were they renting out their beach house and moving to a smaller apartment?

"And why," the girls asked one morning, "was Dad on a business trip when he was also in jail? And now he's in Texas. Is that a business trip too?"

Gemma set down her coffee.

Doreen smiled and cocked her head at Gemma. "Yeah, Mom, explain that."

"Who, why, um, where did you hear that?" Gemma managed to ask.

"Mom, we can read."

"And watch TV," Franny said. "Dad was trading something, and they weren't real, so he got in trouble."

"Your father may have broken some rules. Like in a game? So they need to figure out which rules exactly he broke, and then they're going to have to punish him for that."

"But he's in Texas," Ginny said.

"Yes, he is, for a while, but he has to go back to New York." As soon as she said this she realized it was a mistake.

"But we're not there!"

"Well, he's not there now either. He's on this . . . this business trip right now."

She wondered if the girls had picked up any clue that he had been out on bail and was staying with his mistress's family, and that he never even tried to contact them.

It was Doreen who had alerted her to the fact that her husband was now being portrayed as a capitalist hero for losing millions of dollars of his friends' money. Even Doreen, an Arizonan with a libertarian streak, found that idea preposterous. "Maybe he's too dumb to know what he was doing, but that doesn't mean it's not cheating. And to think I almost mortgaged the place to invest with him," she told Gemma.

"We miss Daddy," the girls said. "Don't you?"

Gemma nodded. "Of course you miss him. Of course you do."

WITHOUT UPDATING HER KIK-TOK STATUS or calling a soul, somehow her old high school friends knew that Gemma was back in town. Instead of being furious with her mother for letting out the news, she was grateful for the distraction of a few playdates for the girls. She agreed to meet up only with those of her old friends who had kids of similar age to her own, and who lived within a ten-mile radius of her mom's house. They were lucky Gammer had held on to the place, a generous ranch house on a winding canyon road up from the ocean. So many of her friends' parents had sold out, and she was shocked when she found her former high school pal Sharon living in a mobile home in one of the trailer parks at the base of a cliff above the Pacific Coast Highway.

Gemma drove her mom's old Camry, inching along the PCH, past the oil platforms offshore that she would never get used to, turning off the road in surprise when the GPS ordered her into the old Palisades Bowl. She wound around until she came to Terrace Drive and then pulled up beside a tan-and-brown double-wide.

They sat on the porch, drinking canned iced tea, and Sharon told her how she ended up there, in a trailer, her son and daughter sharing a room the size of a refrigerator box.

"Nothing to be ashamed of," Sharon said. "Divorced, a run of bad luck, crapload of debt. My credit shot. But I've kept out of credit rehab, kept my kids. But, damn, school is short now. They go at ten, back by two thirty. The school year ends May first, Gemma. May first! Can you imagine the hell we would have raised with four-and-a-half-month-long summers? But the kids have to stay real close. Coyotes everywhere."

Gemma hated feeling like a snob, but the surroundings, the urchin-like appearance of Sharon's children, was a shock. The trailer had siding rusted through in patches, narrow slot windows with frayed curtains, wallpaper peeling in strips, shag carpet worn to the baseboards in places. The kitchen sink was piled with dishes, clothes stuffed into garbage bags, all evidence of too many people living in too little space. And the son and daughter, Damon and Dahlia, had something almost feral about them. They were restless, pent up there in a trailer park, their neighbors mostly retirees, their mother seeming defeated. The kids looked bored and angry, unlike the open, smiling, easy sociability of Franny and Ginny.

She knew she had been sheltered in New York, but she had never bothered to consider just how different their privileged lives were. There had been this understanding, unspoken, that life in Manhattan was a precursor to their eventual flight, to a sanctuary somewhere, where they would be even more buffered from the increasingly calamitous global ailings. She and her friends had occasionally exchanged plans about their futures and the sanctuaries many of them had already purchased in preparation for their eventual flight when Manhattan island actually sank and the entire country turned to desert. But Manhattan itself had also been a kind of sanctuary. True, the elements interfered occasionally—the erratic weather, the closing of the FDR and the West Side Highway, the regular suspension of certain subway lines because of flooding—but the city itself was a bubble of relative prosperity compared to the real America of constant brush fires and droughts and heat and desertification. And now, without Arthur, she had nothing with which to shelter her girls from the world.

Sharon asked about Gemma's girls, who were in the next room, playing X³-Box with Sharon's son and daughter. Gemma said they were bearing up okay. "They miss their father."

"That was a hell of a thing," Sharon said. "And I thought you'd found a way out of this mess. Rich guy. Hedge funds or whatever."

"Maybe there is no way out of this mess."

As they sipped from their iced tea, from the bedroom they could hear the exaggerated revving of a computer game–generated engine noise.

Franny and Ginny emerged. "Can we go outside?"

Damon and Dahlia followed.

Sharon looked at Gemma, who shrugged.

"Okay, but stay close. Don't go up into the bluff or into the canyon. Have some water before you go. You'll dehydrate. You have sunscreen on?"

"Yes," all four lied.

Then Sharon turned to Gemma. "There's four of them. Coyotes won't mess with that many."

When the kids were gone, Sharon looked at Gemma and smiled. "Aren't we a sight? All grown up, with kids and no husbands."

"And what a place we've grown up into."

"But I always knew it was like this. Like in high school, it wasn't, like, the prettiest girl would date the handsomest guy. And then the next-cutest, and so on, so that it was all shared equal. It was, the prettiest girl had every guy in the school after her, and the rest of us were left with scraps. And look who I married? John Lapalm."

"It wasn't like that, was it?"

"It was. Maybe you wouldn't know, since you were the prettiest girl, or one of them, but then, throughout life, it just keeps going that way, the prettiest, or the richest, they get more of everything, more life, and the rest of us, even those who start out lucky, like me, born into a good town, parents with good jobs, we get left on the outside."

"I wasn't the prettiest girl," Gemma insisted.

"Okay, but top three," Sharon said and laughed. "And look, you had your shot, you are rich, or were, and you got away from all this, so, my theory holds up. You want a beer?"

"Sure," Gemma said.

They cracked open their beers and drank in silence. "You know, with Kik-Tok, or Facebook before, we see our old photos all the time. Someone is always posting a picture of me from high school, and I look at myself and think, Damn, I was pretty hot. And look at my life back then. I'm at the beach. I'm hanging out with these cute guys at State or by the pier. I'm wearing a Guns N' Roses T-shirt the day after the concert, standing there, posing with Michelle Alpert. It looks like paradise, like we are having the best time ever, and at the time I didn't even know it, so I wonder, in twenty years: Are we going to look at photos of now, of me with my kids living in a trailer, and think, Damn, that looks like the best time ever? 'Girl, you were really living it up then!' And imagine how shitty my life would have to be then, in the future, to look at my life now and think, Hot damn, I want some of that."

Gemma shook her head. "Past performance isn't any indication of future returns."

"What's that?"

"It's something finance guys use, a disclaimer. There are no guarantees."

They heard a scream from down the street. "Mom!"

Both women lunged from their chairs and were down the porch steps in seconds.

They saw three figures down the street, their shadows cast long and inland in the afternoon sun, the light making it hard to see which three of the four children were standing there. Running toward them, the women were already silently wishing their two kids were among the three. *Please, let my children be safe.*

But Gemma soon saw that Ginny was missing.

"Where is she?" she shouted.

The children pointed between the trailers, up toward the hill.

"Coyotes," the boy said. "W-w-we were up the hill, in the bushes, and I heard yipping, so I ran down, told the girls to follow. Didn't see Ginny."

"I told you don't go up the bluffs!" Sharon shouted.

Gemma ran between the trailers and up the hill, climbing the loose-packed and clodded earth in her flats, scratching her shins against the scrub. "Ginny!" she shouted.

"Call someone!" she shouted down toward Sharon.

She ran up a drainage ditch half-filled with dirt and empty, flattened plastic bottles.

"Ginny!"

She stopped and surveyed the bluffs. There was no sign of her. The hill stretched up for a hundred yards and then the angle flattened and she could not see what was beyond. The brush that looked so gentle from the highway was here shoulder high and dense. Her daughter could be anywhere.

How had she let this happen? A child wandering off while her mother drank beer. Why had the rest of the children not kept better track of Ginny? Where was her fucking husband? Where was her pepper spray? Where, where?

She cursed herself for ever leaving New York, for returning to California, and told herself that if she found Ginny, she would never, ever let her out of her sight again.

A trail cut off up the hill and she followed it, through a trash-strewn clearing that looked like a spot where teenagers drank beer, and then up a steeper path over crystalline yellow rocks. She had broken a sweat now, and was bleeding from her cuts, but she still had the energy to climb and then survey the bluff from this higher altitude, the trailer park spreading out below her. Sharon and the kids were no longer on the street where she had left them. Perhaps Sharon had taken the kids back to her trailer and taken up the search herself.

She regretted not having her phone.

The expanse of the area, which from the highway had seemed a deserted strip, now appeared vast and frightening. So many places for so many nasty things to hide. Where should she begin looking? She walked along the trail to a jutting ridge, seeking a clear vantage point around the bluffs that cut north into a canyon. But on the other side was just more brush broken by the occasional copse of oak or bunches of grotesquely twisted cacti. There were acres and acres tucked in here, the land undulating and folding over ridges and points and into pocket valleys and shoebox canyons. The land was divided occasionally by drainage ditches and traversed by animal trails, but despite its proximity to civilization it seemed to Gemma cruelly inhospitable. And Ginny had gone missing in this huge coyote den?

"Ginny!"

She climbed down a narrow track between green licorice-plant spears and followed a ditch, sliding on the rocky scarp, bruising herself as she fell. At one point, there was a concrete platform with a huge pipe protruding out of it and a gauge and metal wheel attached to its side. She paused there before descending, pushing into thicker and thicker brush until she burst through wiry acacia bushes and saw the remains of a camp: abandoned sleeping bags, a tarp shelter hung up between trees, empty cans and water bottles, the remains of a fire, clothes scattered where they had been left, and old sneakers, magazines, and books. She assumed she had stumbled upon an abandoned Ryanville. The sight of this squalor panicked her again. She imagined her daughter abducted by subprimes.

"Ginny! Ginny!"

She followed a trail out of the Ryanville and up another steep path.

"Mom!" She heard Ginny's voice, faint but clear.

"Ginny! I'm coming. Keep shouting."

"Mom, they're all around me."

"I'm coming."

"I can see them, Mom. I can hear them."

Gemma kept climbing. Her own breathing was so labored she could barely hear her daughter's shouts.

"Mom!"

She cut through a thick patch of acacia and a stand of California poppies so woven with spiderwebs that it felt like she was pushing through a closet of silk dresses. Then she heard growling, a snapping noise.

"Mom! They're dogs!"

Gemma was struggling to free herself from the strands and the thick branches, the barbs of acacia leaves and the thistles of sage and broom bushes. She lost a shoe somewhere, and was scraped raw by the flora, but she kept on pushing through to her daughter, finally emerging in a clearing where she saw Ginny, sitting down, blood running down her arm, her face badly scraped.

"Mom!"

There was scurrying in the brush, the scissoring of thin legs and brown and gray fur as coyotes were circling, flashes of silver irises sizing up the little girl, and now Gemma. Gemma could hear the animals breathing, their yips and barks. Where was her pepper spray when she needed it? Ah, wasted on the strange man who had surprised her a few days ago, warning her about coyotes.

Two humans instead of one. What would the coyotes make of that? More daunting, or just more meat?

Gemma grabbed her daughter, hugged her, and winced at the gash ripped into her arm.

"Ouch!" Ginny cried.

"They bit you!"

Ginny looked down at her arm. She had not yet realized she'd been bitten.

Gemma could actually see bone white through the bloody flesh. The scent of the blood had stirred the pack, who were now circling in anticipation of finishing the job. Gemma was too angry to be frightened. If the dogs wanted her little girl, they were going to have to go through her. She didn't formulate this thought, but it was a fact of her current state. Her fear, anger, rage, confusion, all of it coalesced into her being willing to face a charging coyote without hesitation.

The alpha dog leaped up at Ginny. The coyote was going after the weakest, youngest, most vulnerable. The teeth were gray and dry, the mouth angled open and the eyes surprisingly beautiful for an animal trying to kill. Gemma swung a hard overhand right that landed flush on the bridge of the coyote's nose, smashing the canine head downward and changing its trajectory so that it landed on its side on Ginny's legs. The hind legs were scratching into Ginny's flesh as the bitch tried to gain purchase. Gemma struck again, another blow to the head. The dog twisted its head to try to bite Gemma's arm, then backed away.

The rest of the pack was watching with interest, and Gemma heard another dog charging. Again she turned and swung and caught that dog flush on its open mouth, cutting her hand on its teeth but dealing the surprised dog a sharp blow that caused it to turn off into the bushes.

The alpha dog somehow recognized in Gemma an alpha female like herself who would not let her pup be taken.

"Back off, bitch." Gemma lunged, her hands up again, going for the neck, but the animal scurried away into the bush.

Ginny had gone faint, most likely from shock. Gemma put her arms around her, their blood running together. She heard, barely, distant voices, the crackling sound of a radio. She tried to shout but was suddenly so tired she could not raise much voice. The fight had drained her, the adrenaline was no longer surging, and she suddenly felt exhausted, found appealing the notion of a short nap. Just a few minutes' sleep . . .

She roused herself. If they slept, her daughter would lose more blood, the dogs would come back. She pulled off her blouse, ripped the sleeve off, and tied it around Ginny's arm above the wound as tightly as she could. The claw marks on their legs were also bleeding. Her own hand was badly cut and scraped and she could barely bend her fingers.

"Ginny, honey, get up, get up. We have to move."

"Are they gone?"

"Yes, dear, they're gone. Get up."

Ginny rose unsteadily to her feet. Gemma took the girl on her back, piggyback style, and, bent over, marched down the hill. She had no idea she was this strong.

THEY EMERGED FROM THE BRUSH a bloody mess. Their clothes torn, their hair streaked with leaves, twigs, and ticks, and blood everywhere, from scrapes and gashes they did not even know they had.

There was an ambulance waiting for them. And a fire truck had snaked up the hill and was idling, its lights flashing. The firemen were still up the hill searching for them. A police drone buzzed overhead and then was apparently called off, since it banked and headed south along the ocean.

Sharon had taken the kids inside. Franny was hysterical when she saw her mother and sister through the screen door. She charged over but stopped when she was close enough to see all the blood.

"They bit you!"

Gemma shook her head. "Ginny."

The paramedics came over with a stretcher and carefully moved Ginny onto the metal-framed gurney and then slid her into the back of the red-and-white van.

"Ma'am, you're injured as well—"

"I'm fine," Gemma said.

"We have another ambulance—"

"I'll ride with her. Franny? Sharon, can you drive Franny to the hospital? Which hospital?"

"Ma'am," said one of the paramedics, a tall bald man wearing shorts and a blue polo shirt, "we need a valid credit card. And can we ask what kind of insurance you are carrying?"

"I'm . . . I don't know," Gemma said. "My credit card is—it's in my purse." She turned to Sharon. "Can you get it?"

"Can we just *go*?" she said to the paramedic.

"That depends on your insurance."

Gemma had a vague awareness of insurance payments being one among many matters that she had let slide since Arthur's arrest. Now she felt irresponsible, her daughter bleeding from a coyote bite, and she had to admit to the paramedic she was uninsured.

"Look, lady, we don't want to spend the night driving from hospital to hospital, looking for one that'll take you. If you don't have insurance, we'll take you to State Services."

"Where's that?"

"Norwalk. We could get you patched up in outpatient at St. Johns. How's your credit?"

"I can't believe we are having this conversation. She needs medical attention."

"As soon as your friend gives me the card, we'll be on our way."

A fireman in helmet and heavy jacket came down the trail, his boots crunching.

"Did you see them?" Gemma asked.

The fireman shook his head. "But they're up there. Nothing we can do about it. We go out on a half-dozen coyote calls a day."

"Mom!" Ginny shouted.

"A sec, Ginny." She glared at the paramedic.

The fireman nodded. "Is that her? She sounds okay."

"She's a fighter."

Sharon came out with her purse. Gemma took it, found her wallet, and handed the paramedic her one good card. He took it, swiped it on a handheld meter, and nodded.

"Hey, 710! We're good to go."

GINNY SCREAMED AS THE WOUND was cleaned, wrapped, and bandaged ($1,875). The rabies test ($450) was negative. She needed a pint of blood ($1,590). An X-ray ($700) showed no damage to the deltoid, and a range of motion test ($330) was inconclusive. Her bruises were assessed and determined not to be indicative of hemorrhagic distress ($100). Her legs were

swiped and lightly dressed ($420). The doctor ($1,950) determined it unlikely she would have long-term nerve damage from
the bite, and a nurse ($450) showed Gemma how to change the
dressing on the wounds and provided her with bandages, anti-
septic ointment, and wraps ($300). Gemma's own hand required
six butterfly stitches ($600) on the index and middle fingers. Her
own scrapes and bruises were cleaned and dressed ($320).

Franny was in the emergency room with Doreen, who had
brought a change of clothes for them as soon as Gemma called.
By the time Ginny and Gemma emerged from the emergency
ward, Franny was lying with her head in Doreen's lap. Ginny
was asleep in an emergency ward bed, the television tuned to
a muted Disney channel. Gemma came out to see them, and at
the sight of her, in bandages and with her bruises, Franny began
to cry again.

"Mom, are you okay?" she asked.

"I think I am. Ginny is resting up. They want to watch her a
few more hours, but I think we're over the worst. They said they
treat fifteen coyote bites a day."

"Your momma is a strong woman," Doreen said, turning to
Franny. "Now, sit here a bit with Franny, I'm going to sneak
outside." Doreen needed a cigarette.

"Were you frightened, Mom?" Franny asked.

"I wasn't feeling anything. Just these, dogs, circling, and then
jumping, and I wasn't going to let them get to Ginny."

"You were fighting them."

"With my bare hands." Gemma held up her right hand,
stitched up and wrapped.

"Can coyotes get us at Gammer's?" Franny asked.

"Nope."

Franny's eyes welled up with tears. She was sobbing again.
"I'm s-so sad," she said.

"It's okay. Ginny is gonna be fine. I'm fine."

"N-n-no, not you guys. The whales!"

Gemma turned to see on a wall-mounted television Fox News showing footage of the beached whales and a graphic reporting that eight of the dozen whales were believed to be dead.

When Doreen returned, Gemma led them back to where Ginny was resting. They gathered around, smiling, and Ginny said, "This never would have happened if Dad was here."

Gemma stood at the foot of the bed, forcing a smile, silently cursing the world.

WHEN SHE RETURNED HOME, MANY thousands of dollars in debt to MasterCard, and with a daughter who might never want to stray from a paved road again, she found an e-mail from a reporter asking if she would talk for just a few minutes. He said they had actually met, in fact she had pepper-sprayed him just a few days ago. So he was the prophet who had surprised her during her morning run with strange ramblings about coyotes.

You know what, she thought. Fuck Arthur. I'm out here, fighting coyotes, trying to keep my kids alive, and what is he doing? He's hanging around in Texas with über-con assholes who are calling him some kind of capitalist hero? She'd show the world what kind of hero Arthur was. Yes, she wrote to the reporter, yes, I'll meet with you. When? Where?

She slid Ginny and Franny into bed and gave Ginny a slug of the hydrocodone-laced cough syrup ($225). She would have a scar for life. Her shoulder would be sore for weeks. The poor girl. She did not remember the coyote sinking its teeth into her arm, or how she had broken free. When going after larger prey, like a human child, coyotes tended to stalk and strike, and repeat, until the weakened animal could be taken down. Ginny must have fought hard to have survived until Gemma could find her. The pack had been lurking, and one more bite could have pulled her little girl to the ground, where they would have gone for her kidney, liver, heart—Gemma didn't like to think about it.

Nor did she feel ready for social engagements of any kind. She did not want to consider her dating prospects post-Arthur. Her mother was a cautionary tale. In the thirty-five years since she had left her husband—a homosexual violinist who lived in an air-conditioned compound in New Mexico with a dozen stray dogs—Doreen had not had a lover. Gemma shuddered at the thought of that kind of parched spell.

Gemma knew she was not fooling anyone, not after what she had been going through these last few months: she looked her age. But her auburn hair retained its luster, her eyes were still green and bright, her lips full, the skin around her jaw taut, even if there were wrinkles—more every day—radiating from the corners of her eyes and along her forehead. True worry lines, as she weighed in silence the prospects of a single motherhood with a deadbeat con-man husband. Gemma was a handsome woman, retaining her appeal even as her features betrayed the beginnings of the muting and fraying of age, and while men no longer might elbow each other as she passed in front of a bar, every man would be secretly thinking to himself, Hmm, not bad, not bad at all.

She, of course, was too well aware of what she had once been: steadily, dependably pretty. And while she knew she had not lost that completely, she also knew that she was no longer a woman who could compel men to launch proverbial fleets.

Facing the mirror, she cursed herself for her vanity at a time like this, her hand bandaged and now aching (she had Tualaton tablets for that), scrapes and bruises up and down her legs. She'd fought off a goddamn pack of coyotes! Maybe it was being back in her adolescent bedroom, geography reawakening teen worries like *Am I pretty? Do they like me?*

Never, she thought, never again would she be driven by self-doubt and insecurity and teen-girl self-loathing. She would loathe Arthur. She would love herself.

SARGAM HAD QUICKLY EMERGED AS one of the leaders of Valence, in part because of her value as chief mechanic, keeping alive a fleet of battered SUVs that could shuttle the men—and a few women—to work in Placer or Drum. A Pepper Industries subsidiary, HG Extraction, was fracking natural gas from the shale beneath the former agricultural communities sixty miles up the road. They occasionally could hear the convoys of hydraulic rigs rolling by on the highway. There was steady work on the fracking sites, doing the dangerous grunt jobs of cementing, building the casings, and mixing the proppants, and for those who could operate a backhoe or a steamroller, there was work running heavy equipment. The men and women returned weary, but with more money than they would have made day-laboring. They were all eating better. There was a doctor who had turned up in Valence, as well as a nurse. And just a few days ago a former farmer arrived who knew how to maximize crop yields.

Two families a day were now rolling into Valence. They had somehow skirted the border credit checks or found a back road into Nevada, bypassing the gilded tourist mecca of a previous age, Las Vegas, still strobe-lit and neon-suffused but now haunted only by European tourists and those who really did not have much to lose. The serious gamblers, the one-percenters looking to try their luck, avoided Vegas, preferring the legalized gambling meccas now spread across deregulated America.

Sargam noticed that each new family came warily, as if expecting to be turned away, asking humbly for a night's lodging, a place to light a fire and open a can of chili, heat a tortilla. She saw them nod with surprise, their eyes widening, when they were told to pick an empty house and make it their own, offered a seat around a campfire, a cold beer or a mason jar of lemonade thrust into their hands. And she saw hope and confidence restored as the men and women listened to what was offered here: some fracking work if they were lucky; plenty of fieldwork if they weren't. There were green beans, spinach, carrots, and onions to bring in. If they had a few dollars to put into the community fund for lentils, rice, and beans, the community would take it. If not, all they had to give was their backs for an honest day's work.

It made sense in a way that nothing had in a long time. There was no anxiety over credit scores or being hauled in on a collection notice and sent to credit rehab. Nobody had Internet access, and for the first time they did not miss it. Nobody had a working cell phone, but neither did anyone whom they might have wanted to call.

Sargam watched new families settle into abandoned structures and gradually transform them into homes. She saw smiles return to children's faces, the weight lifted from their young shoulders. And she saw the fathers come back from a day's work with some folding money and their wives, those who weren't also working, returning from the marketing with detergent.

Old couples showed up, senior citizens driving beat-up jalopies, asking for water, a place to sleep. There were murmurs in the community about letting in the old and the infirm. Darren was among those who argued that they needed workers and could not support freeloaders. Sargam insisted they take in all who wanted to come, even if they were in need.

"If we reject folks for being old or sick, we're no better than a bank or a credit agency. We need to do the right thing, that's got to be our guiding principle. People helping people."

"Or people dragging people down," Darren said.

"*Or* all we've found is a smaller version of that shitty world we're leaving behind."

DARREN AND SARGAM HAD THEIR first argument over whether or not there should be any governing structure in Valence. They were sitting on her sleeping bag in her house, both freshly washed after trips to the pump. Darren was pointing out how, for example, the pump was getting so crowded in the early evenings that perhaps they should assign different time slots to different streets. Sargam urged against it. And while Darren had initially been opposed, he said he had begun to see the need for some organization. Despite his own status pre-Sargam, he now said he believed that the number of single, unattached men should be kept to a minimum. There had to be strict prohibitions against fighting. And each family had to contribute four days, or nights, a week to farming the parcels. The Commons, as Darren had taken to calling the land, required steady maintenance and work. The leafy greens attracted all kinds of scavenging herbivores. The erection of a fence, Darren said, was essential to the community's survival, a project the scale of which required community-wide cooperation. And there had to be designated latrines.

"We have fifty families here, a few hundred folks, we need some way to keep tabs, to encourage participation, to keep the focus on the community," Darren said.

"No, let it evolve. Trial and error."

"We'll be buried in shit."

His night-soil program was his first attempt at community-wide organization. He had five bathtubs broken out of bathrooms, removed to a high point, and then covered with planks. Ripping the drains out of the houses was more difficult, requiring a week of digging in the hot sun and stripping the pipes from the earth, but once he had assembled a few hundred meters, he ran pipe from the bathtub drains into the fields. "You shit in a bucket, you slop the bucket out in the baths," he said. "It's easier than digging a hole." He also wanted the chicken shit scraped up and tossed in, along with any other organic waste.

He had the kids spend the better part of a week looking for earthworms, which he poured into the covered tubs. The worms made a meal of the feces, turning that into soil, while the runoff—worm urine—was a potent and highly effective fertilizer.

He pointed out to Sargam the success of this program, that it proved the community was capable of following a few rules.

"But these are folks who were beaten by rules," Sargam said, "who ran from the rules, who've been told all their lives that they were breaking rules."

"How can we keep growing if folks won't do their part?" Darren asked.

"They will, you have to talk to them. Don't tell them they have to do this or that, but include them."

Darren thought this over. "You mean explain?"

"Yeah, explain what needs to be done, and tell them we have to work together to get it done. Don't become a rule maker, that's like a boss. These folks have had enough of all that."

Darren nodded. "Can't hurt to try."

He took Sargam in his arms, kissing her behind the ear and down the neck.

She pulled away. "Hmm, we gotta go eat."

"You're in such a hurry to get some beans you would leave me all hot and bothered?"

"Trust me, I'm a much sweeter girl on a full stomach."

But Sargam did notice a change coming over her. She was still fond of Darren, found him attractive, but lately she had felt a lessening of desire, a withdrawal from the need for rutting and rubbing. At first she wondered if she was with child, but her period had arrived a few days later. The more involved she was becoming in the community, the more time she spent with the men and women of Valence, talking to them, advising them, listening to them, the less she wanted to be with any one man. If Darren was aware of her decreasing ardor, he kept it to himself. There was so much about Sargam that he didn't understand.

While it was Darren who worried over the technical and engineering issues of their small community, it was Sargam who was emerging as the spiritual leader. The women enjoyed her company, and enjoyed sharing their confidences with her. An Ecuadorean woman, Milla, told her she suspected her husband had eyes for the lady from Hemmet who squatted next door. That bad neighbor had been flirting with her husband at night around the campfire and complimenting him on his appearance, even how he fit his jeans. Milla told Sargam she had not stuck with him through two thousand miles of bad road only to lose him to a pale *gordita*. Sargam assured her that she would talk to the woman and urged her to be patient, to be kind to her husband and give him no reason to stray.

Sargam sidled up to the woman in question the next day while they were on their knees, plucking green beans from the vine, and asked her if she liked Valence.

"It's not a matter of like, is it?" the woman, Maureen, said. "It's a matter of we can stay here. Live here without fear of being run off."

"It is, but we have to work at it," Sargam said.

"I'm working." Maureen showed her apron full of beans.

"Yes, but we also have to work spiritually. To let go of a little bit of ourselves, our ego, so that we can live this way."

Maureen sat up and wiped her forehead. "What are you getting at?"

"What we are doing, making a community, takes great personal strength and character. We have to love our neighbors, to respect our fellow men and women, and perhaps be very sensitive to the feelings of those around us. This isn't just another Ryanville, this is a home. So respect your neighbor."

Maureen squinted, not sure if Sargam was being specific or general, but she nodded. Maureen could see that Sargam was a pretty woman, even beautiful, but somehow she posed no threat and offered no competition. And she now understood that Sargam knew she had flirted with her neighbor.

"I got you," Maureen said. "It's just old habits."

"That's what we need to lose, those old habits. That old world. What we're doing here is for us, people helping people, and if we can make this work, then we'll have done something we can be proud of, without knowing anyone's damn credit score. Let the coasts sink into the ocean. We're learning how to get by on our own."

Maureen nodded, suddenly proud of her little part in this community.

For Sargam, this was one of a dozen visits she would make during the day, bringing peace to squabbling children, calming a woman who was panicky at not being able to call or text her sister, reconciling a feuding husband and wife. She was a soothing presence, and the community waited anxiously for her to turn up at campfire every night, where she would sit down wherever there was space, seemingly unaware of the role she was increasingly coming to play.

When she told Darren that what they needed more than any rules was a proper school, he thought of a few dozen projects he considered more urgent, but then he saw the look in her eyes and nodded, yes, she was right.

SARGAM WATCHED THEM ROLL OFF the ramp and onto Bienvenida, the main street, the Flex listing on an undersized spare, the hood tied down with rope. Jeb at the wheel, and Bailey beside him, Vanessa, looking even more grown in the backseat and beside her the boy, looking about. When he saw Sargam stepping into the street he opened his mouth in surprise.

They had kept this street clear, the house fronts unmodified, the brown lawns unwatered, so that the first impression anyone had on exiting the highway was of an abandoned subdivision, no different from a hundred thousand such wastelands across the country. Sargam was walking across Valence to see a woman worried her son was going too wild. As she approached the curb, the Flex halted and all four jumped out simultaneously, their voices swirling together.

They looked even more bedraggled than when she had last seen them: Jeb in a greasy T-shirt, jeans, and a pair of work boots; Bailey in a blouse and shorts; Vanessa wearing an old sundress she'd found somewhere, one shoulder strap hanging down over her arm; and the boy in too-short jeans, a T-shirt, and a pair of sneakers three sizes too big. They were bonier than Sargam remembered, hunger and exhaustion wafting off them. It was a miracle they had made it this far.

Sargam hugged each of them, and listened to where they had been and what they had been doing: back to Los Angeles, back to Riverside, stops at a half-dozen Ryanvilles, some part-time work building one of the new elevated expressways along the coastal corridor, taking a southern route out of California they had heard about, through Arizona and then up into Nevada. They had heard about Valence, a few folks had, as a place where you could find a little house, maybe some work, and live in peace. No one running you off every three days. And they heard there were dances and good food.

Sargam nodded. "We're trying."

"You're famous," the boy said. "We heard talk about you in the last Ryanville. That you were teaching folks a new way of living."

Sargam laughed. "Not a new way, an old way, a basic way."

"And we never said a word that you were the lady who conked that guy on the head, brained him."

"Quiet, boy," said Jeb. "Don't mind him." He turned back to Sargam. "But we did hear about you."

"About this pretty lady running a community out in the desert," Bailey added.

"They were here before me," Sargam said. "Come on, I'll show you around. There's still a few houses up on Las Lomas, that's four blocks up and to the right."

"My kids are hungry," Bailey said in a small voice.

"Of course." Sargam told them to pull the Flex up to the next corner and turn right. There was a kitchen up there and lunch was almost ready.

They were handed plastic plates with beans, rice, green beans, cooked spinach, and scrambled eggs. The family took seats on long, split logs and ate while other members of the community coming in from the fields joined them. New families came in every day, and sating their hunger set them at ease. There were more Californians turning up, even a couple of families from Riverside. Jeb and Bailey sighed deeply and talked for the first time in months about matters other than who might be hiring or whether there was a water tap or who might have made off with their last good cooking pot. Vanessa sat quietly apart from her parents, but she perked up when a handsome young man, perhaps a year older than she was, dirty blond hair and a gap in his teeth, appeared with a soccer ball and started a little kick-around. Soon, more boys and girls were playing soccer on the scrubby patch between the campfire flat and the fields.

The food was good and filling, and after cleaning his plate and drinking a mug full of water, the boy, Tom, could not resist and ran to join the other children playing soccer. Bailey was about to shout at him not to run on a full stomach, but watching him stalk the ball with his serious, consumed expression, she decided to let him play, for once, just let him play.

SARGAM TOOK THEM TO THE house on Las Lomas. It was not much, three bedrooms that needed a long and hard scrubbing, a living room with filthy carpeting, and a kitchen long ago stripped of appliances and copper piping. But it was a roof and four walls, a front door, the water main down the long, curving street.

They would be sleeping on the floor. Washing in cold water. And Sargam could promise nothing but hard work for little money. They would get what everybody else got, no more, no less. But nobody was going to run their credit or treat them like dirt because they were in debt.

"And," Sargam said, "*you* are going to help me start a school."

Bailey smiled. "You think we can do that?"

"I think we can do anything. That's what this is all about."

Bailey looked around her tattered little house. "I got a lot of work to do. Vanessa, go out to the Flex and bring in all the bedding. I've got some twine rolled up beneath the backseat. See about making a clothesline. Jeb, get that crowbar and rip up this filthy carpet. I'd rather sleep on wood."

She looked for the boy, but he was gone, back to playing soccer with the other boys.

She shook her head, walked over, and hugged Sargam. "Thank you."

FOR THE CHILDREN OF VALENCE, the days were spent shirking work and running wild in the scrubby grassland around the subdivision. The roads had been built on spurs from main thoroughfares, ending in cul-de-sacs, so that when viewed from above, the community might look like the splayed stalks of a fern, stripped of leaves. Within days the boy joined with a gang who ranged through the hills around the subdivision, returning hourly because of the fierce thirst the sun and heat worked up in them. The heat was so intense the boy could actually feel the thirst starting, first as an extra swallow, then as a stickiness in the mouth, and finally a thick, gel-like texture at the back of his throat. In the final stages, he could develop a slight headache, but by then he was back at the pump, guzzling water from one of the plastic bottles that littered the area and were rinsed by the boys and refilled. They ran and they drank, that was the cycle of their days. They played war, capture the flag, ditch, cowboys and Indians, GIs and Vietcong, Navy SEALs and Al Qaeda. They played soccer and football and even a version of baseball with a bat and a tennis ball, which they fielded barehanded. There was always another game, always boys and girls willing to play. A whole desert stretched around them, dry as the inside of a sealed car, but all theirs, every sandy foot of it.

Few of the kids still had bikes, and even fewer skateboards— Tom was one of the lucky few who had managed to hold on to his old deck—and they shared those, playing a game they made up called sweeper, sort of like kickball with bikes and skateboards. They spied on women getting dressed, stole corn from the community stores, caught lizards and garter snakes, and ran from rattlers. Within a week of arriving, the boy had a tarantula in a coffee can that he kept until his mother found it and had him release it far from the house.

He had friends within a day, and knew their names within two. Ted, Juaquin, Emmett, Yuri, Vito, Yoshi, and Juan were the boys; Emma, Nathalie, and Maya the girls, and soon it seemed he knew them better than he had ever known anyone. After a few weeks he even stopped worrying that his family would be moving on and that he would lose his new friends, because nobody was leaving, and in fact more kids kept coming.

He came home filthy every night, his mother ordering him to the pump with a bucket, and not to return until he had scrubbed himself, which he did in the encroaching darkness and the first chill of night air, shivering and not getting himself clean in the cracks and hard-to-reach spots and drying himself too fast and then running home because he did not want to miss supper or the campfire or the DJ parties on Friday nights.

Vanessa, now above these childish games, was only too aware of what she was missing. She had seen enough movies and read enough books to know that teenage life in America was supposed to involve cars and kik-toks from cute boys and dates and a prom. She should be shopping in malls and flirting with boys, but here she was, in this desert, with, like, nothing to do. She helped her mom, cleaning the bedding, airing out sleeping bags, and hauling water in buckets from the pump. Jeb had nailed the bottoms of coffee cans over the gaps in the floor, boarded up the windows, and duct-taped a seal where gaps had opened between the sill and the wall. The house was dark, but Jeb found a clear plastic tarp that he laid over one window to let in some light. The nights were cold, but more comfortable than sleeping outside. Though the boy slept soundly, issuing occasional soft murmurs that sounded as if he were playing even in his dreams, Vanessa would lie awake, recalling boys she knew when she was last in school, and wistful for missed opportunities, such as a date with Manny Bramford, who had told her friend Tobin that he liked her, but then she and her family had moved away before they had even had a conversation.

Her mother showed her how to soak up her monthly blood with a rag when they ran out of tampons in Arizona. When they arrived in Valence, Sargam gave her mom a box of tampons for which Vanessa was grateful. But here she was, a woman in a place surrounded by wild boys and old men. What was there for her?

Part of her wanted to be running the hills with her brother and his friends, and another part wanted something brighter and more exciting. She had an idea in her head of sitting in a car, a boy in the backseat next to her, the weight of his body in motion. She remembered hiding beneath a mattress as a little girl, and the feeling of evenly applied pressure that left her with a novel wetness between her legs.

I DON'T LIKE TO REREAD my old work, especially my first book, my only book that received some acclaim and notice, which, at that time anyway, made me feel as if I were making a difference. But I'm stoned and feeling nostalgic, so I take an old hardcover edition of *What You Wish For* from the bookcase in my office and I begin reading and I am taken by the energy, the anger, of the prose. This writer—was it really me?—is caring so deeply about the fate of the world, rooting so hard for our better natures that he—I—told the story so that it reads like an instructional manual about how to live virtuously: We must care, it makes clear, about our neighbors. For our fates are inseparable.

But who was I to stand in the way of regress? I was just one man. What could I do? I still care, I really do, but my concerns are more parochial. I'm trying to hold my family together, or the rump version of if that remains, raise my kids to ride bikes, swim, read, all that old-fashioned stuff nobody does anymore. I see what we've become—I wish I could say I was blinkered— but I just don't know what to do about it. There's no one really standing up and saying, "What the fuck are we doing?" Give me something or someone to believe in, and, well, I don't know if I would actually believe, but I might write a hell of a story about it.

There is a knock on my office door. I put out my joint and wave an old tablet computer around to try to air out my office.

There's Ronin, on his way home from school and stopping by, presumably to get money for a snack.

I worry that my office reeks.

"Hey." He tries to brush past me.

"Wait, wait." I won't budge. "You hungry? Let's go eat."

"With you?"

"Why not?"

He weighs the idea. How embarrassing is it to be seen with your father in the middle of the afternoon on a weekday?

"How about you just give me some money and I'll go to Panda and get some food and eat it here."

I give him a twenty. This buys me time.

When he returns with his food, glutinous heaps of sugary, corn-starch-coated chicken and greasy noodles and a huge waxed cup of pink drink, he sits on my office sofa and begins chewing with his mouth open, chicken and noodle and pink drink sloshing around behind retainered teeth.

"How is school?"

"Sucks."

"You dealing with Freaks?"

"Sucks."

"Math?"

"Sucks."

Ronin has cycled through various expensive tutoring programs in an attempt to boost his math scores, which persist in the range typical of underperforming Caucasians. Mathematics instruction, bewildering in the best of times for me, is the educational Mordor of my son's life. What his middle school is teaching, and how they are teaching it, does not resemble what went on in the classrooms of my youth. What stops me from outright rejecting these new methods is my own feckless academic record. Who am I to have deeply held opinions about what works or doesn't work in the classroom?

Still, what's happening in my son's middle school is a microcosm of our era's preferred method of fucking up. Three years ago, after a bitter court fight in which the teachers' union was stripped of collective bargaining rights, every math teacher in California was fired and public school math instruction throughout the state was privatized. Enhanced Quantitatives, or EQ, a division of a private equity firm that has contracts with numerous state boards of education, claimed to have cracked the code of Asian math dominance. EQ's software-based learning system was supposed to bring American seventh- and eighth-graders up to the level of their peers in Singapore and Shanghai. What this meant was hours of watching instructional videos and PowerPoint presentations by EQ specialists who were themselves barely numerically literate—and would have been earning minimum wage had that not been abolished. The students were ordered to memorize a host of materials that I had never

learned: perfect squares to 1,600, times tables to 40 x 40, *pi* to ten
places. I had trouble seeing what purpose all this rote memory
served, and for Ronin, who seemed to have not yet developed the
part of his frontal cortex that dealt with retaining data beyond
social network passwords and *Call of Duty* cheats, these strings of
numbers might as well have been distant planets for all the like-
lihood he ever had of reaching the required goals. Even with EQ
now designing the state exams, the students' scores had dropped,
which the EQ specialists had blamed on our children failing to
memorize what their peers in Singapore and Shanghai memorize by the time they are seven years old. The solution: sign our
kids up for expensive EQ extra sessions, which are proving as
fruitless as the actual classes themselves.

I went to school to meet one of these EQ specialists—Barry,
who wore a microphone headset the whole time we spoke because
every conversation he has with a parent is recorded by EQ.

I asked about Ronin, and why, after all these extra EQ sessions, he was still struggling in math. Barry answered, "The
EQ learning experience has been assembled from thirty-six
semantic differentials and cross-referenced with best-practices
standards from the top-five-performing academic systems in the
world. The EQ learning experience has been proven to increase
test scores in simulated test takers by eleven percent per year of
implementation."

I realized he was repeating words that were being spoken into
his earpiece.

"What about Ronin?"

"Of course, the performance of each individual EQ subclient
may vary."

"But Ronin—"

"The subclient, even after purchase of additional EQ products, may still deviate from the statistical norms—"

"Can we just talk about Ronin?"

He held up a finger to silence me.

"—may still deviate from the statistical norms and simulated test-taker results for a variety of non-EQ-related causes—"

"Stop talking."

"—for a variety of non-EQ-related causes, including but not limited to non-EQ-controlled events. If, for example, the EQ subclient fails to process EQ-designed and -assigned units in the required time, then that subclient falls out of the EQ Learning Experience statistical normatives and cannot be included in any EQ Learning Experience assessments."

"This is supposed to be a parent-teacher conference."

"A parent-*specialist* conference," he corrected me.

"About why Ronin is screwing up in math."

"And I've explained, that if the subclient fails to process EQ-designed—"

"Could you just talk like a normal person?"

He listened to the voice in his earpiece. "As an EQ specialist, I am free to discuss the EQ Learning Experience and related products, and to direct you to our website, or smartphone app, or Kik-Tok, or, if you prefer, to provide you with a hard copy catalog, and there you will see the various EQ Learning Experience options that are available to you."

"So the solution is to buy more crap from your company?"

And that was when I decided that if Ronin was ever going to learn basic algebra, I would have to teach him myself.

I'm an awful teacher. Yet I've always believed every father has three responsibilities: to teach his children to swim, ride a bicycle, and master the multiplication tables. (Though my own father failed at all three.) But somehow, through teary afternoons during which any witness would have called Child Protective Services for how I shouted at my children, they learned to ride and swim. And Ronin, miraculously, had committed his multiplication tables to memory, up to 12 x 12. Maybe there was hope.

I look at Ronin. So fragile in his skinny jeans and high-top Converse and hoodie with a broken zipper. I want to give him a big hug and tell him, Fuck those people and their fucking lame math. He seems so vulnerable, a little kid, trying to act big and unafraid, and failing at both. He chomps his Chinese food and grins vacantly, confused by the awful education he is receiving and further embarrassed at being labeled a youthful sexual predator. I want to drive with him to a cabin somewhere—in one of the few national parks not yet ruined by shale oil extraction rigs—and just let him be a kid and screw up in all the ways that kids are supposed to screw up.

I get up and lumber toward him.

"Dad, what are you doing?"

"I just want to give you a hug."

"Um, weird," he says. But he lets me engulf him.

Later, as we're walking up Bashford toward our house, the sidewalks empty and Ronin stomping alongside me in his impatient lope, he asks, "Why don't you drive, like normal people?"

It's not a question that merits answering, so I ignore it and we continue our trudge up the street.

We round the corner onto Iliff, and we can hear coyotes howling—the sun is nowhere near setting—but instead of frightening, it is somehow beautiful and we feel safe even if it's just the two of us against the dogs of the world.

ABOUT A BLOCK UP ILIFF, we come upon something remarkable: a half-dozen boys between the ages of eight and puberty, playing a game of football over two stretches of lawn bisected by a driveway. They are playing three-on-three, a self-hiking quar-

terback and two receivers versus a rusher, who is counting—
and I love this—in Mississippi, and two pass defenders. The
game bears no resemblance to the football played on television
or the Gruden NFL computer game. This is padless, helmetless,
in flat-soled sneakers on patchy grass, and it is beautiful. They
are tackling each other on the hard earth, wrapping each other
and collapsing to the ground in piles of boys. How many hours
had I spent playing like this? One end zone a driveway, the other
a flower bed. This feels like time travel. I look at Ronin. He
seems fascinated by the game, by kids playing a game in their
own front yard. It is something he has not seen before, not in
our neighborhood, where children are driven to and from games
and practices in armored vehicles.

"What are they doing?" he asks.

"They're playing football."

"Where are the uniforms? The, you know, helmets and stuff?"

I tell him that you can play football in whatever you are wearing. You just need a ball.

One of the boys, tall with black hair that falls to his eyes, completes a long pass to a teammate, who runs through the driveway
for a touchdown and then is tackled by his opponent anyway.

"Let's play," I say.

Ronin shakes his head. "That would be weird."

"Come on," I say. "There's two of us. It'll be even."

"Dad, come on, don't—"

Maybe it's because I'm still stoned, but I step out onto the
lawn and ask if we can join. "One and one?"

The boys look at each other and shrug. How weird is this? I'm
having trouble figuring that out, but I realize I'm going to have
to ignore my perceptions of any reactions to my weirdness and
just have fun. As soon as I pick up the football, I feel better. I toss
it to Ronin, who drops it.

"Hey, Ronin," says the dark-haired boy who threw the touch-down pass.

"You two know each other?" I ask.

Ronin nods.

Two of the other boys whisper something to each other, and I believe I hear the word "Freaks" hissed in their exchange, but I choose to ignore it.

"Okay, Ronin, you play with them"—I point to the dark-haired player's team—"and I'll play with these guys."

I receive the punt to start the game, and I hand it to one of the boys on our team and he runs alongside some ice plants before being shoved into the patch of dirt around a lemon tree. We huddle up. The biggest boy on my team is named Martin, and he is the quarterback. The other two, the two who were whispering about Ronin, are named Brian and something that sounds like Fizz. Martin gives us each a pattern. Brian and Fizz are going to run a crossing pattern, I'm to go deep. We break and I look over at Ronin, standing with his hands in his pockets at the line of scrimmage, looking down at the grass. I want him to be more engaged, to be in an aggressive-looking crouch like the other defenders, or with a knee-forward, legs-bent stance like the pass rusher, but his body language is of total indifference.

"Come on, Rone. Ready?" I say.

He shrugs.

"Hut, hut, hike!" Martin fades back, the two boys run their crossing pattern, and I begin to lope downfield, looking back for the ball, which is on me surprisingly quickly. The kid has a good arm. I catch it, and take a few slow steps, not wanting to take too much advantage of my size, when I am gang-tackled by three defenders—they are fast little fuckers—and the collective weight of them collapses me and I feel for a moment like I am going to vomit. For good measure, Ronin jogs over and jumps on the pile as well, and I feel a sharp cramp running down my side. I should have stretched.

I shake it off and get up.

"Yeah!" I lateral the ball back to the center of the field.

We line up and complete another pass.

Every time I catch the ball, I am gang-tackled, at first by the defense but eventually by everybody. The biggest of these kids must weigh over 120 pounds, and they have heads, elbows, and knees sharp as spikes. I'm sore and bruised, my legs ache, and I feel cramps in places I didn't even know I had. But I keep bouncing up. The kids are giggling and laughing.

"Throw it to him again!" the defense is shouting.

"No, no, no," I beg.

And sure enough, Martin tosses me another one and they gang-tackle me again. It is play that is right on the verge of pure and simple violence, just the way boys like it, and it is infectious enough that even though I am getting brutalized, I keep playing.

More important, Ronin has lost himself in our game, chasing me down and jumping on me along with the other boys with a ferocity and thoughtlessness that I find beautiful and reassuring.

When I am tackled again, I stand up, panting, my jeans and sweatshirt grass- and mud-stained. I'm sweating, and my jaw is throbbing and seems to have lost some mobility.

"Again!" the boys shout.

"No, no, no, someone else," I gasp.

The sky beyond the gray shingled roofs has turned barbecue orange, a cowlick swirl of pinkish clouds rising up into the darkening sky. The receding light leaves behind darker grass, green going blue in the shadows, and the cars driving by beam cones of white light up the narrow, cracked street.

Oh, how I loved playing in the twilight, those last moments of a street football or driveway basketball game before my mother would call me in for the night. And when it was finally so dark we could barely see, then it was "next touchdown wins" or "first to five," this fleeting game suddenly taking on the timed intensity of more organized sports.

We line up again. Now I am defending. The tall boy completes a pass to Ronin. I chase him down, tackle him, and the rest of the boys predictably pile on again. We rouse, dust ourselves off, and then repeat the sequence—vicious tackling, shouts of anguish, screams and giggles, and then another play.

We score hundreds of touchdowns. We gain thousands of yards. We break every passing record.

Finally, when it is so dark we can barely see and house lights have come on up and down Iliff, I call out, "Next touchdown wins."

We are defending. The tall boy completes another pass. I tackle the receiver. We are swarmed with boys. I manage to wriggle free from the pile, then launch myself back into it, driving the crown of my head into another boy's butt and squirming between the boys.

And then the scene is bathed in blue and red light, and I hear an echoed, amplified voice through a loudspeaker, ordering, "Stand up and move away from the children."

The kids are still wriggling, not understanding that we are no longer having fun, and even after I extricate myself from the pile, two of the smaller kids keep charging at me and grabbing my legs.

"No, no," I say and shoo them away.

Through the glare of lights, I can see that a squad car is parked diagonally in the street, blocking traffic. Both the passenger's- and driver's-side doors swing open and two officers walk toward the lawn.

"Are those lights really necessary?" I ask, and I turn to Ronin. "Come here."

"Sir!" shouts one of the officers. "No contact with the children!"

"What's going on?"

The garish flickering of the lights strobes the whole neighborhood, so that trees and bushes and other cars turn shades of pink and blue.

"We've received reports of inappropriate adult-child interaction," one officer says. "Several calls."

"Adult-child interaction? We're playing football."

"Sir, NO CONTACT WITH THE CHILDREN."

By now I can see men and women, and a few kids, standing on front porches, or through opened front doors, watching us.

"The Two-Adult Rule," the officer says, "is that you are to avoid situations where you are alone with a child, or children."

"It's football," I say. "Tackle football? With my son?"

"Football?" the officer says. "Without safety equipment? Helmets? Pads?"

"What the fuck? Nobody's hurt."

I turn to the boys, who are now standing, the ball at their feet, unsure of what exactly is going on. I can tell they are suddenly wondering if they have been playing football with a criminal. "Guys," I say, "tell them what we were doing."

The officer steps forward. I can finally see him fully in the glare of the backlight. He is Hispanic, with a mustache that stops at the lip line and acne scars up both cheeks. "Sir, one more attempt to make contact with the minors and we will detain you. Any additional use of profanity, and we will detain you."

I read the officer's shield, Hidalgo, and below that the gold Los Angeles City Hall logo set amid silver rays with the City of Los Angeles seal centered. On his shoulders are his chevrons, and below that, advertisement patches for Über Justice, Dodge Ram Trucks, and Discover Card Bail Bonds Inc., with phone numbers highly visible. The other officer, Voshkov, comes around. He is clean shaven and wears a policeman's cap. Both men wear radio headsets—like Ronin's teachers wear. "Let's see some ID."

I remove my wallet and hand him my driver's license. He studies it.

"We were walking home and saw some kids playing and we joined in. Nothing strange about that."

"You were walking home? Who *walks*? Do you walk, Officer Voshkov?"

Officer Voshkov smirks. "Negative."

"So you were *walking*, and you joined in?" says Officer Hidalgo.

"Yeah, we started playing football."

"Why would you join a kids' football game?" He turns to Voshkov. "Would you join a kids' football game, Officer Voshkov?"

"No, I would not."

"Would you stop and inappropriately interact with minors without the presence of another adult, potentially endangering them?"

"That would be a huge blinking red light saying 'Negative!'"

"I agree, Officer Voshkov. Yet that's precisely what Mr."—he takes my license from Officer Voshkov—"Mr. Schwab here decided to do."

"Bad call." Voshkov nods.

Some of the boys' parents have come to collect their children. I cannot see clearly because of the glare, but I imagine I see suspicion, fear, concern. There will be careful, measured talks, asking about any unusual touching, about whose idea it was to play tackle, about whether the adult seemed in any way overly enthusiastic about the game.

And I can see the boys gazing back at me, and I hear one of them shout, "It was only a game!" before he is shushed by a parent.

Officer Voshkov takes down the contact information of the parents.

A line of four cars has already formed behind the diagonally parked police cruiser.

The officers either do not notice or do not care about blocking the street.

"Mr. Schwab, please step over to the vehicle."

"This is ridiculous. Nobody saw anything wrong. Or weird."

"We are responding to a complaint," Officer Hidalgo says. "Now, if you'll step over to the car, we can run your license."

"Complaint about what?"

"Child endangerment. Inappropriate interaction with minors. This is—"

"I was playing *football*!"

"So you have said, repeatedly. But complainant mentioned a middle-aged man rolling on the ground with minors. Complainant reported grabbing and fondling. Complainant reported crying and screaming."

"Didn't you ever play football?"

"Not with children. Not without proper safety equipment. Just come over to the vehicle," Officer Hidalgo urges.

I follow him to the car. Ronin is now standing by himself; the boys we were playing football with have left with their parents. He looks small and confused, his pale flesh alternately glowing red and then blue.

"This is just going to take a minute," I shout to him.

I've managed yet again to embarrass my son.

Hidalgo sits down in the cruiser and swipes my license.

"Okay, no outstandings. And your credit score is very good. We don't get many 750-pluses. You are preapproved for an LAPD-branded credit/debit card. You can earn points that can be redeemed to remove traffic violations from your record."

I shake my head.

"No?" Officer Hidalgo says. "You sure? Okay, Mr. Schwab. I'm writing a summons. It's a nuisance citation for reckless endangerment of a minor." He reaches over and switches off the flashers.

He is writing out the ticket.

There is a website I am to go to to find my court date. The range of possible fines starts at $750.

"Are you kidding? Seven hundred and fifty dollars? For playing with kids?"

"Don't play with kids."

"Ronin, come on."

Ronin is silent. He trails a little behind and to the right of me on the sidewalk as we climb Iliff. His hands are stuffed in his hoodie pockets, he looks down at his feet as he walks.

"Wow, that was crazy," I say.

Ronin says nothing.

"I mean, have you ever seen that?"

I hear Ronin stop behind me. I turn.

He is crying. "DO YOU KNOW H-H-H-HOW EMB-B-B-BARRASSING THAT WAS?" He screams through his tears. "WHY DID WE HAVE T-T-TO STOP? WHY?"

I reach out to him. He backs away.

"TO PLAY FOOTBALL? EVEN THAT WAS WEIRD. NOBODY'S DAD JUST WALKS AROUND AND PLAYS FOOTBALL WITH, LIKE, JUST KIDS HE SEES IN THE STREET."

I shake my head.

"WHY ARE YOU SUCH A LAME DAD?" he says. "I WISH YOU WEREN'T MY FATHER."

"Come on, Rone," I say. "I thought it would be fun. And it was, right? For a while?"

"DO YOU KNOW WHAT EVERYONE IS GOING TO SAY? MY DAD IS A CHILD MOLESTER. MY DAD IS A FREAK. JUST LIKE ME."

"What?" I shake my head. "No, this, this wasn't, like, your thing, this was just playing football, and then they saw it the wrong way. This isn't, like, your—"

"WHAT? LIKE WHAT? LIKE MY THING IS REAL?"

I hold my hands out, urging him to keep quiet. "No, it's not real. None of this is real."

His upper lip and cheeks are smeared with tears and snot so that they shine in the streetlight glare.

He wipes his face with the sleeve of his hoodie. He shakes his head. "It'sjustthatIgotoFreaksandeverybodythinksI'mafreakand- nowyoudothisanditwillallstartagainandthoseguyswilltelleverybody- andI'lljustbethatfreakpervertkidwiththefreakpervertdadlike- we'rethepervfamilywholikejustgrabsandmolestseverybody."

"Ronin," I say, "you did not do anything wrong. Well, okay, maybe you did, by pinching that girl, but that was, like, a small mistake, and you learned. And I did not do anything wrong. We stopped to play football, and that's fine. That's just an okay thing to do." I take him by the shoulders. "And you're okay, Rone, you're okay. This is all . . . It's all bullshit."

"I'LL PRAY FOR YOU, DAD," Jinx is telling me. "I'll ask the Lord's forgiveness for your sins."

"No, Jinx," I say. "I don't need you to pray for me. I didn't do anything wrong."

"'Fathers, do not provoke your children to anger,'" says Jinx. "The Bible says to bring them up in discipline and instruction of the Lord."

Our daughter, Jinx, has always been less worrisome than her older brother. Forceful and self-motivated, as well as a pain in the ass, she enjoys long and complicated conversations, which she pursues with Talmudic persistence and a lawyerly appreciation for precedents. She brings up conversations from months prior in an argument about a Halloween costume or whether or not she can have a sleepover, reminding my ex-wife, for example, that she told Jinx she would always support her creative projects and therefore Anya should satisfy her demand to construct a giant mustache out of foam and wire for her.

Jinx usually focused her attentions on making life miserable for her fellow fourth-graders and, periodically, her older brother. But her latest incarnation, as devout Christian, had caught all of us by surprise.

Over a period of ten days, Jinx had turned into a Bible-thumping ten-year-old Baptist after joining an after-school program at the local outpost of Pastor Roger's Freedom Prairie Church called the Captain's Club. Jinx was eager for the high-fructose-corn-syrup candies that CC gave out to students who memorized Bible verses. (Anya forbade anything in her house that had corn syrup, which ruled out virtually every recognizable consumer brand.) Jinx, whose memory has always been elephantine, was picking up four Bible verses a day, spitting them out at the end of CC, and returning home with a sack full of Warheads and Sour Patch Kids. There were other activities at CC, she told us: they could run in the yard—no unsupervised sports, of course—play religious board games, do their homework. But it was the Bible studies that Jinx enjoyed.

"Jinx, please, don't hit me with Bible verses now," I say. "We stopped and played football with some kids. Football, okay? I'm sure Pastor Roger loves football."

Jinx is unsure of Pastor Roger's views on football and returns to eating her mashed potatoes and breaded chicken. Anya is seated at the table opposite me, her purse in front of her, waiting for the kids to finish dinner so she can take them back to her place for the night. She is also unsure about what exactly I have done wrong but has evidently decided to also come down on me for it.

"The police can't just arrest you for playing soccer," she says.

"Not soccer," I correct her. "Football."

"But they can't arrest you—"

"They didn't arrest us, they gave me a summons," I say. "I have to appear in court. Pay a fine."

"But even in this country, they can't do that, not just for playing football. You must have done something."

"THEY DID IT BECAUSE THEY THINK DAD'S A PERV. SOMEONE CALLED UP AND SAID THERE WAS THIS OLD PERV PLAYING WITH KIDS," Ronin shouts.

"What's a perv?" Jinx asks.

"You were playing with children?" Anya asks.

"It's a person who touches other people inappropriately," I tell Jinx.

"Like a molester?" Jinx asks.

"Yes."

"Pastor Roger says child molesters are homosexuals. Because they commit unspeakable acts with others of their same gender, they know no boundaries when it comes to relations," Jinx says and attempts to cut her chicken.

"That's . . . that's ridiculous, Jinx. Child molesters can be all types, gay, straight, anyone. Everyone can be crappy." I reach over, take her knife, and slice for her.

"Like you, Dad," Jinx says.

"I may be crappy, but don't lump me in with the child molesters."

Ronin is surveying the table. I can see how from his perspective our family may have found a new level of embarrassing weirdness.

I turn to Anya. "This was a simple game. We stopped to play a game with some kids. It was a spur-of-the-moment thing. It was fun, Rone, you have to admit."

He nods.

"It was a game of football. We were tackling each other. It's something we used to do as kids all the time. So when I saw the kids playing, I thought, why not?"

Anya is studying my expression. I can see she is wondering if I am stoned but is reluctant to ask in front of the children.

"This doesn't happen to normal people," she says.

"Normal people?" I point around the table. "That doesn't apply."

Anya excuses herself and says she will wait in the living room.

Ronin, who has somehow built up enough appetite for a second dinner just a few hours after his after-school Chinese food snack, sits, chews, and nods. I don't have much appetite, but I sit with Ronin and Jinx until they retreat to their rooms to gather their backpacks.

Anya is in the living room, playing solitaire on her phone.

"This isn't my fault," I tell her.

She keeps moving digital cards on her screen with her thumb.

"I didn't do anything wrong."

She puts down her phone. "You were stoned on marijuana."

"So?"

"So that's why you make strange decisions. Like to play football with children. To tackle them. Nobody else, no other fathers, do things like that. You know? That's why Ronin is the way he is. Confused. Having to go to this sex class. Because you are so messed up and you don't have any boundaries and you—"

"You're blaming me for Ronin? There's nothing wrong with the kid. You yourself said that the school is overreacting. Rone needs to play football, to tackle, to hit someone."

"You were high. That's why you decided to play. You want to be some kind of bullshit hip dad. Like with your ripped T-shirts and jeans and sneakers. Your hair, the way you walk around. And telling Ronin everything is okay, that it is okay to be crap at school. To fail things. And you are always stoned, typical hip dad shit. I never should have agreed to joint custody."

"Don't reopen old bullshit. Smoking had nothing to do with this," I say.

"Of course it did. It's never your fault. You can't take any blame."

"BUT THIS ISN'T MY FAULT."

"See, now you are shouting."

"OH, FUCK YOU," I say and storm out. "I'm sure Florian is a much better father figure."

Florian is Anya's boyfriend.

"Maybe he is," I hear her say quietly.

Jinx is kneeling in her bedroom. I can see her lips moving. I am sure she is praying for us. But when I get closer, I hear her ask the Lord to save the whales on the TV show.

Anya rounds up the kids and they depart, both a blessing and a curse as I immediately miss them and cannot stand staying in the house all alone.

I go out to the Prius—that relic of the hybrid era—and start it up and drive down to my office. I park behind the Chinese restaurant and go upstairs. When I open my computer I see a kik-tok from Gemma Mack.

how are you doing? Boy were you right about the coyotes.
And I'm sorry I maced you. But you took me by surprise. . . .
I'm in santa monica with kids visiting family.

we should meet in person to discuss.

CHAPTER 6

THEY BURIED HER IN A dandelion patch at the bottom of the first foothill at the western edge of the subdivision, a shadeless spot, but pretty enough. In the early morning of the day after Soo passed, Valence gathered for its first funeral, the death of an old Korean lady who had turned up two days before, already in the late stages of terminal cancer. The men dug the hole six feet deep to keep coyotes off the smell, and lowered Soo in an old sleeping bag with photographs of her daughter and granddaughters as well as her own parents. They arranged her on her back, her eyes closed, and with a bouquet of yellow sunflowers atop her chest. Sargam brought Don, her widower, out to pay his last respects before the men had to leave for work and the kids were run down to the school Sargam had opened.

Vanessa watched the service from up the hill, seated in the

dirt, and in particular she noticed one young man, Atticus, whom she had first seen at the campfire the night her family drove in and whose teeth-showing grin she found appealing. He had a short forehead and round eyes, an almost effeminate nose, and shapely lips chapped from too much sun. He was deeply tanned, as were they all, and it suited him, went with his dirty-blond hair.

She made sure to walk past him several times at the camp-fire, to get water from the jug, to get a second helping of beans and rice from the table, and she noticed him noticing her. How long had it been since she felt the excitement of realizing a boy liked her? It had been months, ever since leaving home. (She still thought of Riverside as that, though she knew she would never be going back.) As she watched Atticus help dig the hole and then lower the old Korean lady into her grave, all Vanessa could think about were Atticus's muscles and the way his jeans rode low on his hips. As the mourners were readying to leave, Vanessa came down from her perch to where Atticus was walking with a shovel over his shoulder. She stepped in beside him, as if by coincidence.

"Oh, hey there," Atticus said.

"Oh, hi." She smiled and kept walking.

"Terrible about that old lady," Atticus said.

"She was next door to us," Vanessa said. "You should have heard her carrying on."

Atticus shook his head. "Must have been something. Feel bad for him." He gestured generally toward where Don had been during the brief service.

"Are you going to work up at the sites?"

Atticus smiled. "I am. I convinced them. I told them I'm strong enough and old enough. I'm eighteen."

"Are not," Vanessa said.

"Okay, but I'm sixteen, and I can swing a shovel better than most of these older guys. And you?"

"Seventeen."

"Are not," Atticus said.

"I'm fifteen, and if I could I would go up there with you. Anything to get out of here."

"Aw, it's not so bad. Better than being on the streets in L.A. Where you from?"

"Near L.A. Riverside."

"Nine-oh-niner, huh? Tweakerville. I lived in Malibu."

"Did not."

"I did, for a while, when I was a kid. It was called Malibu Lake, about an hour from Malibu. Was more like the valley. We lost that place and then moved to an apartment downtown."

"What happened to your dad?" Vanessa asked.

"Barely knew him. Last I heard he was in Colorado, I think, and I heard he had a new family. I don't want to know him if he doesn't want to know me." Atticus had to stop himself from running down his father any more.

"Well, I'm bored. We've only been here a couple weeks, but I've never even left Valence."

"It's all right here. We have the dances."

"All right for you. You're going to work. You can stop at a store and buy a, I don't know, Slurpee or something."

They were almost to Vanessa's house, and she could see her mom standing in the driveway, probably looking for her.

"My little brother, he can run around with his friends. They're out playing all day."

"And you're too grown-up for playing?"

"That kind of playing." Vanessa smiled.

"How about after I come back from the sites, we hang out?" Atticus said.

Vanessa shrugged. "This is where I live, for now."

She walked up the driveway to where Bailey stood regarding Atticus with a smile that did not hide her suspicion.

"New friend?" Bailey asked.

THE FIRST THINGS JEB NOTICED every morning as they drove to the fracking site were the vast lakes of untreated waste water that had settled around the raised berms protecting the site, shimmery silver pools that bled to the horizon like a mirage. They didn't have to be told the water was salty and poisonous; the lakes gave off the smell of methane and car exhaust that made the possibility of life seem about as likely as a goldfish surviving in a gas tank. After a few days on the site, Jeb realized that what they were doing was pumping water into the earth, poisoning it, and then dumping it on the surface.

They motored up the circular dirt driveway over the berm and down to the site, where sixty men worked every day. Jeb and his crew had built that berm, with shovels and backhoes, and now the waste water was almost as high as the top, which meant they would have to build the flood wall even higher.

Jeb had never seen this many big-rig trucks parked so close together. He counted sixty-four rigs, slotted in bed-to-bed, their trailer-mounted pumps emitting a deep rumbling sound as they shot the high-pressure boron, zirconium, and titanium fracking fluid down the mile-and-a-half well. They were pumping down 50,000 liters of the water-based fluid a day, splitting open the shale and earth to allow the precious oil to escape through the fissures. The shale oil was pumped back up to the surface with water and then separated from the water in a fracturing tank before it was stored in yet more truck-bed holding tanks. The waste water was pumped through the berm to the waste pools. Whatever had once lived out in that scrub land was gone or dead. In fact, Jeb was sure there weren't any animals besides humans living for a few miles in any direction.

HG Extraction operated the site, which was leased from the town of Placer, a highway rest-stop town that in its prime had been home to twenty-six residents but was now down to zero. The lease paid the former residents of Placer $650 a month each, and they took that money and ran when the first semis hauling the drilling towers rolled up. There were six full-time employees of HG Extraction on the site, and the rest of the workers were subcontracted day laborers from who knew where. Their beat-up SUVs kept showing up every day, and as long as the men could drive trucks and swing shovels and haul trash and operate a sump pump and they didn't complain if there weren't enough hazardous-material masks or that the antitoxin showers that had been promised were never installed, the managers asked no questions. These men seemed happy enough for the six-dollar-an-hour work, and when one of them complained, the managers would tell him there were a hundred men who would take his place.

Jeb started by working with a crew to extend the berm, shoveling black graphite pellets into nylon sacks and then hauling those up to the lip. The graphite pellets were trucked in three times a day and dumped from huge spigots of tanker trucks, the pellets piling up in a massive black mound. They stacked the graphite bags, hundreds of them barely raising the berm. But the waste-water level kept rising every day, the more oil they pumped out, and no matter how hard they worked, they could barely keep pace with the rising waters. Behind him was $40 million worth of HG equipment, and the only thing keeping the flood of waste water from it were two dozen men from Valence hauling bags of pellets in the hot sun.

It was a long, brutal day of unrelenting lifting and tugging, as the men struggled to keep ahead of the pumps. Sixty-four 10,000-psi hydraulic pumps can shoot a whole lot of water down that borehole; twenty-four men had to work double-time just to have a chance at keeping up. By the time Jeb came down the berm for a half-hour lunch, he was aching and sore, his shoulder muscles twitching from the exertion. HG brought in its own food truck; Jeb stared at the cold rice and beans and tortillas he had brought before joining the rest of the men buying burgers and french fries and sodas, feeling guilty about spending $8 on food, but he was hungry from the work and knew he had a whole afternoon to get through. He ate with hands filthy and black from the rubbery pellets and dirt.

The afternoon sun bore down on them, the heat like an actual weight that seemed to be pressing on them so that their shoulders slumped and their knees buckled and their ankles became wobbly. When Jeb drank a liter of water, he knew he would sweat it out in fifteen minutes. The punishing sun seemed suspended in the western sky, never closing in on quitting time and heating them and everything it touched, so that by midafternoon the heat was coming up off the ground as well as down from the sky, and the head of a shovel left out for a short while would burn at the touch.

Finally, a voice shouted, "Time," and the men set down their last sandbag and stumbled down the hill.

"Six an hour? I made more than that inside the Vernon walls," Jeb said to the manager when he was counting his cash after the first day.

"Then why don't you go back there, if you had it so good?" said the manager.

Jeb nodded and kept walking back to his Flex. "By the time we pay for gas, lunch, we're bringing back maybe twenty dollars a day. That's hardly enough to feed a family."

"It's steady," said another man from Valence. "And he's right. There's plenty who'd take our place."

THAT EVENING, VANESSA WAITED FOR Atticus, and then they sat together, beneath a camphor tree, the air cool but the ground still retaining heat.

He had washed after his day's work, and she wore her one clean dress. Despite their eagerness to see each other, when they were alone they were both tongue-tied. Atticus asked if Vanessa had known the Korean lady they had put in the ground that morning.

She told him Soo and her husband, Don, had driven up to the house next door to theirs one afternoon, the lady already near death. She'd been diagnosed with first-stage lymphoma and used up all her health-care vouchers without ever getting cured. When they lost their home, rather than impose on their daughter, who herself had three kids and was barely getting by, they hit the road, figuring eventually to make it back to their daughter's, but Soo had deteriorated fast.

"She looked old," Vanessa said. "And if an Asian lady looks old, then you know she's in bad shape."

They had been run out of Vegas and turned up in Valence, desperate, and Sargam told them to stay, and called for Dr. Alfredo while Vanessa and her mom comforted the old lady and her husband. They were Presbyterians; lapsed, Don had said, but he found the words for a few prayers. Alfredo turned up, examined her quickly, and whispered to Sargam that there was nothing they could do for her. She had lumps everywhere, she was coughing blood. He had a few Opanas that they had taken from some tweakers they had run off, and he gave her those, but she couldn't even get down a sip of water to swallow the pills.

"I never saw a person in so much pain," Vanessa said.

After the sun had set and everything cooled down, Sargam told Bailey and Vanessa they could go home, that she would stay with Don and Soo. But Vanessa secretly sneaked back to watch through the back window. She had never seen anyone die before, not right in front of her, and she was curious.

Vanessa watched as Sargam lay down with the old lady, held her like she was spooning a lover and trying to comfort her. Don was distraught, leaning back against the wall, crying, mumbling in Korean. The old lady was shouting her daughter's name, Eleanor, Eleanor.

"Then this weird thing happened," Vanessa said.

"What?" Atticus asked.

Vanessa said that she saw Sargam lay her hands over Soo's face, her fingers to the old lady's forehead, caressing her hair. It was as if she were soothing the old lady, calming her.

"Sargam's face went, like, all blank, like her eyes sort of, I don't know, rolled into her head? Sort of zombie-like?" Vanessa said.

But whatever she was doing, she seemed to be making the old lady feel better, was alleviating the awful pain she had felt before.

"She was, like, curing the lady?" Atticus asked.

Vanessa shook her head. "No, because we know what happened to her. But, I swear, it was like, this touch she had."

Soo murmured throughout the night, and she seemed to fall asleep, Don also drifting into sleep as well. Sargam watched Soo take her last breath, letting Soo's husband sleep until first light.

"That's creepy," Atticus said.

Vanessa shrugged. She couldn't explain what she had seen.

Atticus laughed and finally summoned the courage to take

Vanessa's hand, and then, emboldened by her squeezing his hand back, he leaned over and kissed her, lips grazing lips, warm soft flesh meeting in the cooling evening.

GEMMA HAS AGREED TO MEET me at the Little Red Bar, the Chinese restaurant and bar downstairs from my office. I change into a clean shirt and check my hair in the mirror in my office bathroom before I go.

I arrive before her and park myself at one of the tables near the bar. There is a flat-panel television tuned to sports, but one of the patrons at the bar asks that it be turned to news so he can see about the whales that washed up on the beach. Gray whales have been washing up on the beach in Santa Monica over the last few days. Their migratory pattern was right off the coast and was disrupted, or so an oceanographer is insisting, by the drilling and extraction platforms now lining the coastline.

Already there was furious bidding under way for the media rights to the whales. The state wants to make a deal, but there is the wrinkle of the Santa Monica Bay Beach Club, which has leased the sand on which much of the show would have to be shot. It seems everyone is enthusiastic about the potential of another *Whale Watch* show, now that the East Hampton whales were all dead. A media expert said that if a dozen whales beached themselves, as happened on the East Coast, a network might pay $20 million for the show.

I see Gemma coming in. She's bandaged, her hands and arms wrapped and bruised. She has a dime-size welt on her forehead, and her neck is red and scratched.

"I thought I saved you from the coyotes," I say.

She shakes her head—"I'm so sorry"—and gestures toward

herself, the sling, the bandages. "I should have listened to you about the coyotes."

"You do seem to attract them. I was actually warning you the other day—they were following you," I say. "What happened?"

"We were down in the Bowl," she says. "They went after Ginny. I got in between them. My hand was, at one point, apparently, inside a coyote's mouth."

"You're a hero," I say. "Who fights off a coyote?"

"Like I had a choice? She was going after my girl."

"Strange, because you usually seem so quick on the draw with the pepper spray," I say.

"Again, I'm sorry, oh my God," she says. "And, of course, because of that, I didn't have any with me when I really needed it."

She recounts the story: visiting her old high school friend, the kids going outside to play, finding Ginny, fighting the dogs, and then the nightmare of the hospital and the bills.

I am strangely inspired by Gemma and her ability to fight off these wild animals. She's a warrior momma, like Grendel's mother, or Joan of Arc, or Jessica Lynch (the first, made-up, heroic version, not the real story that emerged later). I imagine her taking coyotes by the neck and smashing their heads together.

"The fucking coyote killer," I say. "You're so cool. You're, like, I don't know. Forget Tiger Mom. Coyote-killer mom."

I sound like a fucking idiot. Like a ten-year-old.

"Let's get a drink."

"I thought we were having coffee," she says.

"Come on, we're celebrating your successful vanquishing of the beasts."

"Then I'll have a Beefeater martini, up."

"I'll join you."

When the drinks arrive, I ask how she likes being back.

"It's not that different from being back east. I'm a single mom . . . there are whales on the beach."

"Have you heard from Arthur?"

"That asshole? What do you want to know?"

"Um, where is he?"

"He made bail, went down to Texas. He's got some high-roller ultra-cons funding his defense."

"They're talking him up like he's a hero," I say.

"My philandering husband, the hero."

I can't tell if Gemma is wearing makeup around the bruise and the red marks on her chin, the deep, pink racing stripes that run up her neck. She looks, I realize, like a battered woman, a survivor of some sort of awful, abusive marriage, which she is, in a way. Her light dusting of freckles shows a beautiful sort of russet in the afternoon light streaming in through the horizontal window above the bottles behind the bar. I have to stop myself from staring at her.

"How are your girls?"

"Besides being attacked by coyotes?" Gemma smiles. "They're with my mom." She puts down her drink. "Jesus, what is happening?"

"What? Now? Nothing, we're just having a drink—"

"I mean, in the world, coyotes attacking people, and everyone's, like, 'it's normal.' Whales? Whales killing themselves? The West Side Highway is underwater. The prairie is on fire. Rome is burning."

That is true, literally. The Seven Hills are actually on fire. Millions of Italians are fleeing the capital.

"But they're building a seawall in New York," I say.

"We spent so much time thinking about sanctuary, about escape, that I never really thought what all this meant. It's that we're screwed. I mean, aren't we?"

"Yeah, but it will take some time."

"Just enough so that when our kids grow up, they'll die of cancer or starve or drown or get eaten by wild dogs?"

She's pissed off, and I like it. I can see she must spend much of her time around her kids holding it together, and now, with me, she is unloading. I take some pleasure in her seeing me as a confidant.

"We just need to do the best we can," I say.

"Thank you for the platitude."

"I'm sorry, I'm not the best person at figuring out how to save the world. I'm mostly good at fucking it up. But, hey, you know, I bring my own bags to the grocery store."

She frowns.

"Okay, not funny," I say. "What I mean is, it's hard enough just keeping my own shit together."

We order two more, and when they arrive, we clink glasses.

"To what?" Gemma says. "Saving the world?"

"We'll see."

We sip.

"How is it living back with your mom?"

"Ha." She smiles. "You know what it's like, to see, like, an old Duran Duran sticker in your bedroom, and at the same time hear your daughters in the next room, and think, How did I end up back in my teenage bedroom, only with kids? I'm a single mom, living at home with her parent. It's like a KIK-TV reality show, only it's so much sadder than any of those *Sixteen and Pregnant* shows. I'm forty and—"

"Don't be hard on yourself. I mean, *I'd* watch a show where a lady fights coyotes with her bare hands."

"So would I, I guess." She smiles. "So, do you want the goods on my dirtbag of an ex-husband?"

I shrug. "Sure."

"First, I have to ask you: Do you really care?" Gemma says.

"About what?"

"About the world, about what's happening."

"It's already happened." I hold out my hands. "We're not going to go back and stuff all this crap back into the box. I'm not political. Maybe that's my problem."

"But you should write about what's happening. About how fucked we all are."

I tell her that I was looking at one of my old books—my best book, I add—and realize that I miss that guy, the writer who cared, who was invested.

"I want to read *What You Wish For*."

"I'm flattered. I have it in my office. Upstairs."

I pay the check and we go up to my office. When I hand her my first book I have to resist the urge to touch her neck where it is bruised. Instead, I stand there, sort of nodding.

"Hey, do you happen to have a joint?"

"I've stopped."

"When?"

"Last week."

"Why?"

I tell her about the football game, the police arriving, the accusation of inappropriate interaction with a minor, my impending court date.

"So you're, like, a child molester?"

"That's not funny. My ex-wife sees the whole thing as my fault. My son won't speak to me anymore. So I thought I should see about cleaning up my act a little."

She weighs the book in her hand. "That's a good idea."

"Before I get put away for life."

Her phone rings. She ignores it.

Then she receives a text, which she reads.

"My husband is here," she says.

"Here? Like downstairs?"

"No, here, in L.A. He's coming to my mom's house. He's terrible at texting, but look."

She holds her phone out to me so I can read it: "Hney, les get bik together? Pliz!"

A good journalist, a real journalist, would have seized on this opportunity to write a great story about a famous financial villain. Instead, I just stand there, and I'm jealous that Arthur Mack has had this woman, while she remains for me a receding fantasy.

She has to go. "I'm going to tell the kids the truth. And tell Arthur it's over. Again."

I walk her out into the hall and down the stairs to where she is parked.

"So, um, meet again?" I ask.

She climbs into an old Camry. She answers, but I don't quite make it out. And then she is gone.

THE NEXT MORNING IS MY court appointment, downtown on Temple Street. My Über Justice attorney, who according to my Kik map was ten minutes away, turned out to be twenty minutes late, which is not bad considering how difficult it is to move around Los Angeles. What is more worrying to me is that she looks like she is about twenty.

"You're my attorney?" I ask.

"Paralegal," she says. "Almost the same thing."

She is an immense black woman who wears a vast blue jacket over a pink shirt and blue slacks that must take up an entire eight-man tent's worth of fabric. She has a pretty face, long braided hair, and a cheerful smile that fades as I ask my question.

"I'm Miss Glenda Solay, and yes, if you are Richie Schwab, then I am the Über Justice consultant here to represent you regarding your nuisance summons for . . ." She scrolls through her tablet screen. "Misdemeanor Endangerment of a Minor."

Upstairs, the arched hallway is crowded with defendants. Glenda and I have a quick conference, standing inside the recessed area formerly used as a pay phone bank.

"You paid for our Total Innocence and Exoneration package, and at Über Justice there is nothing more important to us than your freedom from unjust prosecution," Glenda reads from her screen. "Now, can you describe in forty words your exculpatory circumstances."

"What?"

"Why you're not guilty. Speak into the tablet."

"I can't."

"You can't speak into the tablet?"

"I can't do it."

"Mr. Schwab, you paid for the Total Innocence and Exoneration package," says Glenda. "If you wish to change your plea, we cannot refund the difference."

"No, not that, it's forty words or less that's hard."

"It's not exactly forty words. It can be forty-three or forty-four."

I try. "I was walking up the street and saw some children playing football and we stopped to join them. Oh, and I was with my son, Ronin. We played tackle football for a while and then—how many is that?"

"Thirty-nine."

"Including 'how many is that'?"

"Now you're at forty-four."

"The important thing is that what we were doing was playing football. Nobody was hurt."

Glenda sighs and switches off the recording. "I can't do my job if you can't explain the exonerating circumstances. The complainant who called the police reported hearing squealing, and then reported seeing you, Richie Schwab, tackling young boys and rolling on the lawn with them."

"We were playing football. That's what football looks like."

"Were you wearing pads? Helmets? Was there a stadium? Because *that's* what football looks like."

"No, we were playing football in the front yard, for fun, without helmets or uniforms because who uses those things?"

"Every time I've watched football, there are helmets and uniforms and, for that matter, commercials and announcers."

"That's professional football, or maybe college, but this was kids—"

"Ah, Mr. Schwab," she interrupts and points to something on her screen. "I have to relay to you a plea being offered by the district attorney's office. If you plead no-contest right now, your fine will decrease to $350."

"What do you mean, right now?"

"You have forty seconds to accept this offer, after that, the fine will increase."

"Wait, what?"

"How do you plead?"

"Not guilty."

"As your Über Justice adviser, I recommend you take the state's plea. The next offer will be higher."

My phone rings. I recognize the number: Ronin's school. I answer.

"Mr. Schwab, this is Vice Principal Nakamura at the Subway Fresh Take Paul Revere Middle School."

Oh no. Not now. "Yes?"

"I'm calling to inform you that the police have been called to the school because a weapon was found in Ronin's possession after he threatened to stab a fellow student. School policy dictates that a law enforcement officer be present when a weapon is found."

"He had a knife?"

"No, it was a comb."

"What do you mean?"

"A comb, but it was a comb in the shape of a flick knife."

"What are you talking about? One of those switchblade combs? Those aren't weapons."

"Mr. Schwab, can you come and pick up your son?"

"Um, I'm a little tied up. Can I talk to Ronin?"

"He's in police custody."

"For a comb?"

"For a knife-shaped comb."

"Jesus, I'm—" I almost tell him where I am but catch myself. "I'm kind of tied up. Let me see what I can do."

I look around the crowded hallway, the attorneys in their suits, the bailiffs standing in a cluster near the window, and the defendants and jurists and families. Next to me is a young tattooed woman handcuffed to a wooden bench, an older, uniformed black woman next to her.

The young woman looks up at me. She's overheard my attorney-client conversation. "Hey, if I had the money, I would take the first plea. After that, they run it up like a goddamn taxi meter."

I turn to Glenda. "I don't want a record as—what is it? Child endangerer?"

Glenda is looking at her tablet. "Mr. Schwab, the latest plea is for $400. As your adviser, I recommend you accept this offer."

"But am I admitting guilt?"

"You are pleading guilty to a misdemeanor of endangerment of a minor."

I think about Ronin. "If I agree to do this, can I go right now?"

"Just sign here." She holds out her tablet.

I look at the e-doc. The plea has gone up to $425. I click on the signature box.

"You're free to go," Glenda says.

CHAPTER 7

A RTHUR MACK WAS NOT A man easily discouraged. He had not built an empire, or a pseudo-empire or faux-empire, by taking rejection to heart. But this was different. For one thing, Gemma wasn't responding to his texts or answering phone calls, and her mother, when he called the landline, would say, "Nobody home for you," and hang up, which didn't make sense but which he generally understood to be unwelcoming. He thought about the girls, and he had to admit a twinge of guilt at their misunderstanding of his current situation. Why, even he had misunderstood his current situation until Pastor Roger and the Pepper Sisters had explained it to him. He wasn't a criminal or a con man or incompetent, he was a job creator, a capitalist, a—what had the Peppers called him?—an entrepreneur in God's free market, and soon his wife and children, or at least his children, would see that they were among the many who had him all wrong, and soon the New York district attorney would be dropping the charges and the tracking anklet would be removed and, who knows, maybe Arthur would even get his broker-dealer license reinstated and he could once again ply his trade.

But he needed to see Gemma, to straighten her out. Like so many, she was mistaking his persecution as being evidence of his wrongdoing, while actually it was proof of his righteousness. Pastor Roger had such a clear way of explaining the upside-downness of it all, that he wished he could remember the exact words, but he had a good enough grasp of the ideas to present a compelling argument. As he drove in the cheap rental, the bubble-shaped compact the Freedom Prairie Church had reserved for him, he admired above him the elevated expressways skying out toward Malibu or arcing in a midair bow up into Beverly Hills. These celestial toll roads were so elegant and traffic-free, and the view from there, Arthur knew from experience, spanned from the mountains to the oil rigs offshore, and he was awash with regret that the temporary diminishment in his circumstances had him motoring with the deadbeats and subprimes on the old, decaying freeway system. If those people knew what they were missing, they too would become job creators. Why wouldn't they?

He was confident that once Gemma saw him, the father of the girls, his long legs and burly forearms and pleasingly dimpled chin—the Arthurness of Arthur would win her over and they could all return to Texas, where he would take up his rightful work with Pastor Roger and the Pepper Sisters. As he nosed the compact up the unwashed masses of the 405, he ran through his new narrative. Of course she knew, as any loyal wife would, that Arthur Mack was no more capable of what the lamestream media had accused him of than he was of shacking up with a mistress upon making bail—or, he had actually done that but was now realizing, from an image standpoint, what a mistake that had been and, really, what a great learning experience that kind of mistake can be in that he wouldn't do it again, not immediately, or not until he had totally won over Pastor Roger and the Freedom Prairie folks, or, no, he wouldn't do that no matter what, and, more relevant, he would be glossing over that part of his recent history to get to the really important parts where he would portray himself as a misunderstood hero. At no point in his cramming for his upcoming confrontation with Gemma did the words "I'm sorry" cross his mind.

He finally merged onto the 10, crossed beneath the Malibu Skyway, and, after forty-five minutes, cleared the tunnel onto the PCH. Where there had once been a panorama of table-flat sand extending from the Santa Monica Pier toward Point Dume, now sat the Pacific Sino Sands Casino and Resort, hunkered along a half-mile of Santa Monica shoreline, its shiny glass arabesque minarets towering over the soon-to-be-refurbished-by-AEG pier complex. The traffic crawled up the coast, the Santa Monica palisades buttressed by cement-and-steel girders on one side, the hastily erected amphitheater around the beached whales on the other. But even Arthur noticed that the drive time between the airport and North-of-Montana Santa Monica now took three hours and twenty-eight minutes. These hardships, he knew, were essential to a well-run economy. Why else would men or women strive to rise out of this class of subprime freeway riders to that of job-creating entrepreneurs who could ride the skyways to their private jets and fly to their sanctuary islands? That class warfare meme about the top one percent was nothing more than the sour grapes of those who did not want to do the hard work of lifting themselves up. Here Arthur Mack's reasoning always broke down. Why, exactly, didn't they want to do the hard work? They were lazy, and they were socialists. But how exactly did socialists make money? From the government, right? That's right, they got those free hotel vouchers and health-care credits from Uncle Sam, and they lived like Subprime Sultans in their fancy hotel suites.

He pulled up in front of Gemma's mother's house. With a wince he recalled, vaguely, the long holiday vacations they spent out here so that Gemma's mother could spend time with the girls. Arthur had to have the house wired for broadband so that he could continue to run his business during those early West Coast mornings. Even so, Doreen always made him feel as if he was doing something wrong, was a fool and a clod and not good enough for her daughter.

He walked up the curling, cracked concrete pathway across a drought-dried lawn. Dusk covered his approach, and through the windows he could see the glow of a television and hear, from the kitchen, the clang of a lid being potted. Gemma passed in front of the living room windows, wearing a green sweater and jeans. But her face? He froze at the sight of her bruises, the black eye. She would have to take him back, considering her unattractive condition.

He knocked on the door, listened at the approach of footsteps. There was silence as he was regarded through the peephole.

"Oh my God, it's the flimflam man," Doreen's gravelly voice called out through an open window. "She doesn't want to see you, Arthur. And I want to shoot you."

"Doreen, I'm the father of your granddaughters," Arthur said. "You can't kill me. That would make for childhood drama."

"You mean trauma, you idiot," Doreen said. "And you've already managed that."

"Is Gemma here? The girls?"

He heard more footsteps and then the door opened. Gemma stood in front of him, her injured face stern and unwelcoming.

"I want a divorce, Arthur," Gemma said.

"No 'Hello. How was jail?'"

"I don't really feel like catching up, Arthur," Gemma said.

"Where are the girls?"

"Asleep."

At that moment, high-pitched voices squealed from another room. "Who is it, Mommy?"

"Ginny? Franny? It's Dad," Arthur shouted.

Little bare feet made wet smacking sounds against the hardwood floor as the girls ran out and hugged their father, who dipped down into a catcher's crouch to return the embrace. "Where were you? Mommy said you were away on business, but Gam said you were in the slammer."

Gemma glared at her mother. Doreen shrugged.

"I'm misunderstood," Arthur Mack said. "I'm an honest businessman caught up in the socialist conspiracy to enflare job creators."

"Enflare?" Doreen said behind Gemma. "You mean ensnare, you idiot."

Both girls looked confused.

Gemma guffawed. "Are you serious? I can't believe they let you leave the state. Or are you jumping bail?"

"I'm legal." He stood and lifted his chino cuff to reveal the tracking anklet. "Vouched for by an American hero: Pastor Roger."

While the particular Arthur Mack thread was finally subsiding into the general, swirled, chaotic weave of the American media quilt, there was now a thick knotting around the completely insane argument that Arthur Mack was some kind of capitalist hero. She had heard Pastor Roger himself making that case.

"Say hi to the girls, explain yourself as best you can, and then be gone."

Arthur Mack squinted as if noticing his daughter's injuries for the first time. "What happened to Ginny?"

"We had some trouble with some coyotes," Gemma said.

"What kind of trouble?"

"Attacked. Ginny got bit. We both got cut up. But we're fine. No rabies."

"Oh my God," Arthur said, "you let our daughter get attacked by wolves?"

"Coyotes. Jesus, don't start with me."

"Mom knocked them out," Ginny said. "She was actually punching them in the face."

Gemma shook her head. "What kind of father—you know what? Never mind."

Doreen went over to Arthur, wagging a finger in his face. "She rescued Ginny from a goddamn coyote. How many women can do that? Do you know how many kids get snatched every day? Every night on the local news they have stories about kids being taken, and your daughter is here because Gemma saved her, you dumb flimflam man."

Arthur shook his head. "Don't say that in front of the girls."

"They don't know what that means," Doreen said.

"It sounds like a candy," Franny said.

Arthur took a step into the house but Gemma blocked him. "You can visit with the girls on the lawn. Mom will step out there with you."

Arthur was angered by the conditions but could see that he had no leverage to negotiate a better arrangement.

He held the girls' hands, and as they all sat down on the wooden bench on the front patio Ginny told him about the coyote attack, and Franny said to her father that if Ginny had been listening like she was supposed to it would never have happened to begin with.

WHEN I WALK INTO VICE Principal Nakamura's office, which has become distressingly familiar to me, I see that Anya is already there, seated with Ms. Ramos.

"Hey, we're getting the band back together!" I lamely joke and am met with the usual stern expressions.

"Where were you?" Anya asks me accusingly. "Your son is taken into custody—"

"I had my court thing, you know about that? My court thing?" I say.

"Ah yes, for molesting the boys."

Now everyone turns to me, suddenly wondering if it is even legal for me to be on school property.

"She jests," I say, only Anya looks very serious. She is squinting with such intensity that horizontal lines are appearing down the middle of her forehead. "Not molesting, no, that's not the correct *English* term. The, uh, actual charges, well, not charges, because they have already been dismissed, were for inappropriate—for causing—they were nuisance charges."

Then I stop myself, because that also sounds bad. "The, uh, there are now no charges, okay? Dismissed! Can we talk about Ronin?"

"Mr. Schwab, Mrs. Moller"—he uses my wife's maiden name—"Ronin's issues are conforming to a pattern. There was the inappropriate touching issue, and now we have his bringing a weapon into school—"

"It was a comb," I say.

"Airplanes have been hijacked with fake guns," says Vice Principal Nakamura.

"The 9/11 hijackers used boxcutters," adds Ms. Ramos.

"But they didn't use combs," I say.

"They didn't *have* combs," Ms. Ramos says.

I look at her. "What? That doesn't make any sense."

"*Exactly*," Vice Principal Nakamura says. "That's why we don't allow students to bring fake weapons onto campus."

"I get that, I totally get that," I say. "But this doesn't seem like, you know, the biggest deal."

"He threatened to stab someone," Vice Principal Nakamura says. "That's not a big deal?"

"But he doesn't have a knife," I say. "So, how is that a threat?"

"What if that weren't a comb?" Ms. Ramos says.

Vice Principal Nakamura nods thoughtfully. "We need to consider all the possibilities."

"But he didn't, he doesn't—he had a comb! We already know that, so his threat—what was his threat, exactly?"

"He and another student were discussing the Youth Sexual Conduct and Guidance Program—"

"Freaks," I say.

"Mr. Schwab, we don't use that term."

"But the kids do," I say. "They call it Freaks. And Ronin should never have been sent there. For what? For pinching a girl's—"

Vice Principal Nakamura interrupts me. "There was a conversation about Ronin's participation in this program, and—"

"You mean another boy was making fun of him, right? Was teasing him."

"Ronin responded by making the threat."

"But Ronin was being teased about Fre—about that program. Ronin should never have been sent there. Have you seen those kids? They're, they're, not normal."

"Mr. Schwab, we don't use that word to describe any of our students, developmentally or neurologically typical or atypical," Ms. Ramos says.

"You must see this, right? How hard it is for the kid, to be in that program, when, come on, all he did was pinch a girl, a girl who, by all accounts, actually likes him anyway, so, and now this, where, he feels bad about himself and a kid picks on him for it so he, you know, makes a dumb threat, but—"

Anya has been sitting uncharacteristically quietly for some time, her black purse on her lap, listening to the conversation and torn between her loyalty to her son and her hatred of me.

"If you hadn't bought him this comb," she says, turning to me.

Did I buy him a novelty switchblade comb? I honestly have no recollection. But does it matter?

"Who cares where he got the comb from?" I say. "It's a toy."

"It's a fake weapon," says Vice Principal Nakamura. "A weapon."

"I couldn't believe that you would buy such a thing," Anya says. "For a child."

Ms. Ramos adds, "Age inappropriate."

"I don't remember when I bought it," I say. "Or if I bought it, but that doesn't matter."

"I would recommend a careful reading of the Subway Fresh Take Paul Revere Middle School code of conduct," says Vice Principal Nakamura, "and Ronin will have to serve a two-day suspension and attend a weekly after-school Youth Anger and Violence Program."

"Great, another program."

"We will release Ronin into your custody," says Vice Principal Nakamura. "The comb will be kept in a secure place until it can safely be destroyed."

"THIS IS YOUR FAULT," ANYA says as we walk down the sidewalk beneath the flat-roofed overhang to our cars. "You talk to him."

"It's not my fault."

"Then whose fault is it?" she asks.

Ronin stands beside me. I can't blame the kid. "Nobody's."

"Then why do I have to do Shooters?" Ronin asks.

"What?"

"The after-school program."

"Oh, the school, oh fuck, I don't know."

"Good parenting," Anya says. "Very good explanation. Ronin, I'll talk to you tonight. For now, you and your father can talk about this incident."

"It's not my fault," I shout after Anya and turn to Ronin. He's developed the first rush of adolescent acne, a faint constellation of zits on each cheek. His youthful gangliness, that quality of a child stretched almost to adult size, is now curving and bowing from the weight he's put on around his shoulders and hips. He's going to be taller than me, I realize, and if his guidance counselors and school administrators are to be believed, my son will soon be a man-size serial rapist murderer. And who will change this trajectory? Who stands between my son and a life of appearances on the National Sex Offender Registry? That would be me, once I get over my own trivial legal issues relating to my own misunderstood behaviors.

We climb into my Prius. The whales, the goddamn whales have made the PCH virtually impassable, production rigs parked up and down the highway and the traffic cops constantly stopping traffic to allow the Fox vehicles to enter and exit the parking facilities.

"Do you think the whales will die?" Ronin asks.

I hadn't really thought about it. "Well, I guess, well, didn't the ones back east die?"

"Yeah. That's why they ended the show. But now they have these whales and, I was thinking, wouldn't it be a better show if the whales didn't die?"

"But don't they always have to be on the brink of death? Isn't that the drama?"

"But, what about happy endings? Aren't those important?"

"Yeah, Rone, they are."

We drive for a while. "Don't let all this shit bother you."

"The whales?"

"No, this crap about the comb, and Shooters, and all that. It's not you, it's the world."

"Don't worry, Dad, this isn't really bugging me that much. Anyway, Shooters is way cooler than Freaks."

"It is?"

"Totally. I mean, what would you rather be? A serial killer who comes to the school and, like, totally kills people, or, like, some perv?"

Traffic lurches forward slightly, but I am so perplexed by Ronin's statement that I don't accelerate.

Cars start honking behind me.

I turn to Ronin. "Neither of them is cool, but, killing people—you can't do that, right? You know that, right?"

"Jesus, don't be a spaz. Everyone's honking. Go."

"But you understand me? That's a scary thing you just said."

"Dad, what am I going to do? Comb their hair to death?"

THERE WERE NO SEASONS IN Valence, there was hot, hotter, and hottest. The exurban structures were designed to be air-conditioned, and like many homes in the American West in the Post-Seasonal Epoch, when winter had shrunk to a sliver of cool mid-February breeze, these homes were not built to withstand a warm climate without 50,000 BTUs of air-conditioning support. The inhabitants of Valence sweltered; on hot nights, you could practically hear the collective sigh of resignation to the heat, residents struggling to find a less sticky spot in the bed, turning over the pillow, hoping to drift into delicious sleep.

But there was also a stretch, a half hour or so of last dark before the dawn, when the still air cooled and the hot hold broke. It felt like a trick of the body, like sweat cooling on the flesh, but it was wonderful, and if you had been stirring and unable to sleep, now you could finally rest, and if you had been asleep, you woke up, and instead of worry or anxiety at what you had left behind and what might lay ahead, you were happy just to be here.

Tom, the boy, stirred and opened his eyes just in time to see his sister, Vanessa, climb out of her sleeping bag, pull on jeans and a T-shirt, and slip out of the room.

For that momentary cool flush was a call to action for Vanessa. The teenagers of Valence were growing up somehow faster than they would have back in their pre-foreclosed homes, where gadgets and television and the Internet would have distracted them and warded off, perhaps for months, the inevitable attraction of the opposite sex, or at least made less insistent the urge to act on it.

Atticus was waiting for her, leaning against a guardrail by a scrub of cotton head near a line of onion flowers, purple petals looking black in the predawn. She saw him first as the outline of a man, rectangular head, broad shoulders, thin middle, and legs pencil straight. Closer, and she could see the boyishness of his slouch, the head tilt and grin as he watched her approach.

She could still return to where her mom and dad slept fitfully, to her sleeping bag across the room from her brother. Could stop, shrug, and then fend off this future. But she was enveloped by the dark, cool air, and, more important, was aware of every step and sound, the rustling in the nearby cucumber plants of some sort of small mammal, the hoot of an owl, the sandy scissoring trot of a coyote's legs, the tingle of soft cool against her arms where they protruded from her white-and-blue T-shirt. She could no more turn and walk away than a hungry dog could stop chewing a meaty bone.

They hugged, not for the first time but with more at stake now, for this was a definite precursor to what they both had planned. He wore a backpack. She felt the straps when they hugged. He took her hand and they walked along the guardrail to a gap where they slipped through, following a trail down a narrow gully and then up into a patch of scrubby sagebrush encircling a bed of rice grass. Atticus walked through the stalks of rice grass, heavy with seed, stamping down a space for them both and rooting out any critters that might be underfoot. When he was finished, he stood for a moment, unsure if he should be so forward as to pull his sleeping bag out of his backpack.

"What are we gonna sit on?" Vanessa asked.

Atticus dropped to one knee and swung his backpack around in one motion, unzipping it and removing the nylon sleeping bag. He unrolled it, shook it out once, and made a place in the grass for the two of them. He looked up at her, still standing, her head silhouetted against the low moon.

"Well?"

She smiled and sat down, removing her sneakers and turning to face him. "You've brought lots of girls up here?"

He snorted. "Oh yeah, hundreds." He pushed his pack aside. "Sure wish we had some beer."

She'd never much liked the taste of beer, the few times she'd had it back in Riverside. "I don't miss it."

Atticus was still kneeling next to the sleeping bag, as if he was about to say his prayers.

"You gonna join me?" Vanessa said. She felt nervous and was surprised by her confident tone.

He walked on his knees toward her, his body jerking from side to side as he came. She lay back and he bent toward her, afraid to put his full weight against her.

That is what she wanted, his heaviness pressing against her, and she pulled him down, taking him by the shoulders with both hands, bony fingers around his upper arms and yanking with such force that he felt her nails digging into his flesh.

"Ouch!"

"Come on." She took him down so they were chest against chest, his hard ribs and pelvis digging into her breasts and hips and she could only take short breaths because of his weight, which brought on a light-headedness that confused and excited her as their lips met and tongues darted. She was gasping, for air and in pleasure, as he arched to bend his head so he could kiss her behind the ear, licking his way down her hairline to her neck, and then abruptly stopping and pushing himself up on his arms. Somehow she knew to extend her arms up over her head so he could wiggle her shirt off.

Later, she would remember enjoying the burden of his body against hers more than the act that necessitated her taking his weight. He had been fast, and while she had been expecting pain, or at least discomfort, there was only a mild soreness, followed by a sensation that felt more like the hint of pleasure than pleasure itself, and after he had grunted and finished he kept lying on top of her, and they stayed like that until he began to move again and they did it again, and this time she felt that hint grow into a wave of pleasure that ended too soon, and then they grabbed at their clothes because the dawn sky was going gray to blue and Valence would soon be waking up.

Atticus tore a handful of grass and used that to wipe their fluid and her blood from the sleeping bag as she slipped on her jeans and T-shirt and stood, feeling awkward about having nothing to do. She took up two corners of the sleeping bag, folding them over and then rolling it up to where Atticus sat, slipping on his boots.

BAILEY WAS SURPRISED VANESSA WAS up, had been to the pump, and brought back a bucket of water without having to be asked. It was often difficult to relate to Vanessa's experience. When she herself was fifteen, she lived in a proper home, in a three-bedroom Craftsman in San Luis Obispo. She lived in the same house, slept in the same room, until she went off to college. Vanessa had not slept in a house with running water in two years. What was happening to us, Bailey wondered, that our children are growing up like animals?

But there was something else about Vanessa, Bailey thought, as she watched her daughter pour the water from the bucket into a pot that she set to boil on a charcoal brazier. She was moving a little differently, was more obviously thoughtful, less briskly dismissive.

"You're up early," Bailey said.

"Restless," Vanessa answered.

Bailey squinted as she appraised her daughter. Vanessa was becoming a woman, too soon, and there was nothing Bailey could do to stem that inevitability but try to love her daughter.

"You know, honey, just because we're here"—Bailey gestured around her at their ratty house—"doesn't mean you can't talk to me about, you know, whatever is going on."

Vanessa said nothing.

"That boy, Atticus, he seems awfully fond of you," Bailey said, watching carefully her daughter's reaction.

Vanessa set down the bucket. Centered the pot. She turned and mentioned her brother was still asleep. Her expression betrayed nothing.

"Wake him," Bailey said. "He's going to school."

Vanessa shook the boy gently by the shoulder, feeling fonder of him for the great distance she now felt from him.

Bailey poured the hot water through the filter, gave the chipped mug to Jeb, and then put another cup under it. She would drink the weaker coffee. Jeb was pulling on his boots.

"You noticed anything about Vanessa?" Bailey asked.

Jeb sipped his coffee.

"She's got a boyfriend and they're up to something," she said. "I feel it."

"Wait, what? Who?"

"Haven't you been paying any attention? Atticus, blond-haired, Irish Mexican or something."

"He works with us up on the site. Good kid."

"Well, why don't you talk to him? Make sure he's got common sense, about rubbers and stuff."

"Jesus, Bailey, you think they're up to that?"

"What else do they have to do?"

Jeb stood up, pulled on his work Pendleton. "Oh man, I'm still sore."

"On the same site? You said they were going to move you."

Jeb nodded. "There's always another wall that needs raising."

He took a tortilla, smeared on some oil, and chewed, downing that with the rest of his coffee. He hugged his wife and was gone, out the front door, where he joined a pair of men walking up the road to where a half-dozen SUVs idled to make the run up to Placer.

Bailey took his cup. Shouted after her son, who now came in, rubbing his eyes and yawning.

"Take this next door to Don, make sure he eats something," she said, holding out a plastic plate of two tortillas and a fried egg.

The boy saw no way out of the chore and took the plate. When he returned, Bailey combed his hair, handed him a notebook, a pen, and a pencil, and told him to follow her.

"Why do I have to be the one kid who's got a mom for a teacher?" the boy said to his mother.

"'Cause you're lucky," Bailey said, closing the door behind her as they both left for school.

SARGAM NOTICED THEM AS SOON as they drove in, three silver-gray SUVs glistening in the sun and bristling with antennas. Trouble was her first thought. They looked like government vehicles. They made their way in a shiny column down the on-ramp and then along Bienvenida, passengers obscured behind tinted windows. They drove slowly and steadily, a sign of the imperiousness of whoever was behind the wheel. One thing Sargam knew: they were not subprimes looking for a night's rest. She ducked behind the house and ran past the cooking fire till she found Darren, kneeling down next to the worm tanks.

"Got visitors," she said. "A whole column of armored SUVs. Looks like law enforcement."

Darren wiped his hands on a rag and stood up. "Did you ask what they wanted?"

"No."

"That's not like you. Shying away like that."

"Let them wait," Sargam said, slipping on her white leather jacket.

As the column wound up Bienvenida and down Las Lomas, the residents of Valence, mostly children and women, with the men away working, ducked into houses or into the lush cultivated rows at the sight of the vehicles.

Sargam cut through the rows of tomatoes, cucumbers, and

sweet potatoes and came up through a backyard and along the side of the three-bedroom ranch where the Korean lady had died and stood by the road as the column slowly drove down the street. She held up her right hand, palm outward, her other hand in her back pocket.

The vehicles stopped, a passenger's-side window rolled down. Sargam stepped around and the gusts of air-conditioning blowing out felt decadent. A man with a thick jaw, narrow face, and sturdy nose looked down on her from his perch in the vehicle.

Sargam could see herself in the man's mirrored sunglasses. She looked tiny.

"Why, hello, missy."

"Can I help you?" Sargam asked.

"Who am I speaking to?"

"Sargam." She held out her hand.

The man ignored her proferred hand.

"And are you the lady we've been hearing about?"

"I'm not sure what that means."

The man nodded. "I mean, are you the queen bitch around here? We've heard about this place. Came to see it for ourselves. Heard about a town full of subprimes squatting in some Ryanville of abandoned homes. Pretty little lady in charge, that must be you."

Sargam did not respond.

"Everyone we see," the man said, "seems to be running off. So, since you came out and hailed us, I figure that you, you must be her, and this . . . this must be your place."

"Not my place. Our place. People helping people," Sargam said. "Can I ask your name?"

"I'm Cord," the man said.

"And you're just sightseeing here?" Sargam said. "What line of work are you in?"

"I work for an investor."

"And your interest here?" Sargam said.

"I could ask you the same question," Cord said.

"We're folks who didn't have any place else to go. And we're not hurting anyone here."

"Be that as it may. We may be at cross purposes here. This land, these houses, I have to hand it to you—Sargam, right?—they ain't worth the wood it took to build 'em. But that's not what we're interested in, now is it? What interests HG is under the land. There's shale oil down there."

"What does that mean?"

"What *does* that mean? I would think it means some changes around here."

The window silently rose and Sargam was again staring at her own reflection in the tinted glass.

THAT NIGHT, AT THE CAMPFIRE, after the men came back and washed and had their dinner, and the kids were out playing soccer, almost every man and woman in the community gathered, sitting on logs or standing, their faces gazing anxiously up toward where Sargam perched on a battered filing cabinet. The transformation of Valence was evident in the size of the crowd; over four hundred adults were now there. Landscaped ground, the terraced fields, the irrigation ditches, the fences built to keep foraging animals off the produce, the heavy cooking pots over a half-dozen fires—that population had required more infrastructure. More houses had been repaired, windows formerly boarded up now open with mesh screens, doors replaced, back porches rebuilt.

The men and women were proud of themselves and of their community. They had accomplished all this without credit ratings or cell phones or the Internet. It was all sweat and toil, but it was theirs. Or so they had come to believe.

Sargam called the gathering to attention and began speaking, her words echoing outward so that everyone could hear her report of the interaction with the men in the armored SUVs. That HG Extraction, a division of Pepper Industries no less, seemed interested in Valence. But so far, that was all just talk.

"Until we hear further," she said, "we don't assume anything. We keep working up at Placer. And we keep bringing in the harvest and working on the pump and the fields. The kids keep going to school. Valence is our home now, and I don't know about you, but to me it feels good to have a home."

There was cheering, followed by the DJ starting up the wheels of steel with the old Primal Scream track "Come Together," and Darren brought out a few trash cans full of ice, cold beer, and wine. Solar-cell-powered lamps cast the area around the DJ in yellow light. Artificial light was a special treat in Valence, and immediately suggested festivities.

Sargam shot him a look. "You're blowing our money on booze?"

"It's Friday night. Let them have a party," Darren said. "We may not have one for a while."

"Some of these guys have to be at work up at Placer tomorrow," Sargam said.

"Come on, dance with me," Darren said.

THE KIDS HAD PLAYED SOCCER until it was dark and come up to where the campfire was blazing and the grown-ups were drinking and dancing in the flickering light. There were pitchers of lemonade for the kids, but a few of the older ones stole beers from the trash can and made shandies. Most of the adults

were themselves too tipsy to notice, and in the firelight and the
shadows cast by the dancers, it was hard to see who was doing
exactly what. Atticus helped himself to a few Coors, and even
though the men noticed and knew he wasn't legal, they had
put in enough full days with him up at Placer to know he did a
man's work, so they wouldn't deny him a grown-up's pleasure.
He made his way down the side of the house and around to the
front, where there had been DJ parties back when the community was small enough to fit in a front yard. Vanessa was
waiting for him by the front step, sitting beneath where there
had once been a light fixture but was now nothing but a red-
and-black exposed wire.

"Hey, babe," Atticus said. "Did you miss me?"

Vanessa smiled. "You wish."

He sat down beside her on the step.

She tensed up.

He turned toward her and bent down to plant a kiss.

Vanessa was not expecting the gesture of affection, and when
she turned to see if anyone was watching, her forehead collided
against his chin.

"Ow," she said. "God."

Atticus mumbled, "Sorry," and handed her the can.

She sipped it tentatively. She'd never been fond of beer, but
tonight seemed special. The DJ parties were the only time when
Valence felt like a real place. You could squint and sort of imagine you were at a real party somewhere in the hills above Los
Angeles or at a rave out in the desert.

"What did you do today?" Atticus asked.

"Helped my mom. Cleaned. Brought in about a ton of carrots.
Look at my hands. They're orange."

He took her hands, smiled at her, and then held them up to his
mouth and licked her palms.

"Atticus! Eeeww," she shouted. But she did not pull her hands away. His tongue was cold from the beer.

He laughed, released her hands, and took a sip of his beer. "You should see this berm we've built up there in Placer. It's as high as those hills," he said, pointing to the foothills to the west, near where they had been lying that morning. "A pile of black pellets, like a castle wall, keeping out the muck they're pumping from that well."

"What do you do?"

"I haul sacks of this stuff, shovel it out, bag after bag. They haul them in by the semi. No matter how high we dig and haul, the next day, we have to dig and haul more. It's hot. Hot as hell. But they say they're building a new tracked rig, a monster on tank tracks that they can roll right up to a site, then bore, drill, and pump. I don't know."

Vanessa didn't seem interested.

"Hey, let's take a walk."

"I know what you want to do."

"And you don't?"

She did, actually. What they had started that morning was a project of sorts, and she felt the more they worked on it, the better it would get. But she wanted to talk a bit more first.

"Let's take a walk," she said. "An actual walk."

They stood, brushed off their butts, and strolled down the dirt path that would have been the paved walk from the front door if this house had ever been finished. They turned away from the noise, the DJ beats, and the whooping of people drinking and dancing. As they drifted farther away from the noise and artificial light, the desert night closed in around them, with only the canopy of white stars, a half-moon, and the whitewash of house walls to guide them up the street. They walked toward the off-ramp from the highway, Atticus already thinking of how he would loop them around and then come down Las Casas, back up to the hills and their little spot in the rice grass.

They saw the flashlight beams swaying with the strides of men and assumed, at first, that these were fellow residents making their way to the gathering. Then they heard a dog barking, followed by a grunted shushing and the crunching of boots against rocky dirt.

Finally came the silhouettes of thick-shouldered men walking along the front yards of Bienvenida. Vanessa and Atticus froze, hoping they hadn't been detected.

"Cops," Atticus said.

"What are they doing here?" Vanessa said. "We never have cops here."

"We have to get back to tell everyone," Atticus said.

But the lights were already upon them, a half-dozen bright yellow beams causing them to shade their eyes with their hands.

"Stay right there, subprimes," said one of the men. They were in black uniforms with reflective lime-green piping up the sleeves and down the pant legs.

Atticus and Vanessa were struck silent by the apparent authority of these men, and they both had been on the run with their families long enough to know that these encounters with police, private or public, always ended badly for subprimes.

"We're not doing anything," Vanessa said. "We have a right to be out walking."

A voice behind the lights grunted. "They're just kids."

"This one looks like a woman to me."

"Hey." Atticus stepped forward. "Watch it."

"Or what, subprime? What are you gonna do?"

Vanessa took Atticus's hand to hold him back.

"Stay here, subprimes, we're taking a stroll ourselves."

The men filed past them, their black uniforms and German army–style riot helmets scratching and clicking as they went.

SARGAM SAW THE MEN IN uniform march in, a half-dozen in riot gear, and the dog on the leash. One of them, a large dark-haired man with a mustache, his helmet strapped tightly, ordered the DJ to cut the music. When the DJ didn't comply, he found the power cord and ripped it from its connection to an extension cable. The music died and those few who had not yet noticed the uniformed intrusion now did.

Sargam stepped forward. "I'm not sure you were invited to our little party."

"This is private property," the Hispanic man said. "This is HG Extraction land. And you subprimes have got to go."

"We're not hurtin' anyone," shouted a woman.

Sargam asked, "What are they aiming to do with the land?"

"Not your business," the officer said. "They have clear title. They don't owe you, or me, an explanation."

"When you say 'they' . . . you mean you aren't HG Extraction?"

The dark-haired man pursed his lips. "We're doing our job, lady."

Another of the uniformed men stepped forward. "We don't have to explain nothing. We've been hired by HG, which is all you need to know. You, all of you, have got to go."

"Or what?" Sargam said. "You're going to run us off? There's six of you. And look at us, we are a community . . ."

She held her arm out behind her to indicate the hundreds, staring in angry silence at the uniformed men, who suddenly became aware of how badly they were outnumbered. Even the dog took on a less menacing posture, slinking down onto its stomach.

Darren, the DJ, Jeb, and a few dozen men were inching closer to the campfire, closer to the uniformed men, who began staring anxiously at each other.

"You're not doing anything tonight," Sargam said. "Nobody is going anywhere. I expect we'll be hearing from you again soon. But for now I think it would be best if you return to whoever sent you and told them there's nothing in this here desert but a few thousand rattlesnakes."

The crowd around her began cheering and whooping. Atticus had returned and reattached the power cable and the music came back up, the same Primal Scream song again, "Come Together."

The community resumed dancing and the guards departed, followed by a few dozen men, as well as a several kids, all tracking them to the highway. Atticus and Vanessa walked with them, and before the column ascended the off-ramp, the large dark-haired man turned toward Atticus and said, "We'll be back for you subprimes."

While Jeb watched the men go, Bailey was watching Atticus and Vanessa, and noticed the ease of their manner with each other, and Vanessa's greater confidence and swagger.

"Honey," she said to Jeb, "we need to have a talk with our daughter. And you need to have a talk with Atticus."

Jeb still saw his daughter as a child. "Why?"

"Because your little girl is becoming a woman, and fast."

CHAPTER 8

ARTHUR MACK SAT IN HIS rental Ford at the end of El Medio Avenue, staring at the waves breaking near Gladstones and the oil platforms that clotted the whole bay from Point Dume to Palos Verdes. At one point he had taken pride in his involvement in that great American industry. By selling those futures swaps, those C3DS3s, he helped enable great companies like Pepper Petroleum and HG Extraction to erect those oil rigs and extract that precious oil and gas and coal and all that great stuff that we need to keep driving our cars and invading other countries and, hell, to keep making great TV shows about beached whales. Arthur didn't quite get the connections between Pepper Industries and Pastor Roger and himself, except that they were all on the same side, and that that side was *winning*. Now the important thing was to stay on Pastor Roger's winning team, because that team would keep him out of jail and set him back up in business and allow him to become, as Pastor Roger would say, a victor, not a victim.

He dialed Steven Shopper.

"I've made contact with my family," he told the Texan, "and my wife, she isn't so happy to see me. I saw the girls, though, and, well, there's a lot going on, but they're okay. There's been some issues, with, like, they were attacked."

"Attacked?"

"By a coyote. Ginny was, and Gemma, she was attacked too and bit. She's got a shiner and some scars, and you have to wonder, you know, if a woman who lets her daughter get attacked by wild coyotes is such a great mother, and if that is such a great place for the girls to be, right?"

"You make a valid point."

"So, I'm trying to fix this, and put my family back together like Pastor Roger wanted, and I thought maybe if Gemma and the girls, if they could just meet Pastor Roger, then they would understand that we all need to be together and how important family is, right? Because it's really important to Pastor Roger."

"And to you," Steven Shopper said.

"Yes, to me, of course. Family is everything. I mean, I miss my girls and all that."

"The pastor will be in Nevada this week."

"He's going to Vegas?"

"He will be blessing the good work the Pepper Sisters are doing, extracting fuel from God's bounteous Earth. He blesses the sites before they frack."

"So he's not going to Vegas?"

"He will be blessing some new fracking sites."

"Oil!" Arthur said, finally understanding.

"Yes," Steven Shopper explained and then mentioned a few sites, including towns called Placer and Valence, which Arthur had never heard of.

"I'll send you the information of where the pastor will be. Perhaps your family could join you and experience for themselves the blessed wisdom of Pastor Roger."

Arthur drove to Bowdoin and then down to Temescal Canyon and the Pacific Coast Highway. There they were, those damn whales, and all the tourists flocking to see them. Arthur had missed most of the first season of *Whale Watch*, but he knew from listening to Pastor Roger that the whales were making a gesture of surrender so that we could drill wherever we wanted in the sea. More oil! What could be wrong with that?

He dialed Gemma, surprised when she picked up.

"Hey, babe," he said.

She was silent.

"Um, well, I was thinking I'd like to take the girls out for dinner. Buy them a steak."

Gemma said, "I should say no. I should tell you to go fuck yourself. You've left us broke, Arthur. You're a deadbeat. You—"

"Let's not revisit the past," Arthur interrupted. "I'm trying to be forward facing."

"What does that mean?" Gemma said. "I can't believe I married you. I'm being punished for my superficiality."

"How can you be punished for something good?" Arthur asked. "But, the girls? I'd like to take them out for dinner."

"And when are you leaving?"

"First thing," Arthur said.

"You sure?"

"Yes."

"Okay, take them to dinner. One hour, and then I want them back."

"I'm on my way."

Arthur was preparing his pitch. He would tell Gemma to just come with him, to Nevada, mainly to have Pastor Roger convince her to give their marriage another shot. Then she would return with Arthur to New York, or, even better, move with him to Dallas, where he could resume trading and being a job creator.

He pulled up in front of his mother-in-law's house and immediately saw her glaring at him from the front porch where she stood, banished by Gemma for smoking menthol cigarettes.

"He's back," Doreen growled. "I assume you have a great investment opportunity for me."

"Well, yes, as a matter of fact I do. But that's not why I'm here. I'm here to take my kids out to dinner," Arthur said.

"I know. I'm coming too," Doreen said, smushing her cigarette out in a white ceramic ashtray.

"Daddy!" the girls shouted, running out the front door.

"Hey, cuties. Now, talk to Gam for a few minutes while I have a quick word with your mom."

"She says she doesn't want to see you."

"Shhhh, she's just being mysterious."

"Ha!" Doreen said. "The only mystery is why she ever married you."

The screen door made a quiet creak as he opened it. It took a moment for his eyes to adjust to the interior darkness. "Gem?"

He remembered the way through the living room, past the piano and into Gemma's old bedroom.

"Hello, baby doll," he said.

Gemma was lying in bed, reading a magazine. "Look, it says here that you were in Dallas at the Freedom Prairie Church, and, oh look, Faith Hill was there too!"

"Gem, you need to come with me."

"To dinner?"

"To meet with Pastor Roger. He said we should be together. That if we're together, there is nothing we can't achieve. You can go back to being a great mom—not getting attacked by coyotes and stuff—and I can go back to what I'm good at."

"And what is that, Arthur?"

"Entrepreneuring. We'll move to Dallas!"

"Dallas? Arthur, I'm never going anywhere with you. Do I really need to go through the list of fucked-up things you did? Starting with cheating our friends and ending with living with your fucking mistress, and, oh yes, didn't you also cheat *her* friends and family?"

"Cheat is not really the right word," Arthur said. "I was mis-understood. I was building a small business and the socialists came and they regulated me because they hate entrepreneurs—"

"You don't really believe that, do you? Socialists? In America? There are families living in caves. And socialists are the problem? You know how much it cost to see the doctor after the attack?"

"The market, um, isn't always, um, sufficient?" Arthur said. "Efficient!" He was so pleased when he came up with the correct word that he smiled, as if expecting Gemma to get back together with him as a reward.

Gemma shook her head. He was still a handsome man, with his thick lips and new goatee. Even now, she found herself drawn to Arthur's physical charms, but the weight of repulsive behavior had tilted the scales permanently toward disgust.

"Arthur, I made a mistake marrying you. We have two won-derful girls and so we have to find a way to be civil, but we aren't getting back together. Now, when you go back to New York for your trial—"

"Pastor Roger says they are going to drop my case."

"Of course they will," Gemma said. "Well, after whatever happens happens, then we'll figure out how you can see the kids on alternate Sundays or something like that."

"Alternate? You mean once a week?"

"No, Arthur, there's just one Sunday a week. But that's a discussion for later. Right now, see our girls—my mom is going to ride along and sit in the car while you dine. And have them back in an hour."

"Doreen is coming?"

"I don't trust you, Arthur, so take it or leave it, that's how it's gonna be."

HE DROVE THE GIRLS DOWN to the Golden Bull, recently rebuilt after the Pacific had flooded lower Santa Monica Canyon. The restaurant bar was crowded with various grips and techs from *Whale Watch* unwinding after their shift. Doreen stayed in the car in the valet lot with a paperback novel and a pack of menthols to bide her time. They were given a booth in the front of the restaurant and each ordered a surf and turf—the hotter planet, warming oceans, and vast unregulated agro-fecal runoff from man's shores had made the seabeds grotesquely fecund with lobsters, which seemed to be living in a perpetual state of overabundance. There were lobsters on every menu, in every sandwich, as the basis of every stuffing and starchy crust. The rubbery meat was tasteless, but still, with buttery sauce, palatable enough. Franny and Ginny dunked their tail-meat into the butter and ate with grim faces, deciding to take this opportunity of alone time with Daddy to make their case that the current state of affairs—Daddy gone—was not acceptable to them.

"I know, I know," said Arthur, sipping a margarita. "Tell your mom. Hey, I'm here, right? I want to get back together with Mom, but she won't have it."

"That's because you committed securities fraud, among other charges."

"Mom told you that?"

"Gam."

"Well, there are other people, really cool smart people—do you know who Pastor Roger is?"

"He's on TV."

"That's right. And he believes in Daddy. He says that what I did was really important. For the economy, for American energy independence."

"Is that why you have to wear that bracelet on your ankle?" Ginny asked.

"What's energy independence?" Franny asked.

"Yes, well, no. I wear this so that people can keep track of me," Arthur said. "Energy independence is when, when we drive our cars or fly in a big airplane, or we cook those lobsters, you need gas or oil or something, and we want to cook that stuff ourselves, not let the Arabs or Chinese cook it for us—"

"Or Mexicans—" Ginny said.

"Exactly, or Mexicans. Because Americans, we want to cook our own food." Arthur wrinkled his brow. "Or, no, we don't want to do that. But we want to have our own fuel to cook our food."

"Gam cooks our food. She made us a pot pie. Is that energy independence?"

Arthur sipped from his margarita. "Um, yeah, no, that's not really it, but sort of."

"You're not making any sense," Ginny said.

"But we still love you," Franny added, with a rolling of her eyes toward Ginny.

Arthur tried to change the subject. "Ginny, how is the arm?"

"Itchy, sometimes."

"Are you, like, freaked out about the coyotes?"

"I was, but Mom was awesome. You don't even know."

Yeah, yeah, yeah, Mom is so awesome. But what about Dad? Dad who got them their summer house and private school tuitions and a million ballet, ice skating, gymnastics, and God-knows-what classes? Sure, it had gone a little off the rails the last few months, but was that his fault? No, he had already established that.

He watched the girls chew their lobsters. They needed to be together again as a family. Pastor Roger was right. It was all about family, family and energy independence and entrepreneuring and job creating. If they could just be together again, then Arthur was sure they would have a bright future. He needed Gemma and the kids to see Pastor Roger, to meet with him. Then he would be able to make everything understandable in a way that made sense, even to Gemma.

THE GIRLS SHARED A QUEEN-SIZE piled high with the same stuffed animals and quilts that had surrounded Gemma when she was a little girl, the old clean smell of the fraying cotton somehow as comforting to them as it had been to Gemma. The little room faced Adelaide, and the cliff beyond that, and when Gemma was a girl, before the oil rigs and the flooding of Santa Monica Canyon, the ocean, the curve of the shore past Jetty, up toward Sunset, the dusty tan and drab olive of the cliffs— relatively coyote-free—all of that had been her true north, the sight reassuring, particularly after her own handsome rascal of a father ran off with a German exchange student named Arnold when Gemma was just nine. What was it about their line of women, always falling for good-looking idiots?

Her own wounds were healing, the horror of the coyote attack still fresh in her mind, if less immediate. But still, she *had* fought off the dogs, hadn't she? She took some renewed confidence in her ability to be a mother. If the dogs could not get her girls, then no one would, not that idiot Arthur, not this cruel, unfeeling world of men.

She lay down in bed, for the first time in months with a sense of possibility. Nothing would be easy. A woman, crowding forty, two kids, no degree, having to start over in a country where underclass and overclass were as divided as serfs and nobles, on a planet gone awash in melted arctic ice and broiling in 130-degree summers, where there was no collective idea about how to fix any of this, much less any acknowledgment that there was even a problem. She could not believe that finding sanctuary in some kind of postapocalyptic housing for the wealthy once seemed a plausible solution to her. Was that really the best they could do? A few thousand years of civilization was going to end with bankers and lawyers and movie stars and tech-company C-suiters living on islands while the rest of humanity parched or drowned? Yet that's what passed for forward thinking among her former friends in Manhattan. Of course, the sanctuaries were always described more as contingency plans, like fallout shelters during the 1950s, something you didn't want to use but it was reassuring to have, just in case. But there was no other course; this was exactly where they were heading.

She heard her phone buzz and saw a kik-tok from Richie.

"Hey, you—talk?"

She hit the call-back button.

"Hey," she said. "How did it go?"

"Well, I took a plea deal."

Gemma wasn't sure what that was. "That doesn't sound like a great idea."

"I was in a hurry. Ronin's school was calling. There was a weapons issue."

"Weapons?"

"He had a switchblade comb."

"A comb?"

Richie grunted. "It became a huge thing. More counseling. The poor kid. How are you?"

"Arthur came by. Took the girls out to dinner."

"You went?"

"My mom monitored."

"So, you guys aren't—"

"Back together? Are you serious? He's my—I can't really explain what happened to me with Arthur. I liked him, and I missed the obvious problems: like, he's a sociopath. Please, just let this slide. But no, not together, no chance."

"That makes me happy," Richie said.

"That's not the reason for my decision, but fine, be happy."

"I have to go to meet my ex-wife for lunch tomorrow, but, later, do you want to get a drink or dinner or something?"

She nodded even though he couldn't see her. "Come by the house."

CHAPTER 9

T TAKES ME ONLY FIFTY minutes to get to Santa Monica, where I'm supposed to meet Anya at a vegan restaurant. She says she has a solution to our problems and she wants to talk to me about it in person. I let the valet take my car and go inside, where Anya is seated by a window, sipping from a mug of roiboos tea. She is still beautiful, and for a moment I imagine she wants us to get back together; she will tell me she acknowledges her role in our marital crisis, is, in fact, contrite about what she has done, and now seeks reunion.

There is no chance of this, of course, and as soon as I approach her and she presents me with a cheek to kiss, I am saddened by the thought that we are now reduced to this. But ours was never a happy marriage. It was mutually assured destruction from the start. Of course, now, I wish we had tried harder, but when we were in the middle of the fighting, the silence, the contempt, there were plenty of moments when I felt I couldn't bear any more of the same.

Separation hasn't been bliss. Anya, not surprisingly, has adjusted much better than me. She's pretty, and, at least until you get to know her, and maybe even after that, for the right type of man, i.e., one who is superficial enough to put looks before everything else, easy to get along with. I always assumed I was that superficial, but it turns out I was wrong about that, as I have been about so much.

Anya is the embodiment of a certain type of reaction to our national orgy of self-centeredness disguised as free market economics: she has withdrawn, totally, into her own self, via yoga and juice cleanses and shaman therapy and the picayune specificity of the foods she will put into her body. It's a response I might belittle but at least it is a response, as opposed to my own inactivity.

Anya's boyfriend, the German architect Florian, lives in an eco-friendly house made of sod somewhere in the Hollywood Hills. The house has been featured in various magazines. It looks like an igloo covered in grass, an abode fit for a Hobbit, but it has become a popular form of architecture for those who profess to care about the environment: many of the über-wealthy are seeking to build such structures on their sanctuary islands.

Florian is smart, practical, physically fit—he bicycles fifty miles a day, wearing an oxygen tank as he pedals—and an epicurean chef who has fed my children molecular gastronomy brownies and sprayed chocolate milk alcohol-free martinis into their mouths. Florian has even bought Ronin a turntable.

Like most fathers in this situation, it drives me a little crazy thinking of Florian with my kids. But there's nothing I can do but subtly remind my children that Florian is a fucking asshole.

I take a seat. I'm hungry after the long drive. For some reason, I am careful not to tell Anya about my plea.

"How are the kids?" I ask.

"Ronin is getting over the comb issue. I could have killed you for causing that—"

"Come on!"

"—and Jinx is still gaga for God. Captain's Club today."

I look through the menu. It's high-end, hydroponically grown organic produce: kale, squash, spinach, pureed and blended and sprinkled with imported vinegar. I hate this stuff.

I order some roasted yams and a cup of coffee.

"They don't have coffee," Anya tells me before the waiter can scold me.

"Then some ice water," I say.

"We have room-temperature water," the waiter says.

"Fine, water."

Anya says she is worried, not just about our kids, but also about the planet.

I agree. Though my worries tend to be more local, I agree that on a planetary level we are in trouble. It's just such a large problem I don't ever really try to acknowledge it, comprising, as it does, so many constituent smaller problems like traffic, weather, coyotes, assorted species die-offs, that I seldom have time to work my way up to the actual large problem of we're all fucked. I think that's the appeal of the Pastor Rogers of the world, they reassure us that we're not all fucked because God has a plan. God wouldn't have put all this shit into the earth if he didn't want us to abuse the fuck out of it.

"I'm worried," I say. "But, you know, what am I going to do?"

Anya says she would never expect me to do anything, but in a resigned tone that makes me feel like this is my shortcoming. I let that slide, but too quickly I see where this is going.

Florian, it turns out, has built one of his eco-sod-igloos on an island off Lombok, near Bali. Various developments in and around Bali have become popular sanctuary spots, the higher end of them built and developed by resort firms like Aman and the Soneva Group, and others in descending order of opulence by other scaremongering developers eager to sell into the Chinese and Japanese markets. Florian has secured himself a little sanctuary compound, and he wants Anya to come with him.

"California will be under water," Anya says, "and what's above water will be a thousand degrees and so polluted you can't breathe and the UV will give you cancer in a few minutes. We can't stay here. You can't stay here. You know that."

So Florian has himself a sanctuary. Good for him. "Isn't Indonesia, like, the highest-population-density place on Earth?"

"Not where Florian's compound is. An island, average elevation one hundred meters, protected. And here's the thing. They've built these wonderful schools—"

"Oh no," I stop her. "No. You're not taking Ronin and Jinx."

"I didn't say that. I'm just thinking. You should think."

My yams arrive. A plate of root vegetables, drizzled with vinegar and some sort of kelp flakes. It looks awful.

"You can't take my kids to Indonesia, like a million miles away."

"Sooner or later we all have to go, somewhere, and you don't have any plans."

I take a bite of my yams. They are delicious. I realize I'm hungry.

"But this idea everyone has, of escaping. I mean, unless you can escape the actual Earth, I don't think it's really a plan. It's more of a holding action."

"Life is a holding action," Anya says.

"But, going away like that, giving up. It's selfish."

"Like you're trying to save the world?" Anya says. "You write for a business magazine that glorifies the greediest oligarchs on Earth."

"But at least my heart isn't in it."

"Your heart isn't in anything. That's always been—" She stops herself, wisely deciding she doesn't want to go down old warpaths.

I swallow yam. "Shouldn't we be doing something here? To make our world more livable, instead of running away to some resort?" I'm not sure I believe what I'm saying, but the words sound good to me. "We should make a stand, not hide. That's not even going to work anyway, this whole sanctuary idea. It's just buying time."

"That doesn't sound bad, buying time," Anya says. "But anyway, don't be selfish. Your children can have this great life. I'll send you the link to the website for the school they are building. It's a green school. It's beautiful, like a paradise for kids. And I think Ronin could use a change, don't you?"

"No."

"Will you at least think about it?" Anya says.

"Do you understand what you are asking me? To let my kids go to live on the other side of the world?"

"You'll see them," Anya says.

"When? Christmas? I suck at Christmas. You know that."

"You can visit. And you know, you definitely know, that this is their best chance."

"Best chance for what?"

"For staying alive."

WE ARE A LITTLE DRUNK, Gemma and I, standing in the alley behind the Little Red Bar. The red glow of a cocktail sign above us lends Gemma a pinkish tint. I don't know about second or third chances or how I might be able to save my own life, but I still know something about desire and feeling like if I can somehow make this work, with this person, then who knows what else might work? Every winning streak has to start somewhere.

We kiss at the top of the jog of stairs, where the pavement is gouged and rutted. She is soft-lipped, reluctant at first to part them, but then she opens up and I am intoxicated by desire and hunger and escape. Because for a few moments, while we're making out in a back alley, we are removed from time and the world stops ending, just a little bit.

But as much as I am taken with her looks and confidence and character, what really made me want her was when she told me how much she liked my first book. No matter how much I tell myself I'm a hack, I harbor my old dreams, and it is lovely for a moment or two to have a beautiful woman tell me I'm talented.

"You should keep writing. I mean, writing real stuff," she says. "Not stupid stories about stupid people like Arthur."

Later, we are walking along the cliffs over the Pacific, down by the bluffs, the twinkling oil rigs offshore looking like distant Christmas ornaments. In just a few years, we've mucked up one of the most beautiful coastlines in the world, with casinos and hotels, an elevated skyway. But at night, the glistening lights shine through the marine mist, the neon softened by the moist air.

It feels too soon to take Gemma back to my place.

We stop at a bench and sit down.

"It's so pretty," she says. "You can almost forget how it's all coming to an end."

"Because it's incremental, right?" I say. "A little bit each day, a degree or two a year, a few gutted regulations or new laws per term, and it's not enough for most people to make a stink."

As I say this, I realize I am changing, I'm feeling it, I'm coming to believe that we have to make a change. But how? Should we start giving out bumper stickers or something?

"It took my husband going to jail for me to realize how insane the whole sanctuary plan was," says Gemma. "But I woke up. And you?"

"I think I'm waking up."

We watch the oil rigs flicker in the distance, talismans of our doom.

THE BOY WAS EXCITED BY the preparations, the activity, the sense of purpose among the grown-ups that even the children tried to mimic. Tom had overheard, at a meeting held by the campfire, that they would refuse to vacate. They were tired, Sargam told them, tired of being driven off, of being pushed around, of being told they were not good enough, of being called subprimes.

"We aren't sub-anything," she shouted. "We are just as good as anyone who paid their goddamn mortgage or student loans. You don't judge a person by their credit score."

The grown-ups cheered. And there had been reporters there, filming Sargam, interviewing members of what they were calling a commune before they were corrected by the residents of Valence. "This ain't no commune. There wasn't anyone living in these houses but a bunch of drug addicts, and we ran them off and turned this godforsaken foreclosure-ville into a community. People helping people."

This wasn't some Ryanville, they kept saying, where kids were hungry and sleeping in the open. Where they couldn't get a bath or a hot meal. Where they could be run off by some security tech. Our kids have a school. We have a doctor—he could use some medicine, supplies, equipment. But no one goes hungry. No one is turned away.

The boy would run up behind whoever was being interviewed

and jump up and down, and smile and wave, excited to be on TV, thinking maybe some of his old friends back in Riverside, maybe Daniel and Terry, would see him. And he felt proud to be living in a place important enough for TV cameras to be covering it.

More people were arriving, in better trucks and vehicles, sometimes loaded up with gear—generators, schoolbooks, computers, and, one notable afternoon, toys for the kids, skateboards, bikes, soccer goals. That was the best day since Tom had arrived, and he and his friends had spent the next two afternoons inventing a new game called helicopter, involving bikes, skateboards, and a soccer ball. It was a brutal, violent game with numerous collisions and hard falls on the pavement.

They loved it.

Where was all this stuff coming from? Why were TV cameras suddenly here?

He and his friends discussed Valence's sudden prominence.

"We're like pirates," an older boy said, "like outlaws. And so we're interesting, because there aren't many folks like us left in the world."

"Like when there used to be native tribes, those one's where the women show their tits all the time, and they used to show them on TV."

"Before they were extinct?" the boy asked.

There were nods. "We're savages."

But who was giving the stuff?

"People who support us. People who think what we're doing is cool."

The boy thought about that. "Are we going to get extinct?"

The boys shook their heads. "Hell, no. Who wants this place, anyway?"

BUT THAT WAS PRECISELY WHAT was so compelling about the Valence story. It came to represent the battle of the small against the big, the underclass against the overlords, the subprimes versus the primes. Here was a group of dispossessed families who were not only making their little community work—it was quaint how they had their little school, their fields, their communal mealtimes—but was refusing to flee in the face of the largest privately held petrochemical conglomerate in the United States, one of many owned by the Pepper Sisters.

They were led by a telegenic woman who wore a white leather jacket and repeated that this community had been here long before HG Extraction had been granted the land by an act of eminent domain, promising the state a few percentage points of the value of whatever shale oil they extracted. She was mesmerizing as she condemned the Pepper Sisters, the greedy one-percenters, and a government that would give away a thriving community so that it could be turned into a fracking site. She urged the television crews to head up to Placer and see what those sites looked like. Eight square miles of toxic sludge, she said. Look around, this ain't much, but families can live here, happy families.

Sargam rejected, outright, those inquiries that came in from talent agencies and management companies. She talked to reporters, even encouraged other citizens of Valence to speak to the few who made their way out here from Las Vegas, but she would not make herself a hero, wary lest anyone in the community see her as setting herself apart in any way.

She had known it would come to this, and one evening, as she and Darren were talking in their refurbished house, they discussed the community's options. There was no doubt that HG Extraction, with the full force and weight of the state, would come to move them out. This whole community was but a speed bump between HG and its precious shale oil. It was dirty the way they used eminent domain to take back the land, paying nothing and driving off a few hundred innocent families, but that's how they operated.

"That's capitalism," Sargam said. "That's the system we got. The big, the rich, the powerful, they can take whatever they want. There is nothing to stop them."

She was slipping off her jeans and cotton socks, wiping her feet with a washcloth wet in a bowl.

"It's, like, we're all of us, the millions, the billions who live in the red, subprimes—God I hate that word—but all of us are waiting for something, someone to stand up to them, to say no, enough. You can't just take and take," Darren said.

"You know who we're waiting for?" Sargam said.

He was standing shirtless in his jeans, resting his butt against the kitchen counter. "Who?"

"We're who we've been waiting for," Sargam said. "There's no one but us. You and me. All these good people."

Darren smiled. "I like that. We are who we've been waiting for."

"It's been said before, but that's what we are. There's no one but us. If we go, all these families are going to go back to living in some Ryanville. Kids hungry. No schools. Dirty. Goddamn, that's no way for families to live, for good people to live. Look, we gave them—no, they gave themselves a chance here, took a ghost town and made a community. And now these cursed Pepper Sisters, who already have so many billions, who see the whole planet as a gigantic pit mine, they want to take this from us too."

Sargam sat up then. "It's not just the shale oil."

"What?"

"Why they want to run us off so bad. It's us. They can't stand the idea that people like us could have found a way to live that's fair, dignified, outside their system. They need to prove, to every subprime out there dreaming of a way out, that there is no way out, that no such freedom exists, no such dignity. So they have to crush us, drive us out. That's what matters to them. We can't go."

Darren nodded. He knew better than to disagree with Sargam. And he wasn't going anywhere either.

SARGAM COULD TELL JUST WITH a glance at Vanessa that she had been plucked. The girl was walking with purpose, her gaze intent, even her hips seemed fuller beneath the black sweatpants she was wearing. She couldn't have been more than fifteen, Sargam guessed, but, then, she'd been younger, and it hadn't been with a boy like that Atticus, a good boy with ready smiles and broad shoulders who doted on Vanessa whenever he thought Bailey wasn't watching.

"Vanessa, come here, girl," Sargam said as Vanessa strode by, a basket full of dishes and cups dangling from her narrow fingers.

The sun was so bright some mornings it was like a third person in the conversation, the stinging rays like the hot breath of the eavesdropper. Vanessa held her other hand up over eyes, the blues of which shone through the little pocket of shadow like something precious lost, then found at the back of a dresser drawer.

"How are you and Atticus doing?"

"Fine, I guess."

"He seems like a good boy, well-spoken and mannered. And the way he dotes on you, it's wonderful to watch. Reminds me, reminds us all, of something. Well, something maybe we never even had."

Vanessa was sure she didn't know what Sargam was talking about.

Sargam was so pretty, with her black hair and amber skin, but she wasn't pretty in a mean-girl way, but pretty maybe in the way a favorite teacher could be. You wanted her not just to like you, but to protect you.

"Atticus is really nice," Vanessa said, hoping she wasn't revealing too much.

"You don't have to be shy with me. I know you two . . . you know," Sargam said.

Vanessa averted her blue eyes from Sargam, held her hand lower so that Sargam would not see that she didn't want to meet her gaze.

"I'm saying," Sargam said, "that you're going to need to take some precautions, to take care that you don't get with child."

Vanessa blushed, her skin pinkening and then going vermillion around the freckles on her forehead.

"Don't be bothered, darling," Sargam said. "I'm not judging you or lecturing you. You're young, who knows what you can be, what you can do. You don't need a baby now."

Vanessa looked away, then the slackness of her features tightened and her expression became pinched. "What am I gonna do, huh? I'm living in this, this, whatever this is, and I don't have anywhere to go or anything to do, and yeah, maybe I got a guy and I like him and we have some fun, but don't tell me I'm saving myself for anything or that I got any future or anything like that, because I've seen what's out there."

Sargam held out her arms and pulled Vanessa toward her. "Girl, I'm not saying don't have some fun, but I'm telling you to make sure you get some protection. We can get you something, you know, for that."

Vanessa smiled. "Oh, okay, for that. I'll come by later."

"No, tell that boy of yours, Atticus, to come by; he should be taking some responsibility."

IT'S GONNA BE A WAR, thought Tom. We've got hundreds of men, strong ones, like my dad, and they will fight and fight and fight for us because we're right. The boy was walking along the rows of sedge and onion, beneath the stumpy juts of dried cypress, and up a hill to where all the other boys would gather in the afternoon. Tom considered what a battle might mean. He had seen movies and TV shows, the bombed-out cities, the bundled-up old women pushing carts, the girl running naked down a dirt road, the soldiers wearing night-vision goggles searching through a house for the terrorist, and he had trouble transposing that to this little elbow of the world and to the people he knew. They had no tanks, no airplanes, no bombs, there was just his dad and Sargam and Atticus and a few more men and boys who would be armed with nothing more than righteousness, and was that really enough?

The grown-ups talked about nonviolent resistance. But he was a boy, and caught up in the excitement of conflict and the thrill of potential combat. He had been watching the preparations, the supplies laid in, the gas masks and chemical suits, the food and water that were being stored in every home as Sargam warned they would soon be cut off from the outside world. The boy found in this great excitement and understood that he was seeing things that he would never have seen back in Riverside. Like every boy, he was in a hurry to jump his boyhood self and land squarely in manhood. This great upheaval set to occur seemed to provide precisely that possibility. All that time riding in the rear passenger seat of the battered Flex when Tom felt he had not grown or learned a damn thing, and here he was, on the cusp of real, live war.

He saw Emmett and Yuri and Vito and Ted and Juan, seated in a circle under the shade of a skinny pilitas sage. They had with them the usual writst-rockets and baseball bats. Yuri, the luckiest among them, was the owner of a Crossman pump-action pellet gun. Tom sat down. They shared what they knew, what their parents had been doing, preparing in their own small ways for how they envisioned the cataclysm would go down. They agreed to meet up by the shade tree every afternoon of the war, and they talked about what they would do if they came upon an enemy soldier in their midst.

This last question was the most vexing: What would the enemy look like? Would they be American soldiers? Or cops? Or security techs? Or some combination?

"What did it matter?" the boys said. "When has a uniform ever been good news?"

But armed only with slingshots and BB guns, how would they be able to tangle with Kevlar-coated gladiators sent to uproot them?

Yuri had the answer. They would turn their weaknesses into their strengths. He talked to them about "gorilla warfare," about insurgency, about how a few kids with slingshots had driven the United States out of Iraq—or something like that—and though he didn't know the correct spelling of the term, what he was proposing was radical. Boys with rocks against men with guns, drones, gas, and grenades.

He proposed they gather here, and use their size and the knowledge of the trails leading to various parts of Valence to stage strikes against the enemy, sneak attacks using wrist-rockets, rocks, and a pellet gun that would stun and weaken the enemy, would—he searched for the word.

"Immoralize him!"

The boys liked the sound of Gorilla Warfare.

They would be the Gorillas.

The soldiers would never even see them, swinging through branches down trails they didn't even know existed, until the Gorillas were upon them, teeth gnashing, claws grasping, tearing their hearts out.

They had to gather equipment, water, food, knives, rocks, enough to survive out here for weeks if they had to, so that while their parents were engaging the enemy from the front, they would be attacking where he was weakest, in the rear.

The Gorillas!

THERE WOULD BE NO ACTUAL winning, Sargam knew, there would only be a moment that might look like winning that had to be fixed in people's minds. Eventually, the weight of the forces coming to bear against Valence would be too great. There was no way that a few hundred families in a forgotten property development who happened to be situated above a few million tons of shale could triumph over centuries of capitalism.

The media were gathering, eager for a showdown between the telegenic warrior momma of the have-nots and Pastor Roger and the Pepper Sisters. Pastor Roger was on all the networks, intoning in his soft, mellifluous voice the spiritual mission of the Pepper Sisters, and the socialist, progressive dystopia that would ensue if Valence was allowed to continue eking out its existence.

"People helping people?" Pastor Roger would ask. "I don't hear any inch of room in there for God. This is secularism run amok, the gravest threat to God's fabric since Joseph Stalin and Adolf Hitler and Osama bin Laden themselves."

His position was simple: we can't have a socialist enclave in the middle of America, a town of God-hating progressives who don't believe in private property or the individual's right to exploit that property.

"Where would it end?" Pastor Roger solemnly queried. "Could the socialist dictator come to your house and tell you how to arrange your furniture, tell you not to build a modest six-thousand-square-foot home on your blessed plot, tell you to put illegal solar panels on your roof?"

This was a holy battle, Pastor Roger preached, prophesying that as soon as the legal system allowed, the Pepper Sisters would begin moving their extraction equipment into Valence and break ground on what would be a vastly profitable shale oil field. "Isn't that what God intends? And I will be atop the first truck, blessing the drill bits."

While Pastor Roger always appeared in his climate-controlled studio in his vast domed football stadium, Sargam did her interviews standing against white Sheetrock or framed by the vegetables growing behind the tract rows. When asked what gave her and the people of Valence the right to violate a court order and stand in the way of American energy independence—which had been achieved, by the way, a decade ago; the U.S. was now the world's leading energy exporter—she would respond that she was only doing what the folks of Valence wanted. "We've been running for so long," she said, "in ragged vehicles, sleeping under overpasses, on the side of roads, told to move on from every faucet and tap and bathroom, and denied every service, and so we finally find a place and we make a home of it—"

An interviewer cuts in. "As subprimes, you had no choice but—"

"We don't use that term here," Sargam said. "We don't judge a person by his or her credit score. We've made our home here, using that simple credo, and we don't need credit or cell phones or the Internet, not if we have each other, and that's what the one percenters can't stand, that a fulfilling life is possible without any of that stuff. But it is, and we are living it."

She came across as thoughtful and pretty, and despite the media's attempts to ferret out her "story," there was no story to be found. She had simply appeared, as if from nowhere, in her white leathers on a motorcycle. There was no record or photographic image of her from before, no credit history at all, which further fueled Pastor Roger's rants about Sargam—the foreign name itself was suspect—being some sort of sleeper progressive, a socialist plant from abroad who would undermine America's strength by denying her energy independence.

"I've lived and seen enough to know," Sargam would say when pressed about her past.

To her people, she projected a steady confidence. They would prevail, this was not a last stand, but rather a beginning of a new way of living. If all those millions could just see what a difference people helping people made, then they all had a chance. If that seed could be sown, then anything was possible. But lying quietly on her bedroll, with Darren snoring beside her, she would consider the most likely outcome: an army of security techs, a battalion of bulldozers, and a squadron of drones driving them off, and in the fog of tear gas there might be nothing for television viewers to see, beyond a demolished, abandoned exurb. She knew she must never show this fear or doubt but convey complete faith that the great arc of history would bend toward something like freedom.

It was not much, she knew, to stake people's lives on. But she had also seen the eyes of the men and women who worked with her every day, and she had read, correctly, their desire to flee no more. This was the rock they chose to stand on.

ARTHUR MACK WOKE HIS DAUGHTERS with kisses and nose rubs against their soft cheeks. The girls slept together on a queen-size four-poster, and when they opened their eyes, their first thought was how happy they were to see their father, and their second was what exactly was he doing in their Gam's house?

"Let's go, girls," he whispered. "Do you want waffles? Do you want to meet Pastor Roger?"

"Um, I dunno," said Ginny.

"I'm sleepy," said Franny.

"Let's just go and have a quick breakfast and meet with Pastor Roger, and that'll be all nicey nice, right?"

"Does Mom know?"

"Shhhh"—he held a finger up to his lips—"let her sleep."

He gathered up both girls and a down comforter. "You girls can sleep in the car, on the way to the waffles."

This didn't seem to the girls a good idea, or in keeping with the recent pattern of their days, but they were tired and he was their father.

"Don't you guys want to be a family again?" Arthur asked.

They agreed. It was what they wanted.

"So let's do that, and that starts with us leaving right now."

He had them padding out the door and down the stone path to Adelaide before Gemma had even stirred. She heard whispers and little feet against the path and thought it sounded strange, and then she sat up with a start, tossed her bedding aside, and was out the front door in time to see Arthur's taillights heading down the street.

I SIT WITH RONIN AT the dining table, his algebra book open between us, a dozen sheets of blank scratch paper, pencils, and erasers spread out on the table in the cone of yellow light as we both ponder the mysteries of polynomials. We are supposed to reduce $(-18 \times^2 n)^2 (-1/6 mn^3)$, sets of numbers and letters so alien-looking and -sounding it hurts my eyes and mouth to look and say them. But the only chance Ronin has of passing seventh grade, I realize, is if I sit down with him and both of us, inch by bloody inch, advance up the Omaha Beach of middle school algebra. It is a first time for both of us. I myself was so stoned in seventh grade that I doubt I grasped this material, but that was in my youth, before the waves of numerically literate Asians, both at home and overseas, became the officer corps of capitalism. Now, the only hope our children have of achieving a life of 750-plus credit scores is to be able to go polynomial-to-polynomial with those East Asian kids. Of course, if Enhanced Quantitatives were doing what the state was paying them to do, I wouldn't be sitting here, struggling to wrap my middle-aged brain around these strings of hostile numbers and letters.

Ronin shows me what he knows so far. How to simplify inside the brackets, then find like terms, push those together, remember the order of operations, then exponents, but no, I think, this has to be wrong. Shouldn't exponents be first? Or is it brackets? I flip through the textbook, looking for the correct order.

"That can't be right."

Ronin sulks beside me.

I worry I am undermining his self-confidence. Am I being too harsh? If I were more confident myself, then wouldn't I be able to gently nudge him to the correct simplifications? Where is his Danish mother and her numerically hyperliterate architect boyfriend? Why aren't they helping Ronin with his math?

"PEMDAS." Ronin sounds this alien word out slowly.

"Is he Greek?" I ask.

"No, it's 'Please Excuse My Dear Aunt Sally,'" he says, recalling a mnemonic that he has obviously heard repeatedly in his EQ sessions. "Parentheses, Exponents, Multiplication, um, something, Addition, Subtraction."

"Division?" I say.

"That's it!"

And we set to work with our simplifying. Reducing $(-18 \times^2 n)^2$ $(-1/6mn^3)$ to $54m^5n^4$ is a pleasing and logical operation that makes us both happy. We each do a dozen of these problems, and both come to the same answers eleven out of the twelve times we try. We are making something work, together.

"This isn't so hard, is it?" I ask.

Ronin is concentrating, and I imagine that he is making a breakthrough, right here, at our dining table. Why, we may have the makings of an Ivy Leaguer after all.

"I fucking HATE THIS," he says, and puts his head down on his arms.

But no matter, we have completed one night's homework. He is now only fourteen assignments behind.

I'm looking out the dining room window at the empty swimming pool, the pale blue bottom still somehow inviting despite the fact that we haven't had water in it in half a decade. But Ronin remembers swimming in that pool, though Jinx probably doesn't, and how happy it had once made us.

At one point, after we take a break for a few minutes between the algebra and the algebra, I ask Ronin what he thinks about Anya's idea, about going to Lombok with his mother and Florian.

"I dunno," he says, not looking up from his phone.

"But you understand it, right? What this means?"

"I guess," he says.

"Your mom wants you and Jinx to go to sanctuary," I say.

"I'd go with you," he says.

"I'm not going anywhere," I tell him. "I think the sanctuary idea is idiotic."

"Sanctuary doesn't sound so bad," he says. "But I don't want to go with Florian. I think that guy's kind of a dick."

That's my boy, I think.

We get back to work trying to solve the really tough problems.

AT NINE A.M. THE NEXT morning a policewoman arrives and serves with me an emergency court order of child custody. Anya has gone to family court and won immediate full custody of Ronin and Jinx. The family court judge, apparently, agreed that I was a threat to the safety of my children, based on my pleading guilty to Endangerment of a Minor. She informs me that Anya, accompanied by a police officer and social worker, will be at my house in an hour to collect my children and their possessions.

I know if I let them go I will never see them again.

I tell them to pack an overnight bag.

My phone rings. It's Gemma.

"Hey there," I say. "Not a great moment right now."

"Tell me about it," she says. And she tells me her husband has kidnapped her children.

"What an amazing coincidence," I say, "because I'm about to kidnap mine."

I WISH I HAD WASHED my car, or, better yet, had it detailed before my getaway. I hastily cleared the backseat of old man-uscripts and gum wrappers and shopping bags, dumped the kids' backpacks and suitcases into the trunk, leaving space for Gemma's rolling suitcase. I stuffed a few T-shirts and jeans into a backpack, along with my computer. By the time I arrived at Gemma's mother's house, Gemma was already waiting for me, her mother standing behind her with arms folded, studying me with the same scrutiny she probably wished she had given Arthur Mack. I'm not sure if Gemma had told her that, viewed from a certain perspective, I was essentially doing to my wife a version of what Gemma's husband was doing to her. But, bottom line, neither one of us wants to lose our kids. So off we go, driving past the whale carcasses and sitting in three hours of eastbound 10 traffic before we finally leave L.A. County and for a few miles there are up to the startling speed of forty-five miles per hour. I'm amazed the old Prius still has that in her.

It had been easy to convince Jinx to hit the road: we were going to see Pastor Roger. Ronin was delighted by the prospect of missing a few days of school. I sold this like an adventure. We were going east, into the desert, in search of some missing kids. What could be more fun than that?

Arthur had called Gemma, telling her that he had taken the kids for the good of the family.

"Okay, Arthur, I'm not sure I'm following your logic," Gemma said, "but I am going to find you and castrate you for this."

"Ooooh, I love it when you talk dirty." What was alarming was that he actually meant that.

"Where are you taking them, Arthur?"

"The same place I want you to come. We have to go see Pastor Roger. I want the girls, and you and me, all of us, to sit down with him. He's so together, such a dignified person—"

"You're taking our girls to see a televangelist? That's why you've taken them?"

"He's so much more than that. He just has this way of making me—everyone—feel okay about themselves. So that I feel like things can work out. I mean, between you and me, between us, we can all be together. He can do that for us."

"You nitwit, I'm never going to be with you."

"We'll see what Pastor Roger has to say about that. I'm going to see him now."

"Where are you taking them?"

"Wouldn't you like to know."

"To Valence?" she asked. She had been watching the news and knew that Pastor Roger had set up camp near the besieged squatter town.

"Damn it," Arthur said. "Will you at least sit down with Pastor Roger when we get there?"

Gemma hung up.

THE HIGHWAY CROWDS AGAIN AS we near the Nevada border, with hundreds of vehicles pulled off the gray-top into makeshift roadside Ryanvilles, families atop sleeping bags and on beach chairs watching the traffic stream by. There are signs, soaped and water-colored onto rear windows: "People Helping People"; or simply, "SARGAM!" Jinx and Ronin gaze at the masses of families, boys and girls like them, only these are subprimes. I have to resist the impulse to warn Ronin: You see what happens if you don't do your algebra. Whatever happened to these folks, I tell myself, was bad luck, not bad math.

Gemma has been quiet, thoughtful, but careful to engage Jinx and Ronin in conversation. I admire her selflessness in getting beyond her own worries and concerns at this moment as she tries to paint this journey as some kind of rescue adventure.

"We're on a mission," says Ronin.

Jinx thinks this over, asks Gemma, "Do you want to get divorced? Or does your husband?"

I'm worried about where this is going.

"I don't feel like I have a choice," Gemma says.

"Divorce is a sin," says Jinx, "so I think you should reconsider. My father and mother committed the sin of divorce, and adultery, and numerous other sins, and if they don't repent, they will suffer."

"Now, Jinx, remember we talked about how that is one point of view—"

"I'm stating gospel," Jinx insists.

"Jinx, my husband, he committed numerous sins—"

"I know who your husband is," says Jinx, "Pastor Roger has mentioned him from the platform, he's a hero."

"I don't think so," says Gemma. "He cheated people. He cheated me. He committed many sins."

Jinx ponders this. "What sins?"

Gemma thinks for a moment. "Adultery; um, greed; um, sorcery, isn't that one?"

Jinx nods. "Sorcery is a sin."

"Idolatry?" I suggest.

Gemma looks at me, shrugs. "Sure. Idolatry."

Jinx thinks this over. "'So put to death the sinful, earthly things lurking within you.'"

Gemma smiles back at Jinx. "Thank you, Jinx, that's what we need to do."

I hand my credit card to a police officer who swipes it, reads the score, and returns my card. "Welcome to Nevada."

I HAVE TWENTY-SIX TEXT MESSAGES from Anya, nineteen kiktoks, and three voice mails that I ignore.

WHEN WE STOP AT A Del Taco south of Jean, and Jinx and Ronin are eating U.S.-farmed kangaroo-meat tacos in their own red-benched booth, I thank Gemma for being so patient with Jinx.

"She's adorable," says Gemma.

"I wouldn't go that far."

"Don't be so hard on your kids."

"I hate my kids," I say.

Gemma sips her coffee. "I can't imagine how you lost custody."

"You know what I mean. I just—I don't hate them—I just don't know how to fix them, and I hate that."

"You don't fix them," Gemma says. "You just keep them from fucking up too much."

"That's what I'm trying to do."

"Look, I'm glad you're coming with me to look for my kids, but you know that your own situation, in terms of keeping your kids, it's sort of hopeless, right?"

"I like to think of myself as living in denial," I say.

I know how this looks: a father convicted for recklessly endangering minors who then kidnaps his own children is unlikely to come off favorably in family court. The way I see it, I don't have any choice, it's either lose my kids now or lose them later. And I'll take later.

"But you're just putting off the inevitable," she says.

"Isn't that all any of us are doing?" I ask.

WE STOP IN LAS VEGAS for the night, the city a shimmering upward-jutting glow stick of white light in the hazy evening. We're all road weary, our backs aching, our asses sore from riding too long on my old car's sagging suspension. I haven't been to Vegas in a few years, since a story about Steve Wynn's plan to build a full-scale replica of the Roman Coliseum and stage actual gladiator fights—men versus men, men versus lions, lions versus bears, lions versus robots, robots versus men, robots versus robots. It wasn't opposition from environmental and animal rights groups that stopped him, it was the latest spin of the boom-and-bust cycle that undid the plan—at least in Vegas. He built a grand Coliseum in Macao that draws 120,000 Chinese two nights a week to watch fights between men and various wild animals. Chinese convicts are offered the chance to fight for their freedom in these battles.

Vegas has never recovered from the cyclical housing busts, and the whole strip itself has the sickly luster of a grandly renovated McMansion, now a decade out of fashion. The great slot boxes and shopping malls and fountains and fake Paris are all still standing and as gaudily lit and trying-to-beckon as ever, but the true high rollers have long ago forsworn Vegas to gamble instead in the deregulated casinos of Coney Island, on the East Coast, and Santa Monica, on the West Coast. Why fly across country when better action is a few miles away by helicopter?

But the old glitter and heat still excite, though the fountains of the Bellagio no longer spout and the pools at Caesars are empty, Vegas itself having exhausted the central Nevada aquifer a few years back. But for Jinx and Ronin, this skrim of unreality somehow reminds them of theme-park visits and boardwalk afternoons.

"Let's just camp here for the night," I say.

Gemma is reluctant. She wants to continue her pursuit. But I point out that Pastor Roger isn't going anywhere. He's vowed to liberate Valence, and he's waiting to bless the newest Pepper Sisters creation, the 480-foot-high, 125-foot-long, 22,000-ton Joshua Extractor, essentially a deep-sea rig on sixteen-foot-wide treads that requires an additional six lanes of highway on every road it travels. The beast, now lumbering toward Valence, has been giddily featured on the *Today* show as America's latest and greatest weapon in the war for energy independence. A one-stop shale-oil extractor that reduces the number of employees on a fracking site from forty-eight to a mere half-dozen who sit in a climate-controlled bridge high atop the vehicle.

"With the Joshua, all the foreman—that's what he's called, or is he a captain, like on a ship?—all he has to do is drive up and then drop the bit, flip a switch, and then start drilling," the host marveled.

"It's that easy!"

"And then he can pump two hundred and forty thousand gallons of water a second into that hole."

"That's a lot of water!"

WE TAKE A COUPLE OF rooms at Caesars, one for me and the kids and the other for Gemma. My relationship with Gemma is either progressing at surprising speed—our third date and we're already in Vegas!—or is, in reality, a highly awkward courtship, unfolding, as it is, around both a kidnapping and an attempt to thwart a kidnapper. After I send the kids down to the buffet— "Lobster Served 21 Ways"—I head over to Gemma's, where she lets me in while holding a handset to her ear.

"The kids called my mom," Gemma whispers to me.

"No, you don't need to come out here, Mom," she says into the phone. "No, I'm with Richie . . . yes, and his kids . . . no, he's not a child molester . . . no, I haven't gone from an embezzler to a molester . . . yes, that would actually be going down in the world, I suppose, but that's literally the first nice thing you've ever said about Arthur, and you say it now? Good-bye, Mom."

"That sounded like a real vote of confidence from her," I say.

"Don't worry. She'll actually like you. She never could stand Arthur."

She's taken a shower and is in a white terry-cloth robe. I walk over and stand by the windows, looking down at the abandoned courtyard. The huge circular centerpiece pool, with a fountain in the middle—one of about a dozen spread inside Caesars' grounds—used to be full of muscular boys and curvy girls holding large brightly colored drinks shaped like bongs and old dudes swimming lazily between them. Now the pools are bone dry, save for one tiny lap pool about a half-mile away across the compound. They might as well frack here, I think.

"Have you heard from your wife?" Gemma asks.

"Ex-wife," I say. "And, yeah, or, actually, I have received about fifty texts and kiks, but I'm not reading or listening."

I cross the green carpeting, past a velvet upholstered club chair and a coffee table with the top about the size of a CD case. "I don't want to talk about our problems."

"Without those, we are nothing," Gemma says.

"Let's make tonight about us," I say. "Oh, and my kids, who will be back upstairs in about twenty minutes. And I'm sure I'll be hearing from various attorneys who are involved in various legal actions in which I am a defendant very shortly. But besides that, and the fact that your felonious ex-husband has kidnapped your children—who are recovering from a bear attack, was it?—we should be able to free our minds and have totally uninhibited, empty-headed animal-like sex."

I pull her toward me, taking her in my arms, the thick bathrobe making her seem more substantial than she is. She smells of shower steam and sweet soap, the scent coming off her cheeks and sticking in my nose so that whenever I inhale, there she is. Every kiss is with intent, I believe, the desire to push further, to climb into this person, to ravage her, to unload on her, and that is why even in my advancing years, it still causes an adolescent rush, an eruption of ego so that I can fool myself, tongue touching Gemma's tongue, hands inside her robe, on soft breasts, pinching nipples, eliciting moans, hands moving down the robe, toward her uncovered mons, the soft scratch of her pubes, I can fool myself in these seconds, because of the thrill of our kiss, that I am somehow still this bitchin' awesome dude that I never was and certainly never will be again. Making out with a girl for the first, or second, or third time, it makes every rock-and-roll song dead-on accurate, every guitar chord of every rock anthem suddenly hits you square and reminds you how absolutely right Pete Townshend is on every verse, even after decades of crappy TV show sound tracks and car commercials. Because it cuts through—this feeling of being with a new girl—it cuts right through to slice open the closed universe and make everything possible again.

After, we are lying on the scratchy metallic green bed cover. For a few moments, as I pull Gemma close to me and she lies with her cheek against my shoulder, our fears and concerns are at bay. But they come rushing back—I can almost feel the instant a jolt through Gemma's body reconnects her worry circuits: her kids are still out there, somewhere, with her idiot criminal of a husband.

Where are my own children?

I pull on trousers, shirt, shoes, and head down the hall to the elevator and then downstairs, kikking Ronin as I go.

They've forsworn the buffet—the lines are still too long—and instead opted for the shorter line at Shake Shack. When I find them, they are at a table, finishing up their burgers. Ronin is on the phone. I join them, pull up a chair, pick up a leftover french fry.

"Who is he talking to?" I ask Jinx.

"Mom," she says.

"No, oh no, don't tell her where we are," I stage-whisper to Ronin.

"Too late," Jinx says. "He already did."

"You seem happy about that," I say.

"I'm neutral. Between you and Mom? I have to be."

I nod. "Yes, but you know"—I lower my voice so that Anya can't hear me—"but you know that your mom wants to take you to Indonesia. I'll never see you again."

Ronin holds the phone out to me. "Mom wants to talk to you."

I wave my hands. "No, no."

But it's too late, he's put the phone to my ear. "Richie?"

"Hello, Anya."

"What the fuck are you doing?"

"Um, a road trip."

"You are violating a court order."

"That was a cheap shot. Behind my back?"

"It's the best thing for the kids to get away."

"It's not going to happen."

"Oh yes it is," Anya says. "You are so going to regret this. I will find you and—"

"Don't threaten me," I say. "I'm beyond that. I'm—"

"You're right. I'm not going to threaten you. But I will have my children."

I disconnect and hand the phone back to Ronin. "What did you say?"

"I told her we were in Vegas," Ronin says.

"Did you tell her which hotel?"

He shakes his head.

"Good boy. Okay, we need to get a little rest and then we're back on the road."

THAT NIGHT, I'M ANXIOUS FOR my kids to go to sleep so I can go back over and reconnect with Gemma. Jinx senses my impatience and has chosen this evening to begin what she promises will be a life of meticulous flossing. She's carefully sliding the string alongside each tooth, and then rinsing each time.

"Jinx, you have to go to bed," I say.

She ignores me, continuing to floss.

Finally she finishes, and then she starts brushing. She brushes with the same metronomic persistence as she has flossed, and this seems to take even longer.

"Jesus, Jinx, can you fucking hurry up?"

She rinses, puts down her toothbrush, and frowns at me. "Don't curse at me. And DON'T take the Lord's name."

"Whatever, Jinx," I say. "You know, you're turning into a bully about all this God stuff."

"Well, you're rude and abusive."

"Abusive?"

"You shouldn't use profanity with children. That's abusive."

"It's just words, Jinx. Actions are what matter."

"Pastor Roger says—"

"Jesus, will you shut up about Pastor Roger? He's a charlatan. A complete fraud. He's someone morons believe in."

"Who are you to tell me what to believe?"

"I'm your father," I tell her. "I can give you my opinion. Now go to bed."

"No."

"Will you go to bed?"

"No. You can't tell me what to do."

"Look, Jinx, it's been a long day, you need some sleep. We all do."

"I want to see Mommy," she says, and a few tears pop from her eyes.

"You can't, not right now."

She starts bawling.

I know what I should do is go and comfort her, but instead I become angrier. "Damnit, Jinx, you need to toughen up here. You can't be a baby now. Okay?"

"Noooo."

"Toughen up!" I take her by the shoulders, not roughly, I don't think, but I want to focus her, to bring her back. At contact, she starts howling, as if I have injured her.

Ronin, who has been lying on a rollaway, listening to music, sits up and removes his headphones. "Dad? What are you doing?"

"I barely touched her," I say.

Ronin runs over and takes Jinx in his arms. "Leave us alone!" Now he's shouting. "Why can't you be like a normal dad? Like everyone else? Why do you have to be such a freak?"

"I'm not, I wasn't doing—" I am on the defensive. "I'm sorry, I just lost my cool. It's this whole Pastor Roger thing. I know he's a big deal to Jinx, but I, well, I see him very differently. In fact, he's suing me."

"And I hope he WINS!" Jinx says.

I'm an awful father. I acknowledge as much to my children, reciting a litany of my failings in a soothing and relaxing voice, intending to put them to sleep. There was the time I was caught smoking marijuana at a back-to-school night, the time I used profanities toward Jinx's second-grade teacher, the time I started an e-mail chain trying to get Jinx's elementary school principal fired, the time I got drunk and fell asleep in the front yard at the birthday party of one of Ronin's friends, the time Anya and I got into a fight during a parent-teacher conference and the teacher called security, the time the police came when I was teaching Ronin how to ride a bike because my neighbors thought they were watching an act of child abuse, the time I made Ronin play touch football on the street and the police gave me a summons.

There are so many times, and my children find it relaxing to hear me string together my apologies and confessions of guilt, as if they find it reassuring that all our problems, all our family's shortcomings, are the sins of the father.

And when I put it like that, I'm thinking, after both my children are finally asleep, their faces reflecting the desert-night Vegas-strip neon sheen streaming in through the floor-to-ceiling windows, maybe I am a flop of a dad. Maybe Anya taking them away is truly for the best. I'm a mess, a middle-aged stoner who has been lucky making a living—until now, anyway—but a mess of a parent, a shitty role model, and have I conceived of a plan to escape the imminent end? Absolutely not.

I sneak over to Gemma's and for a few minutes again it's like a drug, this fondling and cuddling and intercourse with a beautiful new woman, and I am kept from my own fears and worries and we steal a few hours' real sleep before our fears resurface and we wake, dress, and flee.

CHAPTER 10

I T WAS 120 DEGREES ON God's great Earth today, a sobering temperature, so scorching that three minutes under God's great sun would leave an exposed arm or forehead raw-steak red. That's why God created air-conditioning, of course, and to power those compressors, God made the juice, and to extract the juice God created fracking, and to frack the Earth God begat the Joshua Extractor. As Pastor Roger walked around the monstrous vehicle—the size of a six-story office building on half-tracks, ladders affixed to the sides that climbed up so high into the blinding sun that Pastor Roger could not see where they bowed in at the first platform. The Joshua's superstructure rested on a girded-steel glacis plate forty feet above ground level. Below the telescopic kelly, drill pipe, and casing was a red blowout protector, and hanging between the treads, like the glistening testicles of a Minotaur, was the massive oiled bit, a two-meter-wide toothed and barbed bulb that could cut through granite at a rate of eight feet per minute.

God's vision was great, Pastor Roger reflected, so he sent this shining steed of capitalism to help the Pepper Sisters extract the blessed juice. The pastor stood in the shade, listening to an engineer describe how the Joshua could roll over a shale oil field, drop the bit, wait a few days, release the derrick, casing, and traveling block, after which it was a simple matter of pumping and gathering. Then the Joshua could move on to the next site. The sight of the Joshua lumbering over the horizon, why, it had to be among the most inspiring of God's creations. It could block out the sun; its sound was like thunder and waves crashing, its power like that of an approaching tornado. The massive 46,000-horsepower, 14-cylinder diesel engine could shatter windows and rattle houses miles from its path.

How could this be wrong? How could God have created something this great and unleash it upon the earth if it were not his vision? This was a weapon in his divine hand.

An elevator rises through the middle of the beast, but Pastor Roger preferred to climb the outside, to feel for himself the immensity and grandeur.

But it was hot, the ladder's metal scorching to the touch. He spit once in each hand, asked God to help him deal with the pain, and started his ascent, up past the oily-smelling guts of the beast, up, up, up to the chapel in the sky from which the foreman could survey this earthly kingdom. He climbed and felt the hot wind carry him, lifting him up forty feet from the earth, to the first platform, where he stepped on the grooved steel and walked around a motor room to the elevator to continue the rise to the top.

The television crew—a cameraman and boom mic operator— waited for him on the bridge of the earth vessel along with its six crew members, who stood awkwardly, unsure of how to act before the cameras. Finally, the elevator door opened and Steven Shopper emerged.

"Good, good, now you all do whatever you would be doing if the pastor weren't here. He's going to offer his blessing, and we'll get some footage for the news."

The elevator door opened again and Pastor Roger stepped out, clapped his hands once, and took a deep breath.

"Lovely, lovely"—he smiled at the crew—"great to see you!" And he pumped his fist.

In the distance, he could see the abandoned exurbs with their unfinished ranch houses, now inhabited by the godless progressives who respected neither private property nor God's laws. With the Joshua crew surrounding him, Pastor Roger blessed the Joshua Extractor, thanked the Pepper Sisters for their vision and the members of Freedom Prairie Church for their support, and thanked God for giving them this Earth and the tools to extract the juice upon which they all suckle.

> God, we acknowledge that the Earth and all that is in
>   it belongs to you.
> The Earth is the Lord's in all its fullness.
> Who may ascent into the hill of the Lord?
> Or who may stand in his holy place?
> He who has clean hands and a pure heart,
> Who has not lifted up his soul to an idol,
> Nor sworn deceitfully.

He urged the foreman and his crew aboard the Joshua Extractor to be bold and brave and fearless, to brush aide all who would stand in the way of God's will. He asked the crew to bow down before him, to feel the laying on of his hands. He wept as they looked at one another, the men unsure of the meaning of this prayer. All they had been told was that the pastor would be coming up to offer a blessing. Later, on the KIK News feed of

Pastor Roger blessing the Joshua, the men seemed bewildered as the pastor prayed for them.

FRANNY AND GINNY AWOKE A few miles outside of L.A. and had been complaining every quarter mile since, angrily demanding an explanation of what was going on as regularly as the appearance of the oncoming traffic. Arthur had forgotten how noisy his children could be and for a few moments considered turning around and heading back to his mother-in-law's house to deposit them and good riddance. But he recalled that Pastor Roger would only support him if he could reconcile with his wife and children. Well, he was two-thirds of the way there. He just had to get his brood to Nevada, where Pastor Roger was bivouacked supervising some fight against communists or something, and then his wife would turn up and they would all sit down with Pastor Roger and he would sew them all back up into one happy family. Oh, it would never quite be the way it had been, living in New York, summering in the Hamptons, that had been quite a sweet ride, but living in some nice Dallas suburb, Parker or Highland Park, and perhaps managing some of Freedom Prairie's substantial assets, though even going to work for the Pepper Sisters would be a fine place to start his comeback. In time, the family could even return to New York. Isn't that what disgraced financiers did?

"Will you two just shut up?" he shouted for the twenty-fifth time since leaving L.A. County.

He had reneged on the waffles promise but now had no choice but to stop and feed the girls, who refused any number of fast-food options, citing their unhealthy ingredients and statistics on teen obesity. He finally found them organic turkey jerky and single-serving soy milk cartons in a gas-station convenience annex. At least he couldn't be accused of actually starving his children.

"Mom is never going to take you back," Franny told him. "She hates you."

"We'll see about that," Arthur said.

"She says you're a criminal," Ginny said.

"Well, one person's criminal is another person's Sheriff of Nottingham," Arthur said.

"You mean Robin Hood?"

"Right, Robin Hood."

"So you stole from the rich and gave to the poor?" Ginny asked.

"Well, I stole from the rich AND the poor—NO, I didn't steal. I was making the economy more efficient, performing a function, until the government, the progressives, cracked down on me."

"Why?"

"I don't know. Because they hate success. They want everyone to be poor."

"That doesn't make sense."

"Yes it does, now shut up."

They drove through the hot desert. Arthur had to call Steven Shopper to arrange for temporary credit relief so he could pass the credit checks. Finally, the girls fell asleep again as they crossed into Nevada.

STEVEN SHOPPER STUDIED ARTHUR AND his daughters, the grit and filth of five hundred miles of road staining them so that they looked practically subprime. This would not do. Arthur was happy to be issued fresh khakis and a clean button-up shirt, but the girls objected to the taffeta dresses, complaining the outfits were too girly-girl, until leggings and skirts that appealed to them were produced.

"And your wife?" Shopper asked, after they stepped outside the trailer so the girls could change.

"Oh, she should be turning up at any minute."

"Any minute?"

"She's coming separately."

"What?"

"Well, she's going to follow. That's what I mean."

"Follow you? Do you mean she's in pursuit?"

Arthur shrugged.

Shopper was concerned. "This isn't what Pastor Roger intended. For you to, um, abduct your children, if that's what you've done."

"Come on," Arthur said. "I had to do it. I mean, Ginny was attacked by a coyote. Whose fault is that? I'm trying to work with you."

"The pastor has been generous with both his time and spirit. He's arranged for the removal of the monitoring anklet. And he has been more than fair in terms of easing your passage, but he won't have a home-wrecking philanderer in his flock."

"She'll be here," Arthur said.

Franny and Ginny were seated at a Formica table, eating dry, frosted cornflakes from bowls. The trailer they were in was like a bus, only without the driver's seat. Instead, there was a tinted window that looked out on several other trailers, and beyond them the Joshua Extractor, casting a shadow that left most of the trailers in the shade.

"This is cool, isn't it?" Arthur feigned enthusiasm. "Look at that, it's like the Statue of Liberty."

"Not really," both girls said.

There was a bathroom with a shower, and beyond that a bedroom with a queen-size bed. Arthur walked around the narrow kitchen, opening cabinets, finding water bottles, crackers, potato chips, soap.

"Well, it beats being eaten by dogs," Arthur said. "And that's what living with your momma led to."

"Where are we?" asked Ginny.

"We're waiting for Pastor Roger—and for your mom," Arthur explained.

"Aren't you going to jail?"

"Well, as I told you, probably not, because to some people, including Pastor Roger, I'm a hero. You should be proud of your daddy. What I did helped make this"—he pointed at the Joshua—"made this possible. Or sort of. Now, I'm going to take a quick nap, get rested for Pastor Roger. You two rest up here."

Arthur walked to the back of the trailer and lay down on the hard foam. As he fell into a light, unrestful sleep, he thought about how close he was to rebuilding his life, to vindication.

FRANNY AND GINNY FOLLOWED THE outline of the shadow of the Joshua, not feeling the full intensity of the scorching desert heat until they were out of its shadow and picking their way over the desert scrub. They passed the open doors of other trailers, where they saw cameramen and reporters in polo shirts, some with FP logos stitched on the chest. Next to some of the trailers were piles of refuse, empty cereal boxes and milk containers and potato chips mashed into silty sand. The girls passed through the wheeled city as if they were invisible, the Freedom Prairie officials and television reporters and cameramen too busy to notice them. When they reached the edge of the trailer camp they hesitated at the expanse of open desert before them. They followed their line of sight and could see a village of some kind, a strip of houses in the distance, nestled beneath small hills.

They stopped, shading their eyes from the sun. Then, as if having the same thought at the same moment, they set out, right feet first, into the crab-grassed desert, the heat of the ground pressing up through their thin-soled sneakers.

"It's snowing," Franny said.

Ginny held her hand out. "This isn't snow."

They studied the flakes accumulating on their hands, powdery silver-gray specks soon covering their palms, their arms, their hair.

The ash sprinkled down from the clear sky, trillions of particles, the carbon fallout of vast fires to the east, burning uncontrollably for months. A shift in wind brought the smoke system here, and the flakes were thickening till they partially blocked out the sun and exuded a sickly sweet charcoal smell that left their lungs aching when they inhaled too deeply.

"I don't like this," Franny said.

"It's just ashes. It can't hurt us."

The sooty blanket kept their bare arms from burning in the sun, but it also reduced visibility so the girls were quickly lost in the desert. They walked straight, leaning into the hot wind, their steps making impressions in the sulfurous ground that filled rapidly with falling ash.

"Do you think Mom will come?" Franny asked.

"Of course she'll come," Ginny said. "You can count on Mom."

"And Dad?"

"Dad? I don't know about Dad."

"Is he a criminal?"

Ginny did not want to answer that one, so she continued walking, patting her dress and watching the gray, powdery residue go up in puffs.

THE BOY PERCHED AT THE top of a hill, at the base of a runty barren tree, was gazing through their solitary pair of binoculars at the security techs, who were themselves gazing back. You're watching me? Well, *I'm* watching *you*, the boy thought. About him were a squad of fellow Gorillas—Emmett and Yuri and Vito—lying belly down on the earth, their desert-hue clothing, stained not by design but by boyhood habit, making them almost invisible against the ashy gray earth.

"We've got incoming," said Tom, picking up two figures in white skirts crossing through the ash-fall.

"Hajis?" asked Emmett, loading a marble into a Wrist-Rocket.

The boy squinted through the lenses, struggling to discern the forms. "No, these are . . . girls."

"Girl hajis?"

"No, they look like girl *girls*."

There was disappointment among the Gorillas that the enemy incursion was not only a pair of females but also, probably, not even an incursion.

"Well, we have to do a full screen anyway," said Emmett.

The squad crawled backward down the hill and around the ridge to a crag-protected spot from which they could see the enemy approaching.

"They're kids," said Tom, "a couple of damn girls, just what we need."

"Should we send them back?" Emmett asked.

"Let's see what they want," said the boy. "Maybe they want to parlay."

"Surrender is more like it," said Vito.

"They wouldn't send little girls," said Tom, "for anything."

As the girls drew closer, both now shading their eyes, their faces gray and black from the ash-fall, the boys could clearly see they really were just kids. Like themselves. This was the first time any of them could remember that a couple of kids showed up in Valence without parents.

Tom felt an unwarlike sympathy for these new arrivals. What must they have been through to have arrived here without a vehicle or parents?

The Gorillas stood up, revealed themselves.

"Halt!"

The girls stopped, looking up through the blanket of falling cinder.

"Halt! Where do you think you're going?"

"We're lost."

"Well, you're in Valence now."

"Do you have water?"

Emmett said, "Why should we give you—"

Tom interrupted, "Yeah, here," and held out an aluminum canteen.

The girls each gulped greedily. "We were in a trailer area."

"You came from enemy territory," said Emmett. "We need to debrief you."

Ginny said, "You're not touching us." She held up her scarred arm. "I've fought a coyote."

The boys studied the scar, the tooth marks.

"You were attacked by a coyote?"

"By a bunch," Ginny said. "So don't think you can mess with me and my sister."

The boys were unsure; none of them had tangled with a coyote. Tom stepped back to confer with his fellow Gorillas and came to a decision. "We're going to take you back to see the grown-ups," he said. "Sargam will know what to do."

The boys led the way through the gently contoured earth, behind scrub lines and into the narrow ravines that only they knew, the girls scrambling and struggling to keep up. The Gorillas were as proud as if they had captured their first prisoners, and were about to deliver them to the authorities who would extract valuable intel on enemy troop movements.

As they passed from the outer undeveloped reaches of Valence to the irrigated fields of vegetables, the fruit tree orchards, and the chicken and goat coops, the girls were stunned at the lush wonderland they had wandered into. Even the ash-fall appeared to have abated, allowing them a clear view of what seemed an oasis in the middle of this desert. Men and women working in the fields paused at their pulling and planting, trying to figure who these girls belonged to. The dogs ran out barking from the houses, howling out toward the returning boys. As they drew closer to the ranch houses, they could see women working over tables, chopping vegetables. There were large pots on the boil, children playing soccer.

The boys brought the girls to a pretty woman in white who was removing a splinter from a dog's paw. The woman looked up at the girls and smiled and they smiled back.

"Where are your parents?" Sargam asked.

"Our dad took us and brought us here, well, not here, but over there." Ginny pointed in the direction they had come. "He said we were going to meet Pastor Roger."

"How did you end up here?"

"We got lost."

They had walked across the desert, through the ash, and come upon the boys hiding behind some rocks. They were thirsty, their throats sandpaper rough from inhaling ash, and their eyes stung.

Sargam collected bottles of water for the girls, and a plate of figs, and listened as they laid out a story as bizarre as any she had heard. Their father was some kind of financial criminal—she had heard his name before, she believed—and their mother had taken them to Santa Monica, and he had followed, and, at least to her ears, it sounded as if he had kidnapped them to take them to see Pastor Roger.

The story was complicated and several times Sargam stopped the girls and asked them to back up, but still, she was struggling to put together the whole picture.

"Where's your mom?" she asked.

"Oh, she's going to come get us."

There were already a half-dozen Valence folks waiting for her counsel. She would figure out what to do with the girls later. She saw Vanessa walking by, carrying a bucket of water.

"V, can you take these two, Ginny and Franny, back to your place for a few hours?" she asked. "Tell Bailey to look after them. They came wandering through the desert without any parents but we're expecting their mom to show up."

The girls followed Vanessa down the row of houses, past the kids playing soccer and across a field of onions that smelled faintly of wet dirt, to a house where Tom sat on the back step, shaping sticks into arrows.

"You brought 'em here?" the boy said. "Why?"

"Sargam told me to bring 'em."

Tom looked at the girls. "So I'm stuck with you? Do you play soccer?"

GEMMA DROVE OUTSIDE OF HENDERSON on the way to a place called Valence to get her children back from Arthur. While she empathized with how Anya may have felt about her kids being taken, she resisted drawing any direct parallels between their situations for the simple fact that Arthur *was* a criminal philanderer, while Richie, seated beside her, picking his nose, was, well, what was he exactly?

Not a failure, nothing that definitive could be said about him.

He still had talent, though it was unsteady and too often deployed wastefully, but there were flashes of poetry and insight. Oh, and she had to admit it, she was sweet on him, despite knowing that he was bad for her.

The Prius's air conditioner barely dried and cooled them, so hot was the sun blasting down on the two-lane. They ran up behind another dilapidated subprime vehicle every mile or so, as families were still trying to make it to Valence despite the fact that the entire community had been ordered to vacate. People helping people was a powerful message, and for thousands who had nothing left to lose, it was the promised land.

Her cell phone rang. She picked it up, taking the wheel with one hand.

"Do you have the girls?" Arthur asked.

"No, you dipshit," Gemma said. "You took them."

"Hm," Arthur said. "Are you sure you don't have them?"

"Yes, I'm sure," Gemma said. "Arthur, don't tell me you've lost—"

Arthur hung up.

Gemma turned to Richie. "He's lost them!"

Jinx immediately leaned forward. "He's lost Ginny and Franny?"

"Apparently," Gemma said and began breathing heavily.

"Let me drive," Richie said.

Gemma pulled over. They paused for a few moments, staring ahead at an old Explorer making its way down the secondary, trailing a puff of road dust and exhaust. They could see plastic bins tied down to the roof, a family's possessions mounted on the rack. Around them was the same desert they had been driving through for what seemed like forever. There was nothing but hot road cutting through dry country, a million square miles and not a drop to drink.

"We'll find them," Richie said.

"He really is an idiot. Who kidnaps children and then loses them?"

Richie smiled. At least he hadn't managed that particular fuckup.

He pulled back onto the secondary and picked up speed.

JINX WON'T SHUT UP ABOUT Ginny and Franny. Gone. Vanished. All because of an idiot father.

"We're gonna find them," I tell her and Gemma.

"It's an adventure!" says Ronin.

I am about to admonish him for putting too much of a positive spin on a potentially tragic situation. But I reconsider, because he's right. This is an adventure, or that's how I have to look at it. These may be the last few days of my life as a father. As soon as Anya secures custody, they could be gone forever, tucked away into sanctuary while I sink with the rest of California. How can I make enough memories to last them a lifetime in just a few days of a road trip? I suppose an adventure, a search for some missing girls, is a potentially richer trove of childhood memories than any trip to Disneyland. We must make do with what we have.

"You know," I say to Ronin and Jinx, "I want you two to know that this little trip, my taking you with us, is not going to save you forever. I mean your mother will find us and then, well, I have probably hurt my position more by this little operation here."

"We know," said Ronin.

"I'm sorry I'm not a better father," I say, turning to make eye contact with my kids.

"Watch the road!" Ronin shouts, and I turn back just in time to swerve us back into our lane.

"You ARE a good father," Ronin says. "You try to be."

"You listen to us," Jinx says. "Mom doesn't. She just tells us what to do."

"We need you," Ronin says.

I'm about to cry. I can't imagine these kids being taken away from me. I mash the gas harder. The Prius doesn't have any more to give.

Gemma's phone rings; it's a television reporter who got her phone number through Sargam from Franny.

"Thank you, thank you, thank you," Gemma says. "Tell them we'll be there very soon."

She puts down her phone. "The girls are fine, they're in Valence."

"Let's go get them!" shouts Jinx.

And off we go.

COMMUNE CAMP UNDER SIEGE; PROGRESSIVES VOW
TO STAND GROUND; CULT LEADER: "WE WILL DEFEND
OURSELVES."

The story was being shaped very much in the manner that Pastor Roger and the Pepper Sisters envisioned. A lunatic cult leader convinces a bunch of subprime savages to squat on private property, creating an unsavory, unwashed den of druggie, hippie squalor. This cannot be allowed to stand. State police were arriving, joining the private security forces already deployed by HG Extraction. Reality producers were swarming. Concerned pundits were admonishing. Nothing must stand between the Joshua and its juice. And now that the media narrative was shaping up as People of God versus Atheists, makers versus takers, job creators versus subprimes, the Pepper Sisters would be able to unleash their Valence-clearing operation and wipe away the squalid encampment. Pastor Roger felt it wasn't only that they were obstructing access to shale oil, it was more importantly the principal of the matter: if these subprimes were allowed to set up their own city, then subprimes every-where would feel empowered to undermine authority, and then what kind of society would we have? That would be an under-mining of the basic foundations of capitalism. The dark forces of progressivism never rested. Pastor Roger from the platform had drawn up charts, mapping the direct lineage from William Jennings Bryan to Theodore Roosevelt to Samuel Gompers to Eugene Debs to Leon Trotsky to Ernst Röhm to Adolf himself. History was very clear on where communalism ended. First, the reestablishment of the minimum wage, and then? The par-ticular object of Pastor Roger's sermonizing was Sargam, "the She-devil of progressivism," a leather-clad harlot who came from nowhere to advocate the rise of a new socialist Reich. He warned that we were surrounded by progressives, who con-trolled the media, entertainment, technology, even the military, the forces of progressivism were so powerful they were crush-ing the real America. The evidence: the TV cameras seemed to love showing this Madame Trotsky every chance they got. Even now, as he sat in a rocking chair in his tour bus, reading over the income statements from this week's tithe, he trembled at the thought of this media genic woman who seemed to be on TV even more than he was.

Steven Shopper leaned forward and urged calm. He observed in Pastor Roger an anxiousness he'd never seen before. The pastor was not as steady with his focus on the many, many mat-ters of Freedom Prairie Church, on the finances, the many bat-tles they were fighting on many fronts.

THEY DROVE THROUGH THE MEDIA encampment, Richie slowing down as they passed the Bloomberg satellite truck.

"I could be covering this," he said.

"Maybe you're too close to the story," Gemma suggested.

"Objectivity, or reporting in general, has never been my strength," Richie said.

He wove around the media vans, the Freedom Prairie trucks, the HG Extraction semis all in a row, left wheels up on the pavement. Dead ahead, state police were standing huddled in the afternoon light, the white flaking ash-fall accumulation atop truck cabs and trailer roofs appearing almost as a beautiful snowfall atop some kind of *Dr. Zhivago* village.

Richie slowed to a crawl as a security tech waved at them to halt. The tech approached in tandem with a tan-uniformed Nevada State Police officer. The tech was already making a downward-facing circle with his index finger to indicate that Richie should turn around.

He rolled down the window. "Hello there."

"Nowhere to go," the officer said. "Road's closed."

"We need to get to Valence," Richie said.

The officer shook his head. "No one's going to Valence. It's closed as far as we're concerned."

Gemma leaned forward. "My children are in there. I've come to get them out."

The officer read the concern on her face.

"One way or another, I'm going to get my girls," she said.

The officer looked at Jinx and Ronin in the back, and Richie said, "Those are my kids. I'm just the driver. But, here, my press ID—does that help?"

The officer studied it. "You can drive in, and then you better drive right out. You don't want to be in there too long."

He waved them through.

The visibility limited by the cinders, it was slow going across what seemed a no-man's-land until they saw a few bonfires and the bare outlines of a settlement in the last of the daylight.

DARREN AND THE REST OF the men watched the approaching vehicle, a sedan, the front end casting twin beams closer together than a security-tech SUV. No vehicles had come through in three days, the techs and the cops having shut down Valence in an attempt to restrict supplies and reinforcements coming in from the many well-wishers and supporters that their cause had picked up over the last few weeks. Now they were truly on their own, though a half-dozen reporters, deciding to stick it out with the subprimes, were still inside Valence.

The vehicle, a battered Prius, slowed at the sight of the men waving them down at the head of the off-ramp.

"Hey there," Darren said. "What can we do for you?"

"I'm looking for my girls," Gemma said.

Darren knew about the sisters who had shown up out of the desert. Against his advice, Sargam said they could stay, at least until their mother was contacted. And here she was.

"Okay," Darren said, "keep driving down this road. Stop in at the third house on the first street you come to. Sargam should be in there. But go slow. We got kids running around all over the place."

Richie put the car back into gear, but before he could press the gas, Darren asked, "Hey, what are they saying about us out there?"

Richie thought about it. "They're saying . . . well, the TV is saying how you're trespassing, violating private property, and how the state gave the Pepper Sisters this land."

Darren shook his head.

Richie continued. "But everywhere you go, you see people with signs that say 'People Helping People' or 'Sargam Forever' or 'Valence Rules.' People know what you're doing out here, they do."

Richie steered the car down the off-ramp and stopped at the third house, where four women were sitting on wood and brick benches before a bonfire, knitting in the flickering light. Sargam was framed in the doorway, the flames giving her an orange glow as she studied them.

"Howdy," Sargam said. "I didn't think they were letting anyone in—"

As soon as she saw Gemma and Richie get out of the car she knew they weren't subprimes; their vehicle wasn't packed with a lifetime's detritus the way most folks' were when they rolled in.

Gemma was upon Sargam so quickly that the women around the campfire rose as if to defend her.

"My girls," Gemma demanded. "Where are they?"

Sargam knew immediately who Gemma was referring to, as did the other women, who sat back down.

"They should be over on the next block, at the end of Las Lomas," she said and hugged Gemma. "Those are some tough girls. Survived a coyote attack?"

The tale of the little girls coming out of the desert, one of whom had survived a coyote attack, and had the scars to prove it, had spread through Valence. It was taken as a good omen that with the roads closed and the marshals and state police and security techs closing in, two little girls could just walk right in.

"Leave the vehicle at the end of the block," Sargam said. "It's a short walk, I'll take you."

The figure she cut, the confidence of her stride, the pleasing symmetry of her dark features, the shimmer of her wavy hair reflecting the firelight, rendered her more impressive in person than she seemed on television. As they all followed her down a path through front yards of radish and onion patches, and tomato vines on sticks rising overhead, Richie was surprised at the contradiction between this fertile land and the desert they had just traversed. It was as if someone had figured out how to take what was best about Burning Man, shed all the druggie crap and psychedelic costumes, and somehow make a go of it.

Or was it just his exhaustion—his two days of driving, his intoxication at being with Gemma, his excitement at Gemma getting her kids back?

They saw children playing in the street, riding bicycles and skateboards, the growling sound of bicycles tires on concrete audible before they could see clearly the lithe bodies darting in the half-light of dusk.

"Mommy! Mommy!" From out of the shadows came the two girls in torn dresses, both smiling and dirty-faced but somehow happier than Gemma had ever seen them. "You came!"

She hugged them to her, kissing each on their crowns, and then hugged them again. "You're both so brave," she said.

The girls were giggling, and now all three of them were teary. They held each other in silence.

"We made so many new friends," Ginny said when they released each other.

"Everyone here is nice," Franny said.

Gemma grabbed them again and hugged them, and turned to Sargam. "Thank you."

"Thank *her*. This is Bailey"—and she pointed to a woman with reddish hair.

"Well, then, thank you."

Gemma looked at Richie, suddenly unsure of what they should do. Were they really just going to get back in the car and drive off? And go where?

Ronin and Jinx had both drifted down the block, to where the rest of the kids had resumed playing a game involving skateboards and bicycles. While Richie could not quite figure out the rules, the sight of the bodies in motion, the aggressive pumping and pedaling and chasing and grabbing, the shriek when a child was caught, the wail of a little boy falling off a skateboard and scraping his knee, he found the savagery of the game reassuring. The contest appeared brutal and complicated but had a certain order to it, in the way bigger kids mainly chased down other bigger kids, while the younger kids were spared the worst of the violence. It dawned on Richie why this was so fascinating: he had not seen kids playing with this kind of abandon since, well, since he received a summons for endangering minors after a football game. This was the kind of play he remembered from his own childhood. There was no cell phone or game console in sight. This was good, clean violence.

He watched, amazed, as Ronin, encouraged by the other kids, jumped on a skateboard and navigated between the patrolling bikers to the opposite curb, where he jumped off. Ronin had divined, on his own, the rules, or at least well enough to jump into a game he had never played before with kids he just met. Richie knew that Ronin's doing this back home in Pacific Palisades was inconceivable; he would have been too shy, would have made an excuse about not knowing the rules. He would have been afraid of embarrassing himself.

Gemma observed Richie watching his son, and was about to ask what they should do now, when both her girls started jumping up and down, screaming, "Can we stay? Please, please, Mom, *please*. Can we stay?"

I AM MESMERIZED BY THE sight of my son, who became animated and alive and unaware of himself for maybe the first time in months. And after a few minutes, after Ginny and Franny return to the game, Jinx joins in, and I watch my children play in the dark night in a manner that is at once totally familiar and completely novel. I remember hurried football games and ditch games and capture-the-flag and round-the-block and jailbreak played after dinner on summer nights, the thrill of running in the dark, of hiding in the gloaming. It is novel because I have so rarely seen my children this free.

Gemma and Sargam are talking to each other, Gemma giving Sargam the long story about how we got here, and then they both turn and look at me, and Gemma shrugs to Sargam as if to say, What can I say?

I know before they come over to me that we are spending the night here.

We leave the kids playing their game and wander back with Sargam to the threshold where we first saw her. She leads us to the back of the house, where a communal kitchen is set up, large, scrubbed cylindrical pots are upside down to dry, a few hundred mismatched plates piled on a sturdy plank table, cups and glasses in stacked roller-cases with their tops ripped off. One pot simmers on a fire, and Sargam ladles us out a black bean stew, and as soon as I smell the food I realize how hungry I am.

Gemma and I both sit down on a log bench and spoon the stew into our mouths. The food is earthy and smoky, and while the first bite seems bland, the flavors grow on me, some kind of meat, seasoned with cilantro, onions, chipotle, garlic, and salt, so that after a few mouthfuls, I can't imagine anything I would rather be eating. We wash it down with cups of water.

"What's the meat?" I ask Sargam.

"Rabbit, goat, maybe snake," she says. "Definitely some lobster. Cans of the stuff have been donated—by the pallet."

"Of course," I say. "It's delicious."

"I take it you two are bedding down together?" Sargam says.

Gemma and I both shrug and nod.

Sargam says that we can sleep in one of the houses on the western edge of Valence, on a street called Temecula. It's one of the last uninhabited houses. There are spare sleeping bags and bedding, if that's what we need.

We thank her.

"How long can you hold out?" I ask.

"Forever."

"But how?"

"People helping people," she says.

She can see that I'm skeptical. "This isn't some kind of Masada here," she says. "We're not martyrs. We're families."

"But, Pastor Roger, HG Extraction, they are an army."

She looks at me. "I feel like I'm talking to a reporter."

"You are," says Gemma.

"Sort of," I insist.

"He's a really bad reporter," Gemma says. "Terrible. Lazy. Can't get anything right. Always getting sued. Getting sued, in fact, by Pastor Roger."

Sargam is clearly amused. "Then you can't be all bad."

"Oh, he's not," laughs Gemma. "I'm sweet on him."

She winks at me.

I've never felt so happy.

"I want to write this story, your story," I blurt out. I suppose I have been thinking this the whole time, the whole drive out here, but this is the first time I've put it into words. Suddenly, an old passion and excitement has reawakened and I feel a sense of mission about my work that I haven't had in decades. (Or maybe ever.) I want to tell a great story, a true story, an important story—a story that's messy and beautiful and subversive and uplifting. I now know why I've come.

"I'm not a TV reporter," I say. "I don't have cameras. I'm not even sure I have a place to publish. I just want to stay here and write about you, and about being here."

"Will you write the truth?" Sargam asks.

"I don't know. I'm not sure I know what truth is. I'll write what I see and feel."

She smiles. "That's good enough for me."

After dinner I call Rajiv, plugging my cell phone into the car charger. He's on the heli-shuttle home, and I can barely hear him over the whirring of the rotors.

"I'm in Valence," I say.

"We have two drones overhead and a whole trailer full of terminal guys covering that."

"But I'm *inside*. They're all in their air-conditioned trailer back in Placer. I'm, I just had dinner with Sargam. She'll let me live here among them, tell their story. Access, Rajiv."

Rajiv thinks this over. "It *is* unlikely Sargam would sue you, considering the circumstances."

"Come on!"

"If only we could remove you and replace you with someone more competent," Rajiv says.

"A more competent person would never have ended up in this situation."

"How *did* you end up there?"

"I'm on the run," I say.

"From what?"

I'm not exactly sure. "Everything?"

I realize the true value of what I am offering Rajiv and his magazine. "You should be fucking thanking me for calling you first, you ingrate."

"We do still pay you many thousands of dollars a month."

Oh, yeah. "Fair point."

"And until this phone call, well, I don't need to remind you of exactly why we were doing that."

"Because of the lawsuits," I say. "But now I can make it all up to you."

"We'll see," Rajiv says. "Let me run it by Richard. But, yes, proceed."

AFTER PLAYING THEIR GAME—HELICOPTER, THE kids called it—and then eating their bowls of stew, Ronin headed off with the boys, and Jinx and Ginny and Franny went with Gemma to the house assigned them by Sargam. It was a wreck, of course, but Gemma spread out the sleeping bags in a rear bedroom, rolled up a T-shirt for each to use as a pillow, and the three, exhausted from days of driving and their running and playing, fell asleep as soon as they were horizontal. Gemma walked outside, the faint stirring of a breeze a whisper of relief after the steady all-day heat.

Ronin was crawling along on his belly, following Tom and Juan and Vlad and the rest of the Gorillas on a mission to survey the community's western flank. They paused at the woman standing in the moonlight, the newcomer, and Ronin admired her too as if he hadn't just spent two days in a cramped car with her.

None of the boys said it, for that's not what boys that age talk about, but each thought it: She's pretty. Quickly, however, they returned to the work at hand, to slither into that cornfield and beyond to scout enemy positions.

Tom once read that superior knowledge of the disposition, strength, and location of a formal enemy's organized columns was one of the advantages insurgent forces held in an asymmetrical conflict. The Gorillas already possessed superior geographical knowledge, knowing every culvert and ditch and obscured sightline in the two square miles of Valence and throughout the surrounding desert. They had observed the enemy for days, and as they crawled out to undertake even more recon, a few of the boys were voicing complaints about the rigors of the mission.

"My stomach hurts from so much crawling," said Juan.

Ronin thought the same thing, but found the mission itself exciting. It reminded him of a *Call of Duty* scenario, only without the cool weapons.

"Then turn around and go home," said Tom. "We are going to figure out where they are going to come from, and then how to attack them where they are most vulnerable."

Ronin liked the sound of that. He had already been sworn to secrecy by the rest of the Gorillas, and now he knew why.

The boys crawled through the corn, down a gully, and into a flat-bottomed cement drain with slanted edges. They ran along it for a few hundred feet, until they reached the edge of a field from which they could see the lights of the enemy vehicles, the massing of SUVs parked there in the dark.

"When do you think they'll come?" Ronin asked.

"Soon," the boy said. "Very soon."

I PICK UP MY COMPUTER and dig through my duffel bag for a pack of Cough. I slip out a marijuana cigarette and light it, and immediately I feel a hand on my shoulder.

"Hey!" says the same man who stopped our vehicle on the way in. "That's against the rules."

"Rules?" I say.

"No dope smoking," says the man.

"What are we, in sixth grade?" I say.

"That's Sargam's policy, and everyone supports it. We had to keep out the tweakers, otherwise this would be a haven for meth smokers."

I nod. "Makes sense." I drop the joint.

He introduces himself, saying, "My name is Darren. I live with Sargam."

"She's something."

"She's the fucking messiah," he says, nodding sternly. Then he smiles. "I had you going there, didn't I?"

I shrug.

We are walking through the tomato vines again, and I ask Darren if they can really hold out indefinitely, as Sargam claims.

"Well, we do have one advantage," Darren says.

"What's that?"

"We got nowhere else to go."

I feel sorry for him for a few seconds before I realize that the same could be said of me.

ARTHUR MACK WAS CONTRITE AS he told Steve Shopper the truth. He had lost the girls. They had vanished.

"They couldn't have gone far. There's nothing from this trailer camp the whole twenty miles back to Placer," Shopper said.

"Well, they're not here," Arthur said. "I've walked every foot of this place looking, been asking everyone, the security guards, reporters, everyone. They were last seen wandering across no-man's-land in the direction of that subprime village," said Arthur.

Shopper immediately sensed the opportunity there and asked if Arthur was sure.

"That's what some of the security guys said, but there was that heavy ash storm yesterday, so nobody is sure what they were seeing."

Shopper immediately went to Pastor Roger and told him that Mack's missing daughters were believed to be in Valence. That would make Sargam a kidnapper, practically a defiler of children—good news that gladdened the pastor's heart.

In the past few days, dozens of Valences had been springing up in and around cities across America, as subprimes claimed stretches of foreclosed homes for themselves, and defied the orders of police and federal marshals to vacate. Banding together, they were squatting in these abandoned houses, professing to live by the simple credo of people helping people, and hanging up signs that said: "We Are Valence." They were receiving support from misguided liberals and the progressive media, who could not get enough of this story of nascent communalism. The real story, Pastor Roger lamented, of anarcho-syndicalists seeking to over-throw the government by denying the God-given right of private property, was too often ignored by breathless reporters excited at the simple narrative of subprimes fighting back.

With every appearance on CNN or FOX or KIK-TV, Pastor Roger reminded viewers that this insurgency was proof of the rising wave of progressivism that threatened to swamp our democracy. "Let's talk about the rapes, the sexual abuse, the pedophilia, the public masturbation, the drug dealing, let's remember the unsanitary conditions in which children are living, let's remember what these progressive hellholes really look like and what we are tolerating in letting these subprime, anarchist criminal dens continue to exist."

Then he added during that evening's appearances on KIK, "We also know that here, in the heart of the beast, where the Typhoid Mary of this progressive disease is festering, they have taken two little girls hostage, and who knows what may be hap-pening to those poor little angels right now."

Photos of Ginny and Franny appeared on the screen.

"They were last seen playing in a field near Valence, and we now believe they were abducted by the forces of progressivism. So I shudder, and I have been praying for these two poor little angels, but what could be happening to them in that cesspool of depravity right now? My mind boggles. We have to get in there. Now."

RAJIV CALLS ME AT SIX a.m., local time. I've managed several hours' sleep on the hard floor, curled up with Gemma for a few blissful minutes before we rolled apart because of the heat and discomfort. The girls and Ronin all seem to be catching up on their sleep.

I pick up the phone, which is vibrating next to me on the shag-carpeted floor.

"You know anything about these girls?" he asks.

"What girls?"

"The two missing girls, Virginia and Frances Mack, they're the daughters of Mack's wife. You profiled her."

"They're not missing, they're in the next room, asleep."

Rajiv tells me that overnight, the story of Virginia and Frances has turned into the biggest story in the country, crowding everything else out of the news cycle, with Republican congressmen taking to the floor to demand an immediate drone strike on Valence and Pastor Roger shedding tears on every morning show as he speculated in detail as to what might be happening to those lost lambs.

The missing girls had given the story a human element that dirty-faced subprime children couldn't possibly convey. For Virginia and Frances to have fallen into Sargam's clutches confirmed the deep fears of every law-abiding, God-fearing, bill-paying, 700-plus credit holder.

And I had missed the story, blown it.

"Even a journalist of your incompetence should have a story to file on this. You know the mother."

I tell him that their mom is right here. I don't say I'm sort of in bed with her. But I say that we drove out here specifically because the girls had been abducted by Arthur, her criminal future ex-husband, but now they are safely reunited with their mom.

"Can you get an interview with the mom or with the girls or both?"

I tell him that shouldn't be a problem.

"You realize this is a huge story, a scoop. And you, of all people . . ."

It takes me about an hour to write the single biggest news story of my life, which really isn't saying much. I send it out after tethering my computer to my phone, but I also know that I will soon be out of juice and unable to file anything further. There are a few other reporters still in Valence, independent correspondents who have elected to stay in the community despite the obvious risks of being the target of an army of police and security officers. One of them has figured out who Ginny and Franny and Gemma are, and has sent a kik-tok, but he didn't have an interview or the confirmation—or the photo—that I would send of the three of them, standing arm in arm before the battered house where we were taking shelter.

I also add to the story, in the last few graphs, news that was surprising to everyone, including myself: Gemma intended to stay here with the girls. In fact, she felt safer here than in the rest of the country, where coyotes and ex-husbands were prowling around in the night hours.

"I like it here," she says. "It's sort of like camping."

WHAT THE HELL ARE WE doing here? In this oppressive heat, spending an afternoon bending over a berry patch and plucking runty strawberries that taste sweeter than any hypertrophied hothouse berries I've ever tasted. Sargam told me that I would have to pitch in, do some actual work, a notion that had remained abstract to me until this morning, when I bent over in the furrowed ground and lifted up a stem to pluck, jumping back in terror at the size of the spider that came scampering out of the tangled shadow. It is the sight of me, so slow and unsteady at this backwork, that convinces those skeptical of my presence that I am not a spy or somehow in cahoots with the Pepper Sisters.

It is so hot, and despite my hat and my sunscreen I can feel that I must be burning. I realize I have spent my whole life avoiding this kind of physical labor, the bending, the reaching, the yanking, and for good reason. It is awful. But I understand that it is the price I must pay to stay here. If I had a skill, then perhaps I could work on engineering, or irrigation, or fertilization, projects that have allowed Valence to survive. But I am only a pair of not-very-skilled hands, so I have nothing to offer but my ability to pick berries, or whatever else needs picking.

Thankfully, the short workday ends just a few hours before the afternoon sun makes this kind of work truly impossible. We rise early, at dawn, work till eleven, and then retreat into shade for a few hours of reading. That is when I can talk to the many citizens of Valence about their lives.

They are, though they did not know it until they turned up here, the logical end products of our unregulated free-enterprise system. The privatization of every government service, from education to food stamps to Temporary Assistance for Needy Families to Medicaid, results in a safety net consisting of a few days of vouchers that buys a family maybe a week before they become destitute and hungry. And remember public libraries? The post office? The National Park Service? Lifeguards? The FDA? So much for the quaint notion that the private sector and charitable organizations would step in when the public sector withdrew. The subprimes residing in Valence turn out to be just a few hundred of the millions driving our rutted and potholed highway system looking for work, and even when they find it, it's not enough to pay for food for a whole family for a day. Abolishing the minimum wage with the National Right to Work Act took care of that.

As a cynic and malcontent, my one consistent attribute is my inability to get along in most systems, or with most people. And so as I wander Valence, from Las Lomas to Bienvenida, observing, conversing, interviewing, and also trying to find my son, who, in the glimpses I have of him seems to have grown six inches in stature and self-esteem as he roves this postapocalyptic suburbia turned Walden Two with a gang of boys, I am looking for the flaws, of course, and there are plenty: inadequate medical care, unhygienic sanitation, hours of drudgery, slavish, unquestioning devotion to Sargam. I am wary of falling into a Walter Duranty–like fawning over the socialist miracle unfolding here. This is no miracle, certainly, and it is only the hard-hearted cruelty of the rest of the world that makes this simple community of impoverished farmers seem like any kind of oasis. Having a roof, some walls, enough to eat, and a place for your kids to play is heaven when you've been sleeping under highway overpasses and goaded daily by the end of a security tech's cattle prod.

So what it comes down to, for me, as I wander and process what I am seeing and hearing, is this: Is Sargam for real? Is she a genuine leader who has started a true populist movement that has a chance to survive whatever brutality the Pepper Sisters can

unleash in the name of upholding their legal rights as the benefi-
ciaries of a questionable enactment of eminent domain?

I mean, is Sargam even real? Or is she the inverse of Pastor
Roger? Beautiful, spiritual, egalitarian, radical, redistribution-
ist, she is like the monstrous, collective dream-leader of secular
liberals everywhere. How could someone like this just show up?
She has no past, she comes from nowhere—and becomes in just
a few months a national figure so compelling that the most powerful capitalist forces on Earth are aligning to destroy her? The
last time a political figure appeared seemingly out of nowhere
to mesmerize the population, he ended up steering nothing
more than a slightly less aggressively capitalist course, so that
even while he was still in office there were populist uprisings—
various Occupy movements—on behalf of a cohort similar to
the subprimes. Was Sargam different? Was she the real thing, a
true outsider who believed in nothing more than People Helping
People?

"This is in some ways like a cult," I tell Gemma.

"It is a cult, in that you have to believe, but she makes it easy,"
Gemma says. "She's not asking for anything from anyone. She's
just trying to help folks get along."

"Did you know what life was really like—before?" I ask.

Gemma shakes her head. "I thought about it, but in the same
way you watch people on TV who are starving, or read some
awful account of children who are locked up in basements. You
know it's awful, and you feel bad, but it seems like something far
away. Maybe it's me, maybe it's a flaw in me, but I was somehow
able to live in relative calm even knowing things like that were
going on."

I think I have that same capacity. That's how I lived all these
years, wrote so many stories that were essentially apologias for
a system that fed on human dignity, and never wondered at the

morality or decency of it. I am selfish. I think I always knew that, but only now do I understand that our only way out is if each of us becomes an unselfish version of ourselves. It is going to be a few billion individual decisions, repeated and reaffirmed every day, that will change us, change the planet. Not some great decision by a great leader, or a great law passed by a great Congress, none of which exist.

And I know that sanctuary, if I didn't already suspect this, is just another word for surrender.

"Sargam is a solution," I tell Gemma. "She may not be the best solution, but she is the only one I can see. People helping people is the first step toward wherever we have to go. To freedom."

"Meanwhile," Gemma said, "does freedom have to be so filthy? I'm going to dump a few buckets of cold water on my kids."

"Could you dump one on mine as well?"

HOW CAN THOSE PAGAN SUBPRIMES stand it out here, in this heat, this dust, this ash, this smoke, this hell? Pastor Roger wondered. If we can't extract God's juice here, from this godforsaken patch, then from where could we squeeze the fruit of his loins? We have to grope, to grope down into the earth, to lay man's hands upon the unspeakable, unseeable foundations, the heart, the guts, the snaking intestines of the world. And once immersed, we have to squeeze, squeeze, squeeze!

As soon as the governor gives the order, then we will squeeze them out.

Pastor Roger gave his daily radio prayer and podcast, distributed to millions of devout Freedom Prairie disciples. As always, he thanked the Pepper Sisters, and reminded listeners

of the many hundreds of millions of dollars they were spending
to further the cause of Christianity and Prosperity, not just by
endowing Bob Jones University, not just by creating the largest
and most successful for-profit Christian university system in the
world with Pepper College, but also by endowing the Pepper
Center for Geological Studies at Harvard and the Pepper Petroleum Institute at Stanford. Secular humanism, Pastor Roger
reminded his followers, was another word for progressivism.
Liberal arts was socialism. Art was a hobby for women. Young
Christian men and women should learn applicable skills to avoid
idleness.

He called his wife every morning and evening. Clarissa, a
chunky blonde with a vibrant, rich mane of yellow hair, could
take the platform herself when Pastor Roger was away on mission. She could tend the flock at Freedom Prairie, deliver a stem-
winder of a sermon, cry a Jordan River of tears, and extract a
tithe nearly on par with the pastor himself. Still, she wondered
how long he would have to stay in this desert camp outside Placer.

"When God wills it we will unleash the Joshua!" he told her.
"His kingdom will come."

He blessed her and told her he had business to attend to.

Steven Shopper had brought Arthur Mack to meet with him
on his tour bus, and he studied the energy trader carefully.

Arthur was smiling broadly, leaning forward on the tuck-and-
roll banquette as if awaiting good news.

"Your daughters are with their mother," said Pastor Roger.
"And she, she is in the thrall of a false idol."

"A wrinkle in the plan?"

"More than a wrinkle," Pastor Roger said. "It is a stain, a
dark stain on a pristine white sheet."

Pastor Roger and Steven Shopper had already concluded
that Arthur Mack, despite his unjust persecution and heroic

martyrdom on the wheel of the global progressive movement, did not have the commensurate personal virtue. Why, he was contributing numbers—his own offspring!—to the enemy rather than rallying Christians to the cause.

"It is not our mission to nurture the unclean," Steven Shopper said in a soft voice.

"I can still be of use," Arthur said, panic entering his voice. "I can help you trade the juice, I can hedge the juice."

But Arthur Mack was the vestige of an old news cycle, superseded by the whales and now by Sargam and Valence. He was no longer a useful example of the progressive agenda victimizing a legitimate businessman. He was just another deadbeat dad.

"Mr. Shopper will show you out," Pastor Roger said, turning his back.

And thus Arthur was cast out of the tour bus to wander in the desert, where he offered himself to every media outlet he encountered. The name Arthur Mack was familiar to reporters and producers, but it carried with it no particular titillation, not enough certainly to encourage anyone to offer a helicopter flight or even a car ride in exchange for an interview.

THE JOSHUA LUMBERED FORWARD, A fortress of steel and concrete and polymer and rubber, a beautiful monstrosity and a tribute to God's ingenuity. It shook the ground for a radius of a half mile, the wobble beneath its feet like thunder captured, bottled underground, and then released to roar back up to the sky. The powerful turbines emitted their own heat that made turning toward the sun seem almost a relief. From where the Pepper Sisters sat, in an air-conditioned black SUV, bottles of iced tea in hand, the Joshua resembled the I-beam-and-girder skeleton of a skyscraper in progress. Though they owned it, every bolt and button and knob, from afar the Joshua seemed a force beyond man's control, beyond even God's will. It was like a giant robot. If you gave it arms that swayed at its sides, it would be like a gigantic metal zombie astride the country. Its slow progress made it even more mesmerizing—it moved no faster than a man walking at a brisk pace, and for an object so gigantic, that progress seemed both pitifully meager and utterly unstoppable.

Dottie Pepper sipped from her iced tea. "My my, Dorrie, it's quite a contraption."

"Indeed," Dorrie said. "But, darling, is it a hybrid? What about the emissions?"

Both women started laughing and told the driver to take them back to Pastor Roger's camp.

Pastor Roger welcomed the Peppers, apologized for the state of his immaculate tour bus, and took knees with them as soon as they entered to pray for the well-being of the Joshua and the slaying of progressivism.

"We don't like how this is playing," said Dorrie Pepper.

"That woman Sargam is on every channel," said Dottie.

Pastor Roger urged calm. "She will be forgotten, as every story is. This will become yesterday's story as soon as we evict them from what is rightfully—and legally—yours."

"Yes, but these squatting camps, these Valences everywhere," Dorrie said.

"Terrorists, Muslims, hippies—they are a law-enforcement issue," said Pastor Roger. "Remember Occupy? Of course not. Because it's been forgotten."

"But this woman, she is something different," Dottie said.

"She's a leader," Dorrie said. "Trouble."

"I'm on the phone with the governor every few hours," Pastor Roger said. "He is very sympathetic. He wants nothing more than to restore law and order. As soon as we get the call, we can take possession of your property."

"We can't have children injured," said Dottie. "And the operation has to be done in the dark, like with Occupy; they can't film at night."

"Why, Dottie, I've never known you to take such an active hand in logistics," Pastor Roger said. "We don't want violence, we don't want any injury, we—you—simply want what is your God-given right. The law, God's law, is on our side. This is a holy fight."

"Let's offer them safe passage," Dottie said. "Let's promise them forty acres and a mule if they just load up their Jed Clampett mobiles and ride off."

"That would be succumbing to blackmail," Pastor Roger said in medium-high dudgeon. "That would send the message to every subprime that they should squat and wait for their handout. Why not just bring back the entitlement state? Give them all free health care?"

Dorrie shook her head. "Now, Pastor, don't get all apocalyptic on us. We're just trying to be discreet."

THE SIGHT OF THE JOSHUA lumbering across the desert at first appeared to Jeb and Darren as a dark silhouette against the sky, an Entlike apparition, only here representing the deviltry of man rather than Tolkien's wisdom of nature. Though they knew from extensive media coverage its provenance, the sight was still shocking. Soon, the whole community was gathered at the top of the off-ramp, their eyes focused on the horizon line.

Sargam wondered: Would they just roll that monster into Valence, crush anything and anyone in its way, and then start drilling? Was the battle to end that simply? Men and women with

linked arms crushed beneath its treads? But surely even the klep-
tocratic aristocracy would object to crushing women and children.

She was awed at the courage of the many who had stayed
with her. Only five or six families had chosen to flee. At meetings
every night, Sargam talked about what was at stake.

"This path, this fight, will be harder than anything we have
done, than you have done, and I know you have been through so
much. Every night spent dirty and hungry in some Ryanville has
felt like the absolute limit, beyond what you could take, of what
you could see your children going through. What we are asking
now is even more suffering than that, but at least I can say we
are fighting for a cause. We are sacrificing our comforts, our rest,
even, perhaps, our health and our lives, so that we can somehow
lessen the suffering of so many. That is what we are doing. We
are helping. People helping people."

She studied her fellow citizens: now strong, fed, rested, not
fatigued from months on the road and weary nights in Ryanvilles. They were now proud men and women whose spirits had
soared, their body language revealing them to be unafraid of
what lay ahead.

Privately, when talking with Sargam, Darren voiced occasional doubts about the wisdom of her leadership. Perhaps they
should just surrender, drive away while they still could.

"We have nowhere to go," Sargam said. "We get run off from
each place we set down. If we are going to stand and fight anywhere, it might as well be here, together, for a place we love."

Still, she worried at the wisdom of this decision, even if in
front of the TV cameras or when talking to reporters she never
wavered. She had briefed the citizens on nonviolent resistance,
passed out the plastic cuffs they would fasten around their
arms and each other. She told them what to do when they were
arrested. There were several dozen state's attorneys waiting

in Placer to help process the arrested, no matter their credit scores. Many of the fathers and mothers, she knew, could end up in Credit Rehabilitation Centers, yet they were willing to risk debtors' prison for their cause. Her desire was to live up to their courage.

And at the approach of the Joshua, she could still feel the strongest murmurings of doubt and unease. She turned back toward her people, raised her arms, and said, "There is still time to leave, if that is what you want, but I ask you this: If you leave now, if you run now, when will you stop running?"

I'VE NEVER SEEN MY CHILDREN so engaged—so much like kids. Ronin is gone from first light, playing in the hills with his new friends. When I ask what they have been doing, he tells me they play different games all day, ditch, capture the flag, some soccer, and something they are calling Gorilla. He has never been this long without a game console or cell phone or tablet in his hands. He is rough, scratched, and dirty, his cheeks smudged and elbows scabbed, a feral quality to him that so pleases me.

I know this must end, that this wacky little holiday in the dirt that we've been on will conclude, but I would argue—if I weren't afraid to speak to my ex-wife—that this is ultimately good for Ronin.

And for Jinx too. She is rethinking her opinion of Pastor Roger as she makes friends with people whom Pastor Roger is vowing to drive off or arrest. She insists she is still Christian, but that there are many ways to worship, and she is still figuring out her own. "At Captain's Club it was much simpler," she tells me as she puts on her shoes one morning. "At Captain's Club, if you wanted to go to heaven, if you wanted your family to go to heaven, then you followed Pastor Roger's instructions. But I don't see why just being a good person isn't enough. And if Pastor Roger is so good, why is he so against Sargam, who really is good?"

The evening after the appearance on the horizon of the Joshua, I ask Sargam about her past. She talks about the many foster homes, the abusive foster parents, fleeing when she was a teenager, surviving on the road as a young woman, wandering from Ryanville to Ryanville. It is the same story that has been reported by the media, who harp on the fact that there is no record of Sargam anywhere. She has never revealed her given name. And, most suspicious of all, she has no credit score.

"I'm flawed. By Pastor Roger's standards I'm a harlot. I did what I had to do to survive," she tells me.

"Then what gives you the moral authority to lead all these people?"

"We are doing what is right. That's the easy part. But why me, you ask? Maybe it's because I have nowhere else to go. I come from subprime, I am subprime. I'm not someone who grew up poor, escaped her origins, went to college, joined the elite. I am still subprime. That's what gives me the authority.

"We got played by Washington, by Wall Street, by big oil and the Pepper Sisters. For too long—forever it feels like—we've only magnified our powerlessness by running away. Through bubble after bubble, through the planet heating, burning, flooding, becoming more toxic, for years we've lived with that. Now we have to say 'Enough! It starts here.'"

"But do you advocate the overthrow of the United States of America?" I ask.

She laughs. "As if that were possible. No, we want nothing more than to be able to stay here, in our community, a community that was abandoned and that we remade as a home. Our issues are entirely local."

"And all those other Valences, the thousands, soon maybe millions of people, who are squatting, refusing to move on, trying to build communities. Do you speak for them?"

"My only wish for them," Sargam says, "is that they don't happen to be squatting above a shale oil deposit."

But here is what I notice again: Sargam does emit a certain energy. I guess I would call it a glow, a soothing glow. She's a beautiful woman, initially sexually attractive, though she quickly transcends that and makes you forget it. But there it remains, thrumming in the background, an insistent, steady appeal that keeps you watching and listening. I've never seen a politician quite like her.

I've been around cult leaders and swamis and self-help telemarketers and even Pastor Roger, and I know that Sargam is different from any huckster I've ever encountered.

Jesus Christ, listen to me. Am I losing my cynicism, my natural suspicion of everything and everyone? I don't think so, but what I am witnessing, in Sargam's leadership, in her gentle appeal, her calm approach, her steady character, is as shocking to me as it is unlikely. For the first time in my life I may have found someone I believe in.

TOM AND RONIN STAKED OUT the highest ground they could find, the tufted mounds to the eastern fringes of Valence from which they took turns watching the Joshua as it crawled into position. Both boys were speechless at the sight of the monstrous machine, and frightened by what they were beholding, yet neither would admit his anxiety to the other.

Both boys knew they had no more chance of changing the course of this colossal contraption than they would of changing the weather. But Tom had an idea.

"Inside the machine is a man," he said, "a man who breathes air and bleeds blood, just like us."

Ronin liked the sound of this speech, which Tom was patching together from pep talks delivered in old movies.

"He feels pain, just as we do. He feels fear, just as we do."

"He has to take a crap sometimes," Ronin said, giggling, "just like we do!"

Both boys started laughing, and they crawled back down the mound toward the houses at the edge of Valence. Their fathers, who had already vowed nonviolent resistance, planned to lay down on the off-ramp into Valence before the tracks of the enemy. The boys found such passive resistance unacceptable to their testosterone-driven sensibilities. These were young men, just noticing their first sprigs of pubic hair, their first ejaculations, their first distorted sense of how to be a man.

I SWEEP THE FLOOR OF the ranch house, the broom's soft yellow whisks pushing dust out the open cavity where a sliding window was supposed to hang, so that the motes puff out and up into a brown curl. Gemma is preparing for her daily run, pulling on yellowed sneakers, wrapping a bandana over her sunburned forehead. She is beautiful, my Gemma, and I wonder: If she weren't here, would I still be bivouacked in this utopian work camp? I can't answer that, of course, but I do know that Valence is a wonderful place to be in love. We are surrounded by good, sweet people, all of whom are engaged in a great struggle, so every action feels meaningful. Our love, set against the backdrop of a town under siege, the high drama of it all would bring out the romantic in the most cynical.

These are, I believe, the happiest days of my life, the mornings spent toiling in the fields, the afternoons spent writing about Sargam and Valence, the evenings with Gemma, with Franny

and Ginny and Ronin and Jinx; we are like a postapocalyptic
Brady Bunch, filthy instead of squeaky clean, our ranch house
missing doors, fixtures, and windows, adrift in an abandoned
exurbia, but we are happy.

"We're like a family," Jinx says as she attempts to untangle her hair
before the cracked mirror we've set up on the kitchen counter. She
says this absentmindedly, not considering the weight of the statement.

But Gemma and I are both feeling the same thing, great joy
and hope in this moment.

We *are* a family.

THE RUMBLE WAKES US BEFORE dawn. I climb out of my sleeping bag, straighten myself, and check the bedroom only to find
Ronin already gone. The girls are all up and rubbing their eyes.

"Is it an earthquake?" Franny asks.

I shepherd the three of them into the living room. They huddle
next to Gemma as I pull on my shoes and pants.

"Take them to Sargam's house," I tell her. The fallow fields
behind it have been designated as the meeting place, relatively
sheltered behind two rows of ranch houses. "I'll be up at the off-
ramp."

"Is this it?" Gemma asks, gathering the girls' clothes and
shoes.

"I don't know. I need to find Ronin."

I slip on a hooded sweatshirt, leaving Gemma the big flashlight, and set off down Temecula toward the off-ramp. Other
men and women are marching along the street, their beams
of light bouncing over the pavement. The ground still shakes,
the grumbling growing nearer, and in the distance, toward the
eastern horizon, there is a halogen-white light like an artificial
dawn, so bright it emits a kind of heat, toward which we walk. A

woman begins singing, softly at first, as if she is singing to herself. I can't hear the words or tune clearly, but then she is joined by a few other voices, first the women and then the men, and then dozens of us, tentatively joining and then raising our voices.

As I went walking I saw a sign there
And on the sign it said "No Trespassing."
But on the other side it didn't say nothing,
That side was made for you and me.

In the shadow of the steeple I saw my people,
By the relief office I seen my people
As they stood there hungry, I stood there asking
Is this land made for you and me?

Nobody living can ever stop me,
As I go walking that freedom highway;
Nobody living can ever make me turn back
This land was made for you and me.

Our voices strengthen when we are joined by more fellow citizens, from each of Valence's streets and cul-de-sacs, the chorus rising and the cheers mounting so that we don't hear the grumble or the growl of the machines or the vehicles, just the song. And now there are reporters with video cameras trained on us, and news drones scanning us from above, and we link arms, brother and brother and sister and sister, a human chain a dozen wide across the road, marching toward the off-ramp, where we see Sargam standing in white, backlit by the headlights of oncoming security vehicles. The governor, apparently, has acquiesced to Pastor Roger and the Pepper Sisters and ordered the forcible removal of all who oppose the measure to vacate. The security techs and police are coming, their vehicles stretched out for two miles along the expressway. And behind them, clamorously rolling toward Valence, the beastly Joshua.

We are told to take our places on the off-ramp, arms linked, to block the security techs who will attempt to remove us. The plastic cuffs come out, the men and women fasten themselves to one another, and at the end of each row to the guardrails. We are a human wall, seated on the concrete, heads bowed, a phalanx of scruffy, dirty humanity. Still uncuffed, I break off from the human chain, believing somehow that I am supposed to be covering this, despite not having had a charged cell phone or computer for weeks. My communications with my editor, even my pretense that I am here doing a job, has given way. I am reduced to scribbling notes in longhand: my impressions of what I am seeing here, my hurried notations of Sargam's utterances and sayings, my recollections of my feelings and anxieties about what we are doing here.

Sargam takes her place before her fellow citizens and we wait.

THE NOTICE OF ORDER TO vacate is read out by a Kevlar-helmeted officer in a black uniform and black leather boots. He reads the statement, issued by the governor of Nevada by the powers vested in him, in a disinterested monotone, head bowed in the dozens of lights trained on him. He appears almost sympathetic in the stark light, facing this crowd of seated, chained men and women. But just beyond the luminescent cones stand a few hundred armed, helmeted, riot-geared, baton-wielding techs and cops, awaiting orders to go in and bust heads.

"Will you accede to this request to vacate?" the officer, still reading, asks.

Sargam stands. "We believe that we have established the right to this land, as we made it our home when no one else wanted it. We grew our food here. We built schools here. Free schools. Without vouchers. We are families, men and women and children—you call us subprimes—and we want nothing more than to be left in peace. We do not want to fight—we only ask of the government to be treated as all people should be treated. If this cannot be our home, then let us have a home. Let us be free people, free to travel, free to stop, free to work—"

The officer interrupts her. "So you refuse to vacate?"

"We refuse to be treated as subprimes," Sargam says. "We are free people. If the government—if the governor—truly serves the people, then he will serve ALL the people, no matter their credit scores. We are all Americans, and we will not be judged on the basis of past credit history."

"Occupants refuse to vacate," the officer drones, then walks back to his colleagues and confers with another officer, the two of them gesturing toward the praetorians amassed on the shoulders of the expressway.

The citizens of Valence are seated, arm in arm, ten deep along the off-ramp and in clusters stretching down Bienvenida and into Valence. Men and women are also gathered at key points around the fringes of the community, near the farms, the water pump, the fields, where the children are also gathered.

The officer orders the uniformed columns forward, in a measure intended to intimidate the citizens. The citizens sit and begin singing again.

I stand to the side, resisting the temptation to join Sargam and take up position with the citizens. I need to find my son.

RONIN AND TOM SLIPPED OUT of town, following the culverts they knew so well, and then crawled over the more exposed patch

of desert between Valence and the enemy lines. The cops and techs
were on the move, clogging the highway into Valence, fortifying
themselves on doughnuts and breakfast burritos and coffee for
the invasion ahead. The boys lost count at eighty-five black vehicles, their red taillights a blinking line on the highway, the idling
vehicles emitting exhaust stench that carried over the desert to
where the boys snaked. They were slipping behind enemy lines,
as the Gorillas had been preparing to do. Only Ronin and Tom
turned out to have the courage to follow through on their plans,
and even now, both were consumed by doubts about what they
were doing and only barely resisting the urge to turn back.

Yet neither boy was willing to show his weakness to the other,
so they both crawled on, elbows and knees in the dirt, under the
still-dark sky. They stood when they assessed themselves to be
out of sight, and then marched toward the vast shadowy hulk,
which was so large it never seemed closer despite their progress.

The Joshua was being minded by its engineers and a security guard sitting in a resin chair facing a high-pressure mist-
ing fan. He looked at photos of auto rims on the tablet in his
lap, dreaming of shining silver nineteen-inch wheels—while his
actual thought was to earn enough money to pay the land lease
under his trailer and to keep the air-conditioning on and afford
the monthly fee at his kids' school. The Joshua was so large that
its security seemed to hardly be an issue. How could anyone
make off with something this large? Did anyone worry about the
Rocky Mountains being stolen?

He dozed in his cool column of wind and did not notice two
boys hunched low over the dirt, scampering across the scruffy
flat, just fifty yards away.

The two lean boys looked up at the Leviathan, their first
thoughts being how fucking awesome it was, the dream made
real of every boy who ever constructed a tower from Legos or

blocks. But this beautiful and powerful creature was the mechanical embodiment of their enemy.

All this machinery, darkly gleaming in places, rough and matted in others, stretching up, up, up, failed to fill the boys with dread, evoking instead all the wonder and fear of a television powered down. This was nothing more than another machine in the OFF position, they reasoned, so why should they be frightened? They stood next to the tread, the gear wheels three times their height, the sweet smell of engine grease coating their nostrils.

"Let's roll," Ronin said.

VANESSA GUIDED THE CHILDREN OUT of the fields and toward the three houses that had been converted to classrooms. They were to wait out the siege inside, staying in the shade and near the wet rags and bottles of water stored there in case of tear gas or pepper spray. Some children trembled as they walked. They were used to rising early, with the sun, but not before dawn as they had today. The youngest ones held hands and the oldest tried to comfort them as they shuffled through the onion fields. Once again they were being asked to leave, as each of them had been doing for months and years, as soon as they made a friend. They had been hungry and wandering for so long, that these months in Valence had been a blessing. None of them wanted to go.

They were also mesmerized by Vanessa's stomach, which was now showing. Her posture had changed, her hips and thighs had spread, and now her midsection protruded with what the oldest told the youngest was a baby. Vanessa smiled at the murmurings of the kids, and put one hand over her stomach. The life ahead of her was unknowable, but she had a sense from her mother's warnings, and Sargam's stern, unheeded lectures, that she had complicated her journey, while what everyone around her wanted for her was simplicity. But she wanted complication, wanted the burrs and protrusions that would catch as she fell through this world.

The children came up and touched her belly, asking her what she was going to name the baby. One remarked that she had seen a video of a cat giving birth to kittens and wondered if perhaps Vanessa would have a litter.

Vanessa said she and Atticus did not yet have a name; what she did not say was that her hope was to have her baby in Valence. Her mother, after resigning herself to becoming a grandmother and acknowledging there was no way to fix this situation, actually became excited by the prospect and said this was why they were fighting so hard to stay, so that families would have a place to live secure in the knowledge that their neighbors today would be their neighbors tomorrow.

Jeb and Atticus were gone to resist, and she did not know where her younger brother was, though many of his friends, that band who called themselves the Gorillas, were here. In each child she saw the future for her own unborn child and so now took extra care to make sure that each was tended to and protected and felt safe.

They were ushered into the schoolhouses and urged to sit cross-legged on the floor. Gemma made the rounds, trying to keep the anxiety out of her voice as she reassured them that they would be okay, and asked them if they wanted to sing a song. She began a full-throated "Jimmy Crack Corn," but only a few of the children picked up the chorus, while most looked about uneasily in the dark classrooms.

A few children were crying, and Franny, Ginny, and Jinx attempted to soothe them. When they heard the first shouts, the massed voices, the screams of "NO! Oh my God, NO!" then a gunshot, all the children began shouting and crying, faces glistening even in the shadows, an awful wailing at the unknown.

CHAPTER 11

PASTOR ROGER WAS ON THE telephone with the governor, urging him to give the order to forcibly remove the trespassers. He reminded the governor of the impression it could make on television in the bright light of day. They had to act quickly, before the sun came up. Dottie Pepper herself called the governor's campaign director and read to him a printout of how much money the various Pepper Industry PACs had donated in the last election cycle, and reminded him that there were other candidates who had just as staunchly vowed to fight the progressive agenda, and who the Peppers could back in the next primary.

The governor, after taking five minutes to pretend to consider the matter, issued the order to his attorney general to start the eviction. The state of Nevada had long ago outsourced most of its law-enforcement needs to private security firms, retaining only those officers handing out enough traffic summonses or seizing enough illicitly gained assets to justify their salary. Revenue-positive officers were always looking for new ways to boost their revenue scores, and this assignment—evicting the subprime commune in Valence—was not viewed as a likely high earner. Thus most of the work was being subcontracted to private security firms who brought in low-wage techs receiving the minimum of training in pepper-spray crowd dispersal and a quick course in safe firearm discharge. In reality, all you had to do to qualify as a security tech was have a credit score above 550 and a high school diploma, or pay $500 for a high school diploma equivalency waiver. The Peppers had their own security teams brought in, these being the most muscular and armored, the best trained, though sprinkled among these elite were boys who had never done more than watch over an Arby's parking lot.

While a neat and tidy removal and detention was one possible result of sending inexperienced security forces up against non-violent resisters, a much more likely outcome was chaos, fear, panic, and then violence. Pastor Roger and the Pepper Sisters knew this, and the cover of darkness was necessary to keep any possible mayhem as obscured as possible. The governor, for his part, had made a career of believing his own boilerplate about private-sector solutions to everything: he was actually convinced that his $4.30-an-hour temp cops were every bit as good as the full-time police officers they replaced.

The Pepper Sisters and Pastor Roger retreated to the pastor's tour bus, where he led them in a fierce session of prayer and vigil and Scripture reading. Their fondest wish, as it was for all true Americans, would be for this ugly episode to end without violence, for the rule of law to prevail.

"We worked so hard to avoid this outcome," said Dottie Pepper.

"God, we ask that you grant wisdom to all, to the progressive terrorists and the takers as well as to the Christians and makers, and we seek your patience and counsel throughout," said Dorrie Pepper.

"Now, now," Pastor Roger said. "It's God's will."

He bowed, reached for the Pepper Sisters' bony hands, and held them clasped against his own forehead. "Let this land, let all lands, be restored to their native and rightful state; unshackle the acres from regulators and squatters; get the enemies of your progress out of your way. We have walked so many miles together; nay, you have carried us so many miles—"

Pastor Roger sprung his usual leaks, tears streaming down his face, the carpet beneath him turning dark with his devotion. He cared so deeply about his flock, about his people, that he cried at the sacrifices that job creators such as the Pepper Sisters had to make in order to ensure that America remained prosperous and free.

IN THE DARK, THE SURGE forward of the security techs and cops at first appeared as a shifting of the light and shadow, but to those seated on the off-ramp, the individual uniforms, and then the reflective helmets, coming forward were clearly an army on the march.

"Hold steady," Sargam shouted. "Hold steady."

The faces of the citizens of Valence contorted in grimaces of fear as they stared with opened mouths at the advancing army. At the sound of a whistle, they heard the massed exhaled grunts of the security techs moving forward, and then the sudden, crack of a gunshot. There were screams, shouts—"Oh no!"—and the first fast panic and fear, as some of those clasped together attempted to stand and to crab-leg away from the oncoming wall of black uniforms.

A police officer had shot a dog that had broken loose from where the community's animals had been penned in, and been deemed a threat.

Bailey turned her back to the invasion to address the people. "Stay calm, stay calm," she said. "We have to stay together." She held her hand over her heart as she was captured in a cone of light from a television news drone hovering overhead. "*We shall overcome*," she began singing, and others joined in.

Some of the younger techs saw Bailey standing up, a heavy woman in sweatpants and a hooded sweatshirt reminding them of their own mothers. They stopped their advance, intentionally slowing, and fell to the back of the ranks. Only the most professional techs, those directly employed by Pepper Extraction, willingly took the van, unclasping their pepper-spray nozzles and readying their batons. Behind them, a trio of SUVs equipped with halogen spots strobed the area with bursts of light to enable the advancing techs to see their targets.

Sargam wished for a brisk breaking dawn. Their struggle had to be seen by the many millions, so that there might be some outcry, so that their attempt to hold their plot of earth would at least not be in vain. She put her head down, awaiting the harsh spray she knew was coming, and held firmly the hands of the man and woman next to her to give them her strength and her courage.

Then she stood up tall, raising both arms overhead, as if signaling a touchdown or acknowledging a standing ovation. With her white leather jacket swinging open, zippers gleaming, she effectively stopped the advance yards short of the line of resisters. The techs and cops momentarily paused, silent, while an urgent command "detain and arrest" was shouted repeatedly in their headsets. Still, they were unmoved. The familiar figure captured by dozens of news drones had momentarily delayed the advance of those who, like everyone, were awed by fame and celebrity. She would use whatever tools she had to delay the action, at least until first light.

THEY WERE SURPRISED BY THEIR own courage. The boys climbed, bony hand over bony hand, up a metal ladder designed for longer reaches. Ronin and Tom were making their way up the skeleton of the Joshua, ascending with heavy breaths, their narrow shapes barely standing out from the surrounding infrastructure of pipe and wire and girder. What they were heading toward was unclear to them, but they knew they had to get to the top, sensing that that was where the brains of the beast were, the CPU of the metal monster. They were sweating profusely by the time they were at twenty feet, their hands struggling to grip the cold metal of the ladders. What they saw around them was so far outside their experience that they drew on a computer-game environment to make some sense of it. They were on some sort of final mission, vast, mazelike, alien, presumably full of danger, an End Level destination for any first-person shooter or slasher. Even so, their dripping sweat and exhausted muscles never let them think for long that this was virtual reality.

At the first platform they paused, took deep breaths as if they were surfacing, and looked to the east and to the rising dawn.

"I'm hungry," said Tom.

"Me too," Ronin said.

They both shrugged. There was nothing to do about their appetites. In the dark, they felt gingerly around the checkerboard-plate steel floor. They found the elevator, dumb and inaccessible without the circular keys to operate it. Around the outside of the lift carapace, they followed the floor between hand railings to another ladder and resigned themselves to more climbing, first checking with each other, faces barely visible in the pre-light, exchanging I-will-if-you-will shrugs.

Up they went, another twenty-five feet, their backs catching the very first rays of sun cresting the western desert, but while they were ascending, they heard the crackle and then were enveloped in a powerful hum, their hands almost vibrating off the crossbars.

The Joshua was coming to life, and right in front of them they saw the elevator cab descend, and down below, on the first platform, the shiny, hard-hatted engineers waiting to ascend to the pilot station. They would be invisible to these men in the elevator, and had no choice anyway but to keep climbing as the elevator cab drew parallel and then rose past them.

At the elevator's arrival at the pilot station above them, they heard the doors open, the engineers' heavy-boot footsteps, and the opening of the pilot station doors. The men, chatting casually as people do at the start of their workday, were totally unaware of the two teenage boys climbing toward them.

Arms aching and breathing heavily, first Tom and then Ronin threw their legs over the side of the station platform and paused there, below the slanted pilot's and engineer's windows. They listened as the vast diesel motors down below were fired and set rumbling, the exhaust stench overwhelming. All around them, spotlights and LED strips were turned on, so that the Joshua looked like a Christmas tree, as the desert also lit up in the dawn.

The sun was blistering the horizon, turning white light to yellow, and from where the boys sat, they could see Valence in the distance, looking like any other small town, looking like a place you could call home.

On the highway ribboning toward Valence was a throng of black vehicles that set the gray highway smoking in a haze of white dust and black spent carbon. And at the end of that procession, Ronin and Tom could see where the battle lines were drawn: the citizens of Valence blocking the phalanxes of cops.

The engineers spoke into headsets, confirming that the engines were on, the oil pressure was high, the water temperature not so high, the oil temperature just right.

"We're level," said one voice.

"Let's go," said another.

"Confirming," the first voice said, "Joshua seeking clearance."

I RUN, FIRST BACK TOWARD where Gemma has taken Jinx and her girls, and then I stop, unsure if I should be leaving the scene of a breaking story. The westward-shooting sun is backlighting the cops, projecting their shadows in comically long and skinny shapes toward where Sargam stands with her arms raised. She has put some kind of spell on the security techs. Her face aglow in the dawn, she appears surrounded by light—am I going too far here?—as if in halo. But she has somehow calmed the proceedings, slowed down the advancing forces, so that we are all frozen, suddenly unsure of our actions. This, I realize, was her intention, to drag the proceedings into the light of day so that Americans would observe the removal of good citizens by the dark—literally, dark-uniformed—armies of the oligarchs. She is masterful at manipulating the media, and here she has stopped time for just long enough for the whole sorry sacrifice not to be in vain.

Even more remarkable, a few of the younger-looking techs are shaking their heads, falling back. A handful have even started to come toward Sargam, despite the shouts of their commanders to hold ranks. They recognize, in Sargam, in the lines of mothers and fathers seated, arms linked on the pavement, their own families. Some of these young men are nearly subprime themselves, and those with a conscience must recognize their own hypocrisy. A half-dozen have now lined up alongside the citizens of Valence, eliciting an eruption of cheers, and giving all of us, for a moment, the sense that we may win this thing, that the world is shifting and a remarkable transformation is unfolding. Until we regain our sanity and realize that six kids changing sides doesn't make a difference.

But I'm distracted. Where is Ronin? He still hasn't turned up, and before the pepper spray and batons start cracking heads, I must find my son. To have removed my son from school, to have kidnapped him and driven him to some progressive commune, I can defend, but then to lose him in the middle of the Battle of Valence, that is actually bad parenting. I don't have time to consider the stupid decisions I've been making, but I hate to concede, as I still look around desperately for a glimpse of him, that perhaps taking him from Anya was a mistake. Maybe some tropical island would be better for Ronin and Jinx than spending a few days a week with me? I mean, even if he miraculously passed algebra and then geometry and whatever comes after that, and if he got into an elite college, or even a shitty one, who could afford to pay $185,000 a year to see him through? God, I'm a fuck-up. I mean, even in the middle of a fuck-up—kidnapping my own children—I double the fuck-up by losing one of them.

I just should have left him—

The earth trembles and the SUVs lined up on the highway jiggle on their suspensions at the sound of the Joshua's engines firing. Distant, to the east, an Eiffel Tower on treads obscuring the sky, it rumbles and lurches, the hopes and dreams of the Pepper Sisters and Pastor Roger and every job creator transformed into steel and carbon.

The hulking iron giant grinds over the countryside, churning up the aslphalt highway as it goes, leaving behind tracks surely visible from outer space. The sight is as inspiring for the techs as it is dispiriting for the rest of us. Even if Sargam achieves a stalemate at the off-ramp, how can she hold off this monstrosity?

Gemma runs up, wearing a bandana, T-shirt, and jeans. Ah, here may be the explanation for my questionable actions these last few weeks. A man can lead his children into great danger in pursuit of a beautiful woman. I can even justify it all to myself when I see her.

She tells me Jinx, Ginny, and Franny are safe in the schoolhouse, watched over by teachers. Security techs are advancing into Valence from several directions, their vehicles bouncing over the desert and already in some of the cul-de-sacs.

"Have you seen Ronin?" I ask.

"I thought he was here."

"I can't find him," I say. "We need to look for him." But Gemma starts blinking furiously, her eyes reddening, and for a second I think she is starting to cry. Then I feel the sting myself. The burning around my eyes, in my mouth, down my throat. I know this feeling. I've been pepper-sprayed before.

IT WAS A YOUNG SECURITY tech, watching a few of his colleagues go over to the other side, who felt a wave of anger at his peers. This was not team play! Their betrayal had to be punished by a big dose of pepper spray—a compound named, he mistakenly believed, for the two women whose company hired him. Pulling on a breather mask, he trotted forward, past Sargam, unhooded his nozzle, and fired a stream at the front row of subprimes, dousing a few who could not turn their heads away in time. For those in the line of spray, the sensation of suffocation was dreadful and immediate. Sargam had arranged for citizens to be ready with buckets of water, yet when they ran forward, the other techs interpreted it as a threat and began unleashing streams of oleoresin capiscum themselves.

The assault was captured by the news drones; the footage of the defenseless and seated citizens of Valence being sprayed by uniformed and masked security techs was immediately upsetting to everyone who watched it. Even Fox News could not cut away from the drone footage quickly enough, a newscaster venturing that despite the clear moral and legal justification for their actions, perhaps the security techs had acted prematurely.

The howls of the afflicted were awful, women screaming, men coughing hoarsely. Water washed away the OC, the active ingredient, but not the penetrating sting. They struggled to keep their eyes open, as they had been instructed, to let their tear ducts wash away what they could, but the pain was awful, a burning sensation that seemed to emanate from under their skin.

Bailey and Jeb doubled over where they sat, coughing, trying to spit out as much of the pepper spray as they could. Like their fellow citizens, they had been briefed on this process, but the actual pain from the attack was impossible to prepare for. This was unprecedented suffering, a slicing sensation around the eyes and nostrils and neck and armpits, and even in the groin, every part of the body with a gland near the skin. Yet in their moments of most profound distress, they felt the soothing sensation of soft hands against their skin, this contact of fingers and palms immediately drawing away the pain. They looked up.

Sargam walked down the row of citizens, laying hands on those who had been sprayed. Each of the mothers and fathers along the line felt the relief, immediate and undeniable, and then gratitude that the pain was gone. What had actually happened? Had Sargam healed them?

The veteran cops across from the subprimes, who had rousted Ryanvilles with doses of OC in the past, had never seen anyone recover from a blast this quickly. They had watched Sargam walk down the writhing row, and had seen her laying on hands, but it just didn't make sense.

"Hit 'em again!" shouted an officer.

The uniformed crowd parted, and through the ranks walked a figure in a blue suit and white shirt, wearing a breather mask. His face, showing through the visor, was buck-toothed and red, and it took a few seconds before everyone realized this was Pastor Roger. He came forward, hands clasped, and then waved his arms, as if to quiet an audience. Only no one was applauding here.

He looked at the rows of subprimes who still, miraculously, held their ground, at the woman in white who walked among them, summoning some kind of deviltry to sooth these anti-angels. He saw the magazine writer who had libeled him, and whom he believed he was now suing. The writer was hunched over, trying to catch his breath, and next to him was a woman who looked familiar to him too.

Steve Shopper, wearing a gas mask of his own, ran up, carrying a megaphone, which he switched on and handed to Pastor Roger.

"My friends," he began. "My fellow Americans. Why has it come to this? To your violence? To our having to defend ourselves? To confrontation. That is not our wish."

The citizens of Valence booed the pastor, a few chanting, "*People helping people. People helping people.*"

"—We all want the same things. We all want freedom. We have different ways of expressing that. Now, if you would—"

He paused. Sargam had still not even glanced at him. She was in the distance, still administering to her flock, still with this ridiculous laying on of hands.

Pastor Roger had been warned by the Pepper Sisters not to go to the off-ramp. Yet here he was, drawn by the scene, the news drones circling overhead, the nonstop, cross-platform coverage of the confrontation. If this was a showdown of good versus evil, then he *had* to be there, at the forefront, in the lights. And yet, confronting Sargam in person, and finding that she did not even acknowledge him, he found it . . . emasculating.

He threw down the megaphone and retreated, uttering to the commander, "Smite them!"

As the first row of cops and techs swept forward, Sargam stood her ground. The men were unsure of what to do, until one leaped to tackle her, and then three more pinned her to the ground, ripping off her white leather jacket, her olive-brown arms pulled behind her so that she was facedown on the pavement, her eyes welling with tears.

The broadcast images were close shots of her face. And then a man who would later be identified as a journalist working on a story about Sargam came running into the frame, attempting to pull away the security techs before he was thrown down and kicked in the ribs. These shots were broadcast around the world and went viral with such urgency that they soon superceded even the whales in popularity.

I'M BEING HELD DOWN, MY face stings, my ribs feel as if they've been broken, and I think I'm suffocating because one of these fat techs is sitting on me. I realize they might just let me die. That my impulse to run out and help Sargam could literally have meant the end of me. With my face pressed down against the pavement, I feel the intense vibrations of the approaching Joshua and I wonder if perhaps they will just leave me here to be run over by the giant machine. But of course if Sargam is also run over, then I will be an afterthought, even in the coverage of my own death.

A battle rages, or not really a battle, more like a gas attack as cops and techs spray and march through the ranks of our good citizens, cutting their plastic cuffs with clippers and lifting them off the ground and hauling them away.

Look at me, suddenly passionate and acting impulsively, a lifetime of cynicism overruled as I rush in to defend my idol. And what do I get for my newfound idealism? A boot in the ribs. Around me, I can hear the spraying of the gas, the shouts and screams of the good men and women, and under it all, like the bass line to this holocaust, the Joshua's motors and treads, rumbling closer and closer.

The big-bottomed tech who has been sitting on me leaps up and points in the direction of the Joshua. All the attention has shifted, and a hush settles over the battle. Even the drones are buzzing off to the east.

THE BOYS HATCHED THEIR PLAN: an assault on the pilot station, a decapitation, the ultimate Gorilla attack, as asymmetrical as warfare gets. Two boys barely ten feet tall, combined, taking down a four-hundred-and-eighty-foot monster. The steel latch to the station opened with just a turn, and the men inside the soundproofed station became aware of the change in volume as the external noise of the diesels and treads rushed in. The crew was executing a complicated maneuver, bringing the Joshua up a slight grade while banked to one side, always a dicey operation with a vehicle as unwieldy as this, when they turned toward the open door and were momentarily confused at the sight of a dirty-faced, ragamuffin boy. Was this some kind of school tour they weren't told about? Otherwise, what the hell was he doing here? And why was he so filthy?

Ronin felt as if he'd played this game before, had seized enemy bunkers and command posts and missile silos, had thrown the levers that overthrew an evil empire. He charged toward the vast instrumentation panel, reaching for the long, green-handled levers. There were eight of them, one for each tread, and the boy could not know this but a computerized steering management system distributed power to each tread pod to keep the Joshua both upright and moving forward. The levers allowed for manual overrides to this program, in the event of the Joshua having to reach a certain drilling position or an angled ascent. In reaching for these levers, the boy was changing the power flow, upsetting the delicate balance of the Joshua at the very moment when the vast machine was moving up an eight-percent grade at a thirty-degree angle. Perhaps it was just bad luck for everyone involved, but this was the most vulnerable phase of the operation, and Ronin, leaping at the levers, and actually securing four and shoving them forward, increased the speed of the right tread pods so that the vehicle pivoted awkwardly upward, putting the entire edifice at risk.

The six crew members grabbed Ronin, yanking him away. Meanwhile, seizing the opportunity, Tom charged through the open door, attacked the same levers, manipulating them as crazily as he could in the hope of somehow confusing the beast.

Ronin could see in the eyes of the men the panic at what was happening before he sensed it himself. The Joshua was shuddering in a manner they had never felt before, and a creaking and groaning noise was emitted from the strained metal of the monster. They released Ronin, unhanded Tom, and rushed to the instrument panel, desperate to redistribute power, to level the Joshua, which was clearly listing, perhaps even tipping, to starboard. This allowed the boys to renew their efforts at sabotage; they grabbed at what they could, crawling between legs and reaching under arms, so that the men struggled to operate the Joshua while keeping the boys at bay. At one point, three of them were chasing the boys, while the other three attempted to right the Joshua, and in an effort to escape, Ronin crawled between the legs of one engineer and leaped on the panel itself, stepping over a half-dozen toggles and levers and switches, throwing into disarray everything, from the Joshua's plumbing to the elevator doors, and finally, causing a system shutdown that switched the entire operation to manual.

The sensation of the port treads losing contact with the earth was at first a feeling of leaning to the right, as each man detected his own weight shift, but then there was the unmistakable lightness of the vehicle itself tipping, of the floor shifting, and then the men stumbling to regain their footing as the view out the front window was of the horizon going vertical. The Joshua was falling.

The boys dropped, banging roughly against the control panel, their faces and hands and legs getting cut and scraped as they flew against the side windows. Tom fell so that he was pressed facedown against the window, his blood reddening the glass in front of him as the ground rushed up to meet him. He rolled over and then was facing up, catching for a moment the terrified expressions of the engineers, who were falling past him and out the opened pilot station door. He saw Ronin beside him, whose features were also distorted by the angle and by fear, but who looked back at Tom and whose eyes seemed to widen with a flicker of recognition and satisfaction.

THE UNLIKELINESS OF WHAT THEY were seeing created a sense that this was something they were watching on television or in a movie. Yet here it was, right in front of them, the groaning and clattering confirmation of what they were seeing with their own eyes. The Joshua was tipping over. For a moment, the good citizens of Valence began cheering, but then stopped. They all saw the bodies falling from the pilot station, small, unmistakably human forms, diving, some twisting, but all with the same destination. The battle paused, as the techs and cops and good citizens of Valence all turned to stare.

The bodies fell, each creating a surprisingly gentle-looking puff as it hit the earth.

And then the Joshua came crashing down, all 22,000 tons hitting the desert floor with a massive percussive wallop. Immediately, there were several explosions as live wires sparked the pooling fuel. Next came a rolling cloud of dust and sand, spreading outward in every direction, enveloping them in brown and orange gusts. The air smelled of desert and oil and smoke, and was bitter to breathe. In the chaos, as everyone lost their bearings and froze, losing sight of each other in the brown cloud, Sargam slipped her plastic binds and ran toward the fallen monster.

Pastor Roger, walking east, watched the collapse and the bodies falling and felt, and not for the first time, that perhaps this day wasn't going as God would have wished.

I AM ON MY FEET, accompanied by a massive pain in my side, and looking up at the huge robot keeling over, and my first thought is: This is an amazing story. I scan the sky for news drones and I'm disappointed to see a dozen of them circling the site. I gasp when I see a few figures falling from the command bridge atop the Joshua, tiny figures that immediately give perspective to the massive scale of the thing. These are people, falling, some of them larger than others—

That's a child, a boy, somehow a familiar shape to me, spinning through the air, and it makes me think of my boy.

THE BOY, TOM, THOUGHT HIS last thought. Of his mother, peeling an apple.

THERE WERE NO ORDERS GIVEN but the collective consciousness of both sides dictated action. The uniformed techs and the citizens of Valence all ran en masse to the site. The battle had evolved, in seconds, into a rescue mission.

Their respirators enabled the techs to breathe despite the thick swirl of particles as they ran forward, while Sargam blinked furiously as she attempted to feel her way through. A few of her colleagues came forward with her, and a few confused techs attempted to keep them in line until they realized the futility of the situation and instead cut the plastic cuffs off those they had arrested.

The stricken rig lay on its side, the superstructure above the pilot station having sheared off after the fall so that it lay a few yards from the exoskeleton. The whole mess resembled a building toppled on its side, the vast metal struts and girders still standing, but much of the infrastructure had collapsed on impact, so that the drill and extractor and pumps and tanks were all in a busted, tangled pile visible through the gaps between girders. Several electrical fires were still burning, black smoke pluming upward, and the risk of more explosions kept everyone from going too close to the wreckage.

The techs and cops stood at a distance, awaiting the fire and rescue crew who would have been on-site had the state not stopped funding these services. The Pepper Sisters themselves had long ago lobbied into law the gutting of shale-oil drill-site safety standards, so that HG Extraction did not have a fire and rescue crew anywhere in the area. But running through everyone's mind was the question of whether or not anyone was still alive in the pilot station.

The search for bodies around the rig quickly yielded grisly results. The bodies were all intact, the fall hadn't been from such a great height that they disintegrated, but it was a bloody sight of broken bones twisted at grotesque angles. The techs stood about, unsure of what to do. At first the cops reverted to a kind of crowd control to keep people back, but finally one woman's shrieks became so pronounced that they let her run forward to the body of a small boy. She kneeled down and tore at her hair, shouting, "Why? Why? Why?"

The boy had landed on his head, his autumn-brown hair now soaked red.

Bailey squeezed her eyes and looked around for Jeb, who was stumbling toward them. Neither Bailey nor Jeb fully grasped what had happened—nobody did. The impossibility of their boy being here, amidst the wreckage of this drilling rig, was so incongruous that both kept checking their surroundings and their boy's face in the vain hope that somehow this was not real.

Pastor Roger saw the woman bending over her dead son framed by the fallen Joshua Extractor. In the climactic battle of makers versus takers, a humiliating reversal had occurred, making what should have been a simple nighttime operation into a national spectacle. The optics were horrible. Pastor Roger looked up at a news drone, its camera shooting down at him from a few hundred feet above, giving the world a glimpse of his panicked face.

"What do we do?" asked a security guard in the employ of Pepper Industries.

Pastor Roger shrugged. "Pray."

THE TECHS WHO WERE GATHERED around the wreckage experienced a collective loss of nerve. Some were retreating, slipping back to their SUVs and retiring from the operation. At any rate, it looked like the eviction was off for today, but others surveyed the smoking mess and wondered out loud if anyone was still in there.

But through the crowd came a figure in white, already familiar to everyone, and she did not hesitate to climb over a horizontal girder and slip around a collapsed interior stairwell in an effort to reach the pilot station. Sargam was determined to search for survivors, if there were any, and she was willing to venture into the flaming hulk. The men, standing around, looked down at their feet, unwilling to follow her. Only one came forward, Richie, who somewhat reluctantly climbed over the scaffold and girder to enter into the smoking, stinking ruin.

IT'S NOT COURAGE THAT COMPELS me but shame at my own failings as a man. Shame that no one will follow Sargam into the wreckage to do what obviously must be done. We have to search for survivors. We can't stand around. After I climb in, I'm followed by a few citizens who are waving their hands in front of their faces to fend off the smoke. It is hot from the early-morning sun and the inferno of fuel and electrical fires. We have to skirt vast, smoldering cable nests and even a downed elevator cab, the drill bit and extractor pipes all lying shattered in the sand, the black, tarry lubricant pooling atop waffle-gridded steel.

Sargam takes the lead, climbing, slipping over and under the obstructions. At one point I burn my hand on a piece of rebar that must have secured some cabling and has now turned hot from a fire. This is a miniature hell, I think, a dirty, smoky, toxic industrial waste, and what am I doing here? I've never been a brave man. I've spent my life avoiding these sorts of risks, yet here I am, on a dangerous rescue mission.

I watch Sargam slide under a thick weave of I-beam, shattered carbon and fiberglass, a greenish liquid ominously dribbling down next to her. Without her saying anything we know we have to follow. One after another, we slide under, headfirst, and in the dark we snake our way along hot and oily surfaces, having faith that Sargam has seen a patch of light up ahead.

What else in this crashed Leviathan may still be shifting? My elbow bleeds and my burned hand stings. I continue to climb until I see a triangular opening and can extricate myself from the wreckage. We are in a sort of clearing in the ruins, a hissing chemical fire is burning a few feet to the right of us, and ahead, there is black smoke and a fountain of sparks emanating from what looks like some sort of twisted and blackened junction box.

There is the pilot station, four Plexiglas windows still in place but capillaried with thousands of shatter strands. The boxy structure is propped at an angle because it rests atop a buckled steel platform like an airport control tower dropped on its side.

There are no bodies here. I want to announce this to everyone. We can leave now.

"This doesn't seem very safe to me," I say instead.

She points to a corner of the cracked Plexiglas where I see pooled blood.

Sargam swings herself onto the steel railings of the platform so that she is standing parallel to the grid-patterned floor, her muscular arms reaching up to the door frame to pull herself into the pilot station. She climbs up and over onto a control panel and is gone from our sight, reappearing a few moments later.

"Richie, stay there," she says, and requests a few other men to climb up. "I've found someone."

Two of our colleagues come over and stand on the railings with their feet spread.

"You need more help," I say, preparing to climb up.

"It's a boy," Sargam says.

I know before I know who is going to come down through that door, yet am shocked when Ronin appears, his face bloodied, his upper lip partially torn, his arms limp. Sargam holds him up by the elbows and the two men take his thighs and slide him down as gracefully as they can, considering the situation.

"Is he . . . ?" I say, unable to complete the question.

I take him in my arms and settle him gently to the ground. My boy is rag-doll limp. Please, please, be breathing, I think. Please. I remove my shirt and slide it under his head as the men gather around.

Why did I ever take him away from his mother, from Los Angeles? And what the hell was he doing up there, anyway? I should have been with him every minute. I should have treasured every minute. I should have quit everything and everyone so I could play one more game of checkers with Ronin, sat with him just one more time and lied to him that everything would be all right.

I lift his head up and hold my hand in front of his mouth, hoping for breath, but there is no air. The unimaginable has happened and I start sobbing. I'm on my knees, and looking down at Ronin, and I'm thinking, There has to be a next thing before I let go, even if it is only to arrange for his proper departure. It is so selfish, these first mournings. Rather than think of my daughter and how to tell her, or my ex-wife, who may be watching this live, I'm thinking of myself. I can't get up. I reach out and place my hand on his cheek, pressing slightly, as if checking again to make sure this is really him.

A hand is on my shoulder, and I turn and see Sargam, her head backlit by the burning wreckage. "We don't have much time," she is saying.

I shake my head. What am I supposed to do? Leave my son?

SHE KNEELS DOWN. SHE LAYS one hand on Ronin's forehead, just below his high crown, places her other hand over his mouth, then on his neck, then in through his torn T-shirt and against his chest. She closes her eyes. Is she attempting to comfort him? But that doesn't make sense. He is beyond pain.

Sargam takes my hand and holds it under Ronin's nose. In the heat, I cannot detect any warmth of breath and I start to pull away.

She looks at me with an urgent widening of her eyes. *Stay.*

I hold my hand there and soon I imagine I can feel something, a faint, soft breath against my fingers. This can't be.

She takes my hand and holds it against his chest, and there it is, a heartbeat.

I'm frightened by what seems to be happening here. My son was dead, I'm sure of that, and yet here is some sort of life.

Perhaps he is in some vegetative state, revived but brain dead.

Then his eyes flick open, and I can hear the men around me murmuring, as surprised as I am by what we are all bearing witness to.

"Ronin?" I whisper.

He inhales sharply, as if smelling something and trying to figure out by that where he is. His eyes dart from me to Sargam and take in the wreckage around him. "Where am I?"

I am afraid to think this is a miracle.

WE CARRY MY BOY OUT. Both his legs are badly injured, probably broken, and I wonder why if she can raise the dead, or so it seems, she can't fix his legs as well. I mean, it seems a bit stingy, but then I can't presume to understand what is actually going on here. What I do know is that I have been given a huge gift, a second chance to be a better father. There is a cheer from the crowd as we emerge with Ronin, and he even manages a thumbs-up. Gemma rushes forward with Jinx, Ginny, and Franny, and as we celebrate our reunion. I lose track of Sargam.

THE FOOTAGE OF HER GOING from body to body, seven in all, and bringing each one back to life—even Tom—was broadcast repeatedly and discussed with furious passion. Some newscasters insisted it had to be some sort of progressive trick, some sleight of hand performed by a woman who, let's face it, has never been properly vetted. "Do we know who she is? Where she's from? There should be an investigation of some kind. Homeland Security should be brought in to determine exactly what is going on here."

But even among those most rabidly opposed to what Sargam stood for, there was a murmuring doubt that what had happened out there in the desert was real, that what we had witnessed was some sort of collective mystical experience, a visitation by a person who actually had magical powers.

Sargam became the single most compelling figure in the world, the shot of her standing with her arms raised before the army of techs and cops iconic. Her mantra of "People helping people" appeared everywhere. She became too globally renowned for anyone to even dream of removing her from Valence.

For Sargam, who retreated back into Valence in the immediate aftermath, and retired into her modest ranch house with Darren and avoided the media glare, what had happened was as confusing to her as it was to those billions who would see it. She was physically exhausted by the acts, and as she rested in the dark of her living room, regaining her strength and going over in her mind what had transpired, she tried to understand what she very quickly concluded was not possible to understand.

She was a practical woman, and she resisted the obvious conclusion, that she was somehow magical, or, even stranger, divine. How egotistical to even contemplate that possibility. When she discussed it with Darren, who became a little bit distant since the day of the battle, he did not dare venture a guess as to what this all meant. But he was grateful that the community was, for the time being, going to survive. And there were now tens of millions around the country who believed in people helping people, no matter what their credit rating. It seemed there was hope for subprimes everywhere.

I DON'T BELIEVE IN MISSIONS, or God, or at least I never did before. I have not lived a virtuous life, nor a selfless life, and never gave much thought to concepts like virtue or sacrifice. Yet here I am, living in a community that grows every day larger and more powerful because it is centered around a great woman who may just be the Second Coming. Or she may just be a very talented masseuse. But I know what I saw her do to my son, and I know I owe her my loyalty.

I firmly believe she has broken the fever spell of greed that has blackened our world for too long.

I spend afternoons with Sargam, taking down her thoughts and observations, a project that has morphed into my writing her biography. I type as she talks, and then I go over what I have, organize it into paragraphs and scenes, and eventually turn anecdotes into allegories. This will be a hell of a book.

I walk back up to our house on Temecula, where I will meet Gemma after she is done with her day of teaching. Jinx, Ginny, and Franny are terrific students, inseparable it turns out, so much so that they've become known as "the triplets." Ronin has been very quiet since his near-death experience, as if he is taking stock of the world, and occasionally he will say that he misses Pacific Palisades, our old life, the way things were. Other times he says he just misses his mom.

I know my children will soon be taken from me, I know that this blessed idyll will soon come to an end, that there are great battles, both personal and global to come, and I try to stay in the moment. Sometimes I succeed.

There—I see Gemma and the girls approaching, the three kids skipping up the broken pavement, intent on leaping over cracks, their faces lit by the late-afternoon sun. Gemma is also sunstruck, her brown hair swinging freely over her lightly freckled forehead. She holds her hair up with one hand as she walks, her other holding Ginny's. Then she sees me, smiles, and starts skipping.

ABOUT THE AUTHOR

KARL TARO GREENFELD IS THE author of six previ-
ous books: the much-acclaimed novel *Triburbia*, the
memoir *Boy Alone*, *Now Trends*, *China Syndrome*, *Standard
Deviations*, and *Speed Tribes*. His writing has appeared
in *Harper's Magazine*, the *Atlantic*, the *Paris Review*, *Playboy*, *GQ*, *Best
American Short Stories 2009* and *2013*, and *The PEN/O. Henry Prize
Stories 2012*. Born in Kobe, Japan, he has lived in Paris, Hong
Kong, and Tokyo. He currently lives in California with his wife,
Silka, and their daughters, Esmee and Lola.